DON'T LET HIM KNOW

DON'T LET HIM KNOW

SANDIP ROY

B L O O M S B U R Y

LONDON • NEW DELHI • NEW YORK • SYDNEY

First published in Great Britain 2015

Copyright © 2015 by Sandip Roy

The moral right of the author has been asserted

Bloomsbury Publishing Plc
50 Bedford Square
London
WC1B 3DP

www.bloomsbury.com

Bloomsbury is a trademark of Bloomsbury Publishing Plc
Bloomsbury Publishing, London, New Delhi, New York and Sydney

A CIP catalogue record for this book is available from the British Library

Hardback ISBN 978 1 4088 5663 5
Trade paperback ISBN 978 1 4088 5664 2

10 9 8 7 6 5 4 3 2 1

Typeset by Hewer Text UK Ltd, Edinburgh
Printed and bound in Great Britain by CPI Group (UK) Ltd, Croydon CR0 4YY

For my sister Basabi who taught me the pleasure of reading stories.
For my mother Reba who told me stories.
And for Greg who listened to my stories.

Don't let him know she liked them best,
For this must ever be
A secret, kept from all the rest,
Between yourself and me.

– Lewis Carroll, *Alice in Wonderland*

CONTENTS

I

A Happy Meal

'M A,' SAID Amit, 'I have to talk to you about something.'
Dinner was over. Romola and Amit were alone in
the kitchen. She was putting away the leftovers while Amit
wiped the kitchen counters. June was upstairs with Neel and
his homework. The last traces of a California evening still
dappled the neighbourhood in tranquil honeyed light. Romola
could hear the hiss of a hose as their neighbour, Mr Nguyen,
watered his lawn. Somewhere a little dog barked.

'What is it, son?' She put down the leftovers and turned to
him. 'Is anything wrong?'

She could sense he was struggling with something. She wondered if he was having fights with June. Perhaps June didn't
want her here any more, she thought worriedly, though it had
only been two weeks since she had arrived from Calcutta.

It had been a long time since the two of them had talked
– just her and Amit. Even when Avinash had died and Amit
had made the long journey back to Calcutta for his father's
funeral, they had never really talked. Oh sure, they had discussed Avinash's stocks and shares and what to do with his
bank account and who to invite to the funeral but that was
not really talking.

'What a good boy that Amit is, such a dutiful son,' everyone
told her. 'You are a lucky mother.' She would smile and say,

1

'That I am.' But they never talked, not like they did when he'd come running back from school and plant himself on her stomach while she lay in bed taking her afternoon nap and launch into long stories of schoolyard fights and teacher sagas. She had been his confidante then on lazy summer afternoons, half-listening to his convoluted long-winded stories while the fan whirred sluggishly overhead.

'Ma, remember I brought back a bunch of my old books and diaries from India?'

She remembered. Several years after Avinash died, she had finally got around to going through the closets and had found a shoebox filled with old diaries. They were Amit's and she'd started reading them, smiling at little-boy accounts of school friends and birthday parties until the dust made her eyes water and her throat sore. She'd put them aside for later and had forgotten all about them. She remembered mentioning them to Amit but had no idea he had lugged them back to California.

'Well, there was one of your old address books in there somehow,' said Amit.

'Oh, really?' She shrugged. 'But an address book that old is useless anyway. All the phone numbers must have changed. Half the people are probably dead. Just throw it away.'

'It's not the address book,' said Amit. 'I found this in it. I think it's just the last page. I don't know where the rest is.'

He wordlessly handed the letter to her.

The paper was almost translucent with age, but the handwriting was still clear, the ink Royal Blue. She recognized it with a jolt, even though it had been almost four decades. She remembered exactly where she was the day she had first seen that letter. Funny, she was in America then as well, a newly arrived bride in her neatly ordered kitchen trying to organize her spice jars. Until that letter arrived and turned everything upside down.

I wanted to surprise you by telling you I had finally secured admission to graduate school in the United States. I guess the surprise ended up being mine, getting your wedding invitation. I was hoping that once we were there away from the prying eyes of families we'd be able to live the life we dreamed about during those evenings in Calcutta.

Now it tastes like dust in my mouth. I feel betrayed that you couldn't be stronger. Couldn't you have waited longer? Or did you feel, since whatever we had was a secret anyway, we could just carry on as before? Hadn't we promised to be together, the world be damned? Did you think it was just a phase we'd outgrow like children do with their clothes?

I never asked you to tell the world. I just hoped you might wait for me. I wrote and rewrote this letter three times wondering whether I'd ever send it. I don't really expect you to reply.

Yours
Sumit

Romola sat there in Amit's armchair slightly stunned. After all these years how could she have been so careless? She knew she had saved the letter, unable to destroy it the way she should have years ago. She remembered reading it and rereading it, each word striking her like a sledgehammer, cracking her open over and over again. She had always meant to throw it away, shred it, but somehow she never could. She had hidden it instead – stashed away like a secret pain. But she had never meant Amit to see it. She sat there speechless wondering what to say. This was like one of those terrible television shows she saw during the day where the wife would confess that their little girl wasn't her husband's and the studio audience would gasp in horror.

'Ma,' said Amit, as if reaching across a great divide. 'Ma, tell

3

me about Sumit Uncle. It is the same Sumit Uncle who once came from America to visit, isn't it?'

Romola stared at him shocked. No, she thought, this couldn't be happening, not now. The past she always thought could be wiped clean like a kitchen counter if you were careful enough. She had wanted no shadow of it to fall on Amit, to haunt his dreams. Once he told her that he never dreamed. He said he woke up every morning, his mind as clear as a cloudless summer sky, unremittingly bright in its glare. Was it her, she had wondered. Had she wiped the past clean with such determination that she had given her son only a gift of dreamlessness?

But how could she explain everything to Amit now? Did any of it matter any more? Avinash, her husband, his father, was dead. She was sitting here, a widow in her sixties in a suburban kitchen in California while the late summer evening turned golden. As for Sumit, who knew where Sumit was any more? Was he even alive or, like Avinash, dead from a sudden heart attack?

'It's okay, Ma.' Amit awkwardly put his hand on her shoulder. 'I think you were incredibly brave to do what you did – to give up Sumit Uncle for Baba.' Romola stared at him, confused. She wanted him to stop but he kept talking. 'We don't have to talk about it if you don't want to. But did father know about him? I thought they were friends.'

Romola let his words sink in. She was an adulteress in his eyes, she thought. How had that happened? No, no, she wanted to tell him. You have it all wrong. Anger welled up in her. How quick they were to assume everything was always her fault. Avinash's face floated into her head. And Sumit's. She didn't know who she was angrier with but she clenched her fists to keep her hands still.

She wanted to protest her innocence but the past seemed too complicated to explain now, full of serrated edges that

4

could rip everything to shreds. She twisted the border of her sari in her hand and shook her head, wondering how it had come to be that Amit was asking the questions and she was the one rummaging for excuses.

It was so long ago, she could say. It was just a momentary foolishness, could be another explanation. It's not what you think. It's all lies. You misunderstand. The babble of voices in her head grew louder and louder, their urgent tones more and more shrill, criss-crossing like anxious telephone wires. But nothing seemed right, even to her own ears, each explanation weaker than the previous one, tissue-wrapped in white lies, the cracks showing through the arguments even before she could utter them.

Then she looked at Amit's face and saw something she had not seen for many years in his eyes. He was trying to connect to her, as tentative as the first ghostly little toadstools that sprang up after the monsoon deluge.

He is not angry, she thought in baffled wonder feeling someone had unexpectedly overturned a judgement. He doesn't even seem upset.

'Yes.' She gingerly tested out the legs of each word to see if it could bear the weight of the past without collapsing. 'Your father knew about Sumit, of course. But that was so long ago.'

'I think it's so great we can talk like this, you know,' he said. 'Like adults, one on one. I never thought I'd be able to with you. Now I finally feel like I know you so much better. It's like a huge cloud lifted from over us.'

She stared at him bemusedly. In her son's eyes she was now a mysterious woman with an alluring past, not just his ageing mother with an arthritic knee.

'Well, you know, Amit, your parents weren't always old fuddy-duddies who only cared about your grades. We had our pasts too.'

'I know, but we never talk about it,' Amit sounded almost

excited. 'Ma, I never told you, but June and I were having some problems. I went to see a therapist. It was her idea but I was depressed and felt like I could never hold a relationship together. And the therapist asked me about your and Baba's marriage. And I said I think it was happy but I realized I didn't really know anything. Was it?'

'You went to see a therapist?' Romola ignored his question. 'Why?'

'Oh Ma, it doesn't matter now. But now that I know about all this, it explains so much about you. And me.'

'It does?' Romola was still trying to navigate the unexpected turn the conversation had taken.

'It totally does,' said Amit. 'I know all this sounds like American psychobabble but I needed to know you as a person, not just my mother. But tell me: why couldn't you just marry Sumit Uncle? Did you know him before you married Baba?'

Romola looked at her son. His hair was receding and in the evening light she saw traces of his father in his face. She didn't want to explain anything. She was tired, so tired of always being the one who had to smooth things over, the one who had to keep everything running.

'It just wasn't possible,' she said finally. 'That was a different time. We had to listen to our parents, unlike you all.' But she smiled to let him know she didn't hold it against him for having settled in California, for marrying an American named June, for not naming her grandson Shilajeet as she had wanted but Neel – a name she regarded as bland and colourless, its Indianness discreet as if it did not want to disturb the placidity of their American suburbia.

Amit smiled back and then handed her the letter. 'Keep the letter,' he said. She ran her fingers over it, smoothing out the creases.

'You know,' he leaned forward. 'I've been meaning to tell you something for days and now I think I can.'

Romola looked at him expectantly, bracing herself for whatever it was.

'I am thinking of quitting my job and studying to be a chef.'

'A what?' Romola gasped.

'Chef, you know, like a gourmet cook.'

'I know what a chef is,' she said impatiently. 'I watch TV too. But why do you want to be a cook? You are a computer engineer.'

'I know but cooking is what I want to do,' said Amit. 'It's about following your heart, you know.'

She didn't know, she thought. 'But you studied computer science in America,' she said, as if to reassure herself. Then a dreadful suspicion crept into her voice. 'Didn't you?'

'Yes,' he laughed. 'But that doesn't mean I can never do anything else. Anyway, it's not like anyone ever asked me what I wanted to do. I got into computer science and that was that. You and Baba were so excited and pleased I just went along with it.'

'What does June think?'

'She knows it will be tough. But she thinks I should do what I need to do,' he replied. 'Maybe it will help our marriage even. Things had been tough, Ma.'

What a strange country, thought Romola. He wants to cook his way back into his marriage. And then a sudden lick of annoyance flared up in her. How dare he dig up old infidelities and hurts to give himself permission to quit his good computer job and learn cooking?

'But you never even stepped into the kitchen when you were a boy in Calcutta,' she said. 'What do you even know of cooking?'

'I'd love to cook, Ma, if only you'd let me step into the kitchen,' he said sharply. 'Ever since you came you've just taken it over. I've learned to cook in America and I really enjoy it.'

'You do?' she stared at him as if he was a stranger. Chefs were perfectly coiffed celebrities like Madhur Jaffrey in beautiful silk saris, not Amit. She couldn't imagine him on television with an apron around him talking about sautéing chicken breasts and marinating kebabs.

'It's like meditation,' he said. 'It calms me.' Then he paused and said, 'And maybe you can teach me now. I could watch you and maybe we'll even re-create your recipes, write a cookbook together – "Bengali Meals for an American Kitchen". Wouldn't that be fun, just you and me?'

Romola smiled and shook her head gently at herself. She had been afraid she had lost Amit to America. Who would have thought that accursed letter from so long ago would bring him back to her? They used to call him her little tail when he was a toddler because he'd follow her everywhere. Today he was looking at her with those same eyes again as if she knew the answers and could wrap him in the love of her sari.

She smiled at him and threw up her hands.

'Don't you feel better?' he said. 'Now you don't have to keep all that locked away, a secret any more?'

She did feel better, she thought.

'If you tell me Sumit Uncle's last name and where he lived in America, I could try and track him down on the Internet,' said Amit.

'No, no,' Romola startled herself with the urgency in her tone. 'You must not. Promise me you won't start digging all that up. He might be dead, married, who knows? That chapter is over.'

'Okay, okay,' Amit shrugged. 'It was just an idea. I thought it might be cool. Ma, you know you've done all your duties. You've raised me. You took care of Baba. You wouldn't even take any money for the funeral.'

That American word 'cool' made her shiver. How Ameri–

can her son had become. She wondered if he really meant it. He hugged her before going to bed that night. He never did that she thought as she distractedly put away the leftovers.

All night long she tossed and turned. Once she woke up filled with sharp-toothed anger. Pshaw, she thought to herself. Amit was right. She had done everything everyone expected her to do. If no one had ever asked him if he wanted to study computers, no one had ever asked her if she wanted to do anything at all. All she had ever got to decide was what fish to serve for lunch and whether to have chicken or mutton for dinner. Now after Avinash's death, not even that. Rui, paarshey, ilish, the fish of her childhood, all gone. Who asked me whether I wanted to give them up? she thought angrily. No one. But when she did no one had told her not to.

For a moment that anger rose again, inky dark, from the pit of her stomach, dredging up bits and pieces of the past, like unabsorbed pills, their cheery candy-coloured coating long gone, just the bitterness now, still there after all these years, little pills of bitterness.

By the time the sky turned light the anger had ebbed away and she fell asleep. She tossed restlessly, her dreams full of fish in Calcutta swimming through Amit's giant television screen. The blonde weather person was telling her about fish prices and pizzas and burgers with a fake sunny smile and then she suddenly morphed into Amit, and Romola, startled, jabbed blindly at buttons on the remote control and the whole screen turned solid unblinking guilty blue. She opened her eyes and she saw the blue was the cheerful pastel of the California sky framed in the window by her bed. She sat up in bed and felt for her glasses. As she brushed her teeth she looked at herself in the mirror. There were lines around her eyes, feathery wrinkles. The skin around her neck was starting to sag. She could see the web of wrinkles there as well, like a crushed-crêpe sari. Her hair was turning grey. How thin it had become, she

9

thought. She could see her scalp through the strands. She had never smeared red sindoor on her parting, like some women she knew, as a sign of her marriage. She'd preferred a discreet smudge of red. But without even that her parting looked shockingly naked.

'What are you going to do today, Ma?' said Amit as he usually did every morning. Even though her back was to him as she waited for the water for her tea to boil, Romola knew he was not looking at her. He would be glancing through the newspaper while he absently poured cold skim milk straight from a carton into his cereal, more often than not Rice Krispies.

It was another cloudless California morning, the sky spotlessly blue, laundered by the early morning sunlight as it had been every morning since she got here a fortnight back from Calcutta. But the linoleum on the kitchen floor was cold, seeping in through the hole in her grey sock while the stainless steel kettle purred on the stove. Normally she would never have her tea until she had been to the bathroom and had a wash. But she knew better than to try and insert herself in the carefully timed and choreographed morning drill of getting ready for the day.

Soon Amit would leave the kitchen and she would hear the whine of his electric shaver, the spluttering gurgle of her daughter-in-law's coffee percolating, her grandson chattering through mouthfuls of Froot Loops. As usual.

Except today wasn't usual. Romola curled her foot against the cold floor and pulled her blue cardigan tighter around the crumpled white sari. She stared at Amit, wanting to ask him if last night had all been a dream.

'Why don't you eat some breakfast?' she asked instead. 'How can you survive on just coffee and cereal? Let me make some toast.'

She knew he wouldn't have any. He never did. But it was part of the routine, part of the play of pretending everything was normal. Soon Neel's hair would be brushed and June would have changed into her business suit. Then they would leave. But not before the last-minute instructions: 'Ma, yesterday's leftovers are in the refrigerator. Don't forget to heat them for two minutes in the microwave first. And don't put the plates with the gold rim in the microwave. If anyone calls just ask them to call again and leave a message on the answering machine. Say bye to your grandma, Neel.' The door would bang shut. She would hear the rattle of the garage door opening and then Amit's car coughing into life. She would stand at the window and watch June help Neel into the child seat in her car. She would half-raise her hand in goodbye and then drop it. No one was really looking.

And then for a moment it was silent. The quiet rose warmly throughout the house, rushing in to fill the spaces that had been so frantic and busy five minutes ago. The first time, she had just leaned back against the door letting the quiet curl around her feet and rise around her. But now she hurried across the living room to turn on the TV. It had become a habit. She stubbed her toe on a piece of Lego Neel had left lying on the floor and said 'Uff' but she did not stop till she reached the television and turned it on. The familiar face of that talk-show host with grey hair and glasses sputtered into view.

'Aah,' she sighed and sat down on the couch. The host was talking with a young woman who was obviously pregnant. That's right. She remembered – the show was going to be about young woman who were pregnant with a child by men other than their husbands.

Oh, thought Romola, I hope I did not miss the bit when they bring out the husband to confront the wife. The audience was hissing and booing at the young woman. But she did not seem to care. Romola looked at the carefully-drawn arched brows, the shocking pink halter-top and shook her head. Look at her, she thought. Six months pregnant with another man's child and look how she dresses. She quivered, though whether with righteous indignation or secret relish, she was not quite sure.

But today she felt something was missing. She felt restless and the television couldn't just sweep her away into its brightly coloured world of sordid affairs and illicit sex. She imagined herself in there and a flicker of a smile crossed her face. 'Sons reunite mothers with ex-lovers' could be the theme she thought. Wouldn't Leela in Connecticut get a shock if she turned on the TV and saw Romola there? But the moment passed and Romola realized that today she couldn't blank her head with a remote like she usually did. 'What can I do?' she said, sounding like Amit when he was a little boy on the first day of the long seemingly never-ending expanse of his summer vacation.

'Well, he'd probably know soon enough when the baby is born,' the mother-to-be on television tossed her hair. 'Coz the baby's father – he's black you know.' The audience went 'Ohhhh.' Romola realized she had her hands clapped over her mouth in shock. She had to admit she loved the television. She was amazed at how much she loved it. At first it had scared her – all those channels, and the way Amit and June restlessly surfed through them every time the advertisements came on. She hated that for she loved the ads. She liked watching the car commercials even though they made no sense most of the time. And those beautiful women with sleepy eyes and lustrous hair. But most of all she loved the food – it all seemed bigger and tastier on television – glistening and juicy in eye-popping colours. The fried chicken looked so crisp and brown, the insides so moist and tenderly white, the tomatoes rounder and redder than anything you could get at the supermarket. And those creamy dressings oozing across the screen – Romola had to sit on her hands to prevent herself from reaching out to touch it.

Back in India, she had never bothered to get one of those fancy new televisions everyone seemed to love. Amit kept urging her to buy one. But she always resisted.

'Save your money,' she would tell him. 'Who watches TV anyway? All these stupid, rubbish programmes. Anyway the moment I turn on the television, the maid comes and sits down in front of it. Then next day she brings her friend from across the street and before you know it, my living room is just filled with them. Better not turn on the television anyway.' When Avinash was alive, it had not mattered. He would sit patiently going over his investments while she carefully totalled up the day's expenses. Every now and then she would ask him something or tell him something from her day. He mostly just grunted and she knew he was not listening. But it soothed her – that he was there, working contentedly across the room from her. Now that he was gone, the quiet sometimes unnerved her. It was a dead kind of quiet, musty and dank and it filled her with dread. Sometimes in the evening, she turned the television on just to keep the quiet away from the room. It was like burning incense, she thought ruefully.

Every night she burned one incense stick in front of his framed photograph. Every three days she changed the white garland of tuberose. The picture was from fifteen years ago – he was smiling, his hair just beginning to grey. Sitting in America, she felt a pang as she thought of the picture sitting alone in the dark, shuttered house in India. She had felt like she was abandoning him but didn't know how to say it.

But Amit was right. She had indeed given Avinash a grand funeral – followed every single Hindu rite. She had not taken a paisa from Amit. This she had wanted to do for Avinash. He had had his problems but he had been, in the final reckoning, a decent man. Then after the funeral she had given up meat and fish. She knew in these modern times no one really cared whether widows ate meat or not. Amit had, in fact, asked how she would get her protein.

'I'll eat soya bean nuggets,' she said. 'I hear it's very nutritious.' And that was the end of that. She was a little surprised actually at how easily he accepted her vegetarianism. For a moment she wished he would argue with her, tell her she had done enough, that she didn't need to give up anything like her grandmothers once did. But he had moved on and was talking about closing bank accounts and going through the financial papers.

She wondered if one day she would be able to summon up the tangy taste of ilish in mustard sauce in her head even, or whether it too would fade away like everything else, unused and forgotten.

After Amit had left for America, some days she'd wake up with a craving for fish. But she didn't dare buy any. She was afraid the maid would find out and spread the gossip. After a while, she craved it less. It certainly made her daily expenses much lower. Every day she would hear the neighbours complain about how fish prices were skyrocketing. She'd tell herself she was lucky she didn't have to worry.

Of course, now she didn't have to worry about anything. June was vegetarian too, so she always had some company. Though as they had dinner she sometimes wondered if June ever looked at the chicken curry Amit and Neel ate with a trace of wistfulness.

'This chicken curry is wonderful, just like we used to have at home on Sundays,' Amit would say.

'Why don't you have another piece?' she would reply automatically.

Sometimes she'd wonder what she would do if he suddenly said 'Why don't *you* have a piece?' But he never did. Some days she wanted someone to say, 'Okay, you have followed the rules long enough. You are free now.' But no one ever did.

As she listened to the woman with the pink halter-top talk about her affair, Romola's mind was far away. She got up and restlessly paced the kitchen, looking in the refrigerator. The leftovers were covered with plastic wrap – a little dal and some green beans. She would have to make something for dinner. The ads had come on again. She stood and watched a glistening steak and a pillowy cloud of mashed potato. 'How could they eat such a big piece of raw-looking meat?' she wondered uneasily.

But then the burgers came on – dancing patties of meat, rich brown and succulent, wrapping pieces of lettuce around them like green shawls, hugging giant wheels of tomatoes and then hopping in between two toasty buns as if tucking themselves into bed. Romola stood at the refrigerator staring at the burgers with great attention. Then she put down the little Tupperware of dal and firmly shoved it to the back behind the low-fat no-fat yogurts.

'I am going to McDonald's,' said Romola to the television. 'And no one can stop me.'

She went to the bathroom, opened her make-up kit and first pencilled in her eyebrows. She took her precious Max Factor compact, dark beige, and powdered her face. She debated over the lipstick and decided a touch of lip-gloss would be enough. Finally she looked at herself. 'Presentable,' she said approvingly. 'Quite presentable.'

As the front door clicked shut behind her Romola opened her handbag in a panic convinced she had forgotten the house keys. But there they were right next to the loose change. She really needed to go through her coins and separate out the Indian coins from the American ones. There were even a couple of pennies left over from a long-ago stopover at Heathrow airport. She tugged at the door to make sure it was really shut and then glanced around her as if to see if anyone was watching.

15

It was the middle of the day and the streets were completely empty. A child's tricycle lay on its side on the neighbour's lawn and that was the only thing askew on their little street. Amit liked cul-de-sacs, he said it gave them more privacy. Romola felt if it were not for the television, the privacy would just eat her alive. The houses, neatly painted and shuttered, were like a row of toy soldiers. Each came with its own barbecue grill, a patch of trimmed lawn and a pool in the back. As she walked past them she noticed some still had the morning newspaper lying outside encased in its yellow plastic wrap. She had taken their newspaper in already. She liked to do that first thing in the morning before anyone woke up. Then after everyone had left she liked to read about the sales. There was always a sale on at Macy's.

She walked to the end of the street and then turned left towards the main road. A young man on a bicycle whizzed by. She felt his eyes on her and she suddenly felt conscious of her sari, her navy blue cardigan, her grey hair. She wrapped the cardigan even more tightly around her and started walking. She had memorized the route from all the trips she had made to the grocery store with Amit or June in the car. She knew she would have to walk three blocks on the main street till she came to the first light. Then she would have to cross the street. That light changed a bit too fast for her. She reckoned she had better wait in the middle till it changed again. The flashing little man always unnerved her with his anxious urgency.

Once she had crossed the street she would have to walk by the gas station with its three kind of gas (choices everywhere) and then head towards the shopping centre. She would walk past the supermarket, past the mounds of watermelons piled outside, a pyramid of green with one on top sliced open to show its juicy pink heart. She knew she would be tempted to go in and buy something but not today. She had deliberately left the supermarket coupons at home.

Romola felt as if she was acting in her own play. For a moment she felt a small surge of confidence. Everything seemed to be in place. The dentist next to the supermarket, the nail salon, the chiropractor and then at the end of the block the McDonald's. The golden arches looked just as welcoming as they did on TV. The crayon-bright reds and yellows, brightly coloured and cheerful, made her happy. There was a tiny play area outside with a slide. It was empty and dusty but it still made her smile; the plastic blocks looked like something little fairy-tale elves might assemble. She looked at the windows – the burgers were moist and glistening, the lettuce and tomato looked as if they had just been ripped from the fields. 99c, the signs screamed at her.

Romola stood on the street clutching her handbag. Then she glanced around her and took a deep breath and pulled at the door. Nothing happened. She stepped back, the first wrinkle of uncertainty clouding her adventure. A young boy, maybe twelve or thirteen, came running up casually behind her, pushed the door and loped inside. She smiled. The sign said quite clearly PUSH. She caught the door before it shut fully and with a movement that was both deliberate and steady, pushed it open.

Immediately she felt like she was really, finally, in America.

Everything started to spin around her but at the same time it seemed to all be moving extremely slowly. The restaurant rushed at her in a crazy plastic whirl of reds and yellows and then receded into the walls of pale muted pinks and greens. Rising up on all sides around her, Formica and plastic were bathed in cheerful music as if soaked in sunny syrup. Someone had left their tray on the table and she watched a lonely matchstick of a fry sitting in a smear of ketchup. She heard children yelling and disembodied voices calling out numbers in Mexican accents. Two women unwrapped their burgers in front of her. One had a young girl who carefully ate a fry, dipping its head into a little white container of ketchup, as thick as blood. She could smell it all – a dense low-hanging smell of deep frying that left her both nauseous and ravenous at the same time.

She looked at the confusing array of options on the menu board. Holy trinities of fries, burger and soda beckoned to her. Brahma, Vishnu, Shiva, she thought and chuckled to herself at the blasphemy. $4.89 for a combo. $5.29 for a combo. That was a lot of money, she said to herself. I thought these places were cheap. It took her a while to figure out the difference between the chicken sandwich and the chicken sandwich meal. She hovered at the edges reading everything, squinting at all her options. She wished it explained what a McDouble was.

The kitchen was a hum of activity. It moved briskly like a conveyor belt as people picked up their packets or trays of food and walked away. Giant baskets of fries emerged from vats of oil, plump and golden. Women with white gloves slapped dark brown patties on buns and smeared white mayonnaise with a rat-a-tat-tat rhythm as if they had done this all their lives. Red digital numbers flickered and changed over, always going up, up and up.

For a moment she wished June was there to help her navigate through this. But she knew they would never go there. Neither June nor Amit approved of fast food. Especially now that Amit wanted to be a chef, she thought. They tried to eat everything organic. Romola thought it was a ridiculous waste of money. She had no idea why anyone would pay more for those spindly deformed cauliflowers when they could get those big perfectly round ones for half the money. But she held her peace. She might be the cook but it was not her kitchen.

Every time they drove past a McDonald's, Romola would look longingly at the Golden Arches. They had come to Calcutta she had heard but she had never been to one. To her, they seemed like the entrance to an exotic world. Every time they went out for dinner, Amit would say, 'What do you want today, Ma? Chinese, Japanese, Thai, Mexican, or good old Indian?' and Romola would dutifully answer, 'Whatever you like, dear, I don't mind.' But she looked wistfully at the bright neon-lit procession of fast food places, forbidden and alluring, friendly sirens in the dark night – Taco Bell and Burger King and Pizza Hut. But McDonald's, she knew, was the king of them all. Neel was her only ally in these dinner expeditions. 'I want burgers, Mom,' he might say sometimes but he was easily overruled. Romola once thought of adding her vote to his but was afraid she'd be accused of spoiling her grandson with junk food. Once they went to a cafe that served gourmet burgers. Romola wondered what one might taste like. 'Oh, they are just really bad for you, and anyway it's beef,' said Amit as he ordered a skinless chicken sandwich for himself. Romola followed June's lead and got a spinach salad. She felt like a cow, she thought crossly, when it arrived, a heap of green leaves with little specks of dark-red cranberries and crunchy walnuts. What was this American obsession with chomping leaves?

Now she looked nervously into her bag to make sure she still had the money and walked up to the counter. The woman behind the counter could not have been more than eighteen years old. Romola noticed the big hoops in her ears, the perfectly trimmed bangs of her hair, the swatch of blue eye shadow.

'Can I help you?' Her bored voice sounded anything but helpful.

Romola nodded and then took the plunge. She pointed at a burger on the menu but could not say anything. At the last moment she had thought she would just get some fries or maybe the chicken sandwich. But then she felt that now she was here she had to have a burger. She knew it was beef and it would probably be revolting but she had to have it. It was her only chance.

'A burger – that one,' she pointed at the menu.

'With cheese or without?' said the girl as if reading from a script.

Romola shook her head. The girl looked at her quizzically and then went on to her next line.

'The meal or just the sandwich?'

'Just the sandwich.' Romola had a little more confidence in her voice now. This might just work, she thought.

'Will that be all?'

Romola nodded.

'Forheretogo?' said the girl.

Romola stared at her baffled. This was not a line she knew, there was nothing like that in the script she had carefully rehearsed in her head.

'Forheretogo?' said the girl again. Romola suddenly became aware of other people in the restaurant. She craned forward nervously clutching her half-open bag. The girl looked at her, her plucked eyebrow arched in a question mark. Romola felt her confidence starting to drain away. She felt like she had when she had first boarded an international flight by herself. She'd been convinced she had got on the wrong flight and was on her way to Australia instead of America. The questions and fears and worries bubbled in her stomach but dried in her throat. She shook her head and stepped back.

The girl was still looking at her. So was the man standing next to her.

'Yes,' she said hoping that was the right answer.

'Forheretogo?' said the girl again as if demanding a secret password and Romola lost her nerve. Grabbing the handbag to her chest, she suddenly turned around and started walking as fast as she could towards the door. The girl said something else behind her back but she refused to turn around and face that counter again. She walked past the trash can, its flap swinging as someone emptied their tray in it. She walked past the children with their ketchup-stained faces. She waited for someone to grab her and turn her around and frogmarch her back to the counter but no one seemed to even notice that she was there any more. Her little order had sunk without a trace like a stone in the pond and life went on with not even a ripple to show for its brief, flickering existence.

Before she knew it, she was out of McDonald's, standing in the sunshine on the street, her heart pounding. She put her hand against the wall and looked at the giant picture of the burger and fries and felt an overwhelming sense of failure sucking her down. She wished her maid was here so she could give her ten dollars and say, 'Go get me a burger with some fries. Mind you, make sure they are fresh and hot.' She stood there staring at the playground and the dusty plants that lined it. The clown's painted grin mocked her.

A young boy and his father came out of McDonald's behind her. She stared at the paper bag they held so casually in their hands and wondered what was in it.

As she wandered out into the parking lot a car beeped at her, making her jump. A young couple gestured at her to get out of the way. She stepped back and watched them go towards a sign marked 'DRIVE-THRU'. She could see another menu board there and she walked up to it and started reading again. She stood there, smelling exhaust fumes and drinking in the dizzying array of choices. A truck drove up and stopped. A disembodied voice said, 'Can I take your order please?'

The man in the truck looked liked he worked in construction. She could see white paint spattered all over his baseball cap and shirt. 'Number four,' he said confidently. And then added, 'Could you make that large fries please?'

'Will that be all?' said the voice.

He grunted yes.

The voice repeated back the order and gave him the total. No one said that funny 'Forheretogo'. The truck took off, leaving Romola at the sign. She slowly started moving along the building to see where the food came out. She could hear the bustle of the kitchen from outside, the clamour of voices, the order numbers and the canned music. As she walked to the counter she saw another car pull up. The driver reached out, money changed hands and he picked up his food and left. Romola thought this was a marvellous invention. You did not even have to step out of your car any more. She wished she had a car and could just drive up and drive away with a bag of burgers.

As she came up to the window she suddenly noticed a bag sitting there waiting for the next driver. She glanced back. The car was still parked in front of the menu. The driver seemed to be arguing with his passenger. A child in the back was crying. The packet sat there ready to be picked up. She couldn't see anyone at the counter. Romola had no idea how it happened but as she reached the counter, her hand just crept out on its own. It didn't even feel like her own hand – it was as if she suddenly grew an extra arm, a grabbing arm that snuck out from under her sari, a prehensile limb designed to seize orphaned paper packets. Before she knew it she had grabbed the bag. She thought she heard someone go 'Hey' but she didn't even look back. Clutching the paper bag in one hand, her handbag under her arm, she took off down the street.

She had no idea she could move so fast. She had not run like this in years. Not since they were going to Darjeeling for the holidays and were late for the train. Without looking back she just ducked between two stores and ran past dumpsters, her heart heaving, her legs propelled by pure adrenalin. She was sure the car that had ordered the food was going to mow her down, that police cars would pull up, sirens screaming. She pushed a small child out of her way as she ran on. She zig-zagged without paying any attention to where she was going. Finally when she felt her heart was about to burst she stopped. There was a little park in front of her.

The street looked not unlike the one they lived on. The giant rose bush near the gate of one house littered the sidewalk with blushing pink petals. An American flag drooped in the still afternoon. There was a house for sale across the street. She looked at the street sign. Magnolia Drive it said. She had no idea where that was. But she kept moving.

She entered the park. A lady walking her dog looked at her strangely. Though she was not running any more, Romola realized she must be quite a sight. Her grey hair was dishevelled and coming undone. She could feel rivulets of sweat running down her face and back, trickling down her blouse. Her sari was sticking to her as if it was the middle of a Calcutta summer day. She stopped at a bench under a tree to catch her breath. The McDonald's paper bag still dangled from her hands. She could see the marks of her nails where she had dug into the paper as she ran. A dark greasy stain was spreading along the side like a birthmark.

All she wanted now was a drink of water. But she opened the bag and stared at what was inside. The fries had fallen out of their little packet, now limp and broken-necked. She extracted the burger from its paper wrapping. Squished in her hand, it seemed much smaller and flatter than it looked on television. A smudge of bloody ketchup was oozing from one side and a square of plasticky yellow cheese was coming out the other. The lettuce was falling out as well, protruding from under the bun like a stiff green ruff. She raised the burger to her face and smelled it.

For a while she just sat there quietly inhaling – the scent of burger and fries mixing with the bruised smell of cut grass.

Then she closed her eyes and bit into the burger. She felt nausea rising up but she couldn't tell if it was the beef or all that running. She wondered where she was and how she would ever find her way back home. A bead of ketchup dribbled down from the burger, hovered for a second like a fat red fly and landed thickly on her sari. But for now, Romola realized she did not care.

II

Ring of Spices

WHEN ROMOLA was seven years old her aunt Ila visited from England. She brought her boxes of delicious chocolates filled with strawberries and hazelnuts and pretty dresses trimmed with lace. But what Romola loved best was to carefully open her Ila-pishi's suitcase and breathe in the fragrance of her clothes and cosmetics.

'Lavender, lilac, rosemary,' she would whisper to herself making a daisy-chain of flowers she had never seen.

It was a scorchingly hot summer, even by Calcutta standards. In the afternoons her aunt would draw the blinds and take a nap. Romola would tiptoe into the dark room and carefully open the suitcase. Then she would bury her head in the soft cottons and smooth silks and breathe deeply and surreptitiously. It was like a little corner of England trapped in there. She would feel herself falling through it and leaving the hot parched Calcutta streets and the relentlessly blue Indian skies far behind. It smelled cool and fresh and shaded, so unlike the ripe kitchen smells that clung to her mother's sari – turmeric and sweat and stale talcum powder.

'Foxglove, primrose, daffodil.'

Crouched near the suitcase like a little mouse, Romola wished she could pack herself in with the soft nightgowns and synthetic saris. She imagined waking up and finding she was in England.

She was now walking down a little cobbled street past houses like the picture on her tin of biscuits. She was going home to have scones and strawberries and cream. Her house had a pointed tiled roof and a chimney. And ivy on the walls, or was it honeysuckle?

'Honeysuckle, bluebells, forget-me-not.'

'Romola!' her mother's shrill voice could be heard from downstairs 'Where is that girl?'

'Romola, you haven't finished your rice. Come now or the cat will get it.'

'Romola, check to see the door is closed.'

'Romola, have you done your homework?'

Romola decided that when she grew up she would go to England.

Avinash was not quite from England. He was from Illinois. Romola knew of only one city in Illinois – Chicago – but he lived far away from it in some small university town called Carbondale in the southern end of the state where he was just finishing his PhD in Economics or something like that. It all sounded very difficult and dull to Romola. She liked to read Wordsworth and Keats and Jibanananda Das. But everyone said Avinash was a good match for her. He was serious, academic and sober. Romola's aunt's in-laws lived next door to Avinash's family. Romola's aunt played matchmaker. Avinash's mother had said she was determined to get her son married this time when he visited from America. They wanted a simple, quick wedding before he had to go back. 'You can't do better,' Romola's aunt told her mother. 'They don't want any dowry and she will go to America. And the family is very cultured. Absolutely top class. His mother is recently widowed and anxious to see him settled.'

'My son', said Avinash's mother to Romola's over a cup of tea, 'has always been the top boy in his class. "A model student" his principal called him. Never one to wander the streets like these other roadside Romeos. That was why I never had the slightest fear sending him to America. You know, Mrs Dutt, it's all about upbringing and family. If you bring him up right, then why should you be worried, *na*?'

Romola's mother nodded. She was having a hard time getting a word in edgeways but the boy looked good on paper. She glanced at Romola who was sitting demurely in a pale pink sari ('something that will bring out the colour in your cheeks without being too flashy,' her mother had said). Romola's face betrayed nothing.

'Everyone told me,' continued Avinash's mother, 'see, one day he'll call and announce he wants to marry some American girl. But I said, "I trust my Avi. He would not break his mother's heart." Arrey, he is my only son. He knows his duty. But I had faith and look at him now. Do you know he has had papers published in important journals? Why, my friend Sulata said to me, "Mark my words if your Avi does not get the Nobel Prize one day."'

In the pause that ensued as all assembled digested this piece of information, Romola's mother jumped in. 'So how long before he finishes that PhD?'

'Very soon,' said his mother defensively, 'I've been telling him for so long now – get married, get married. But he said, "First I must finish my master's." Then it was, "Oh I must complete my PhD and get a job, Ma. How will I have a family on a student's income?" So responsible, *na*? But then after his father passed away so suddenly, a massive heart attack, I said, "Enough Avi. Now I have to see you settle down with a good girl. Then only can I shut my eyes in peace." He said, "But I am not done with my studies yet," and I said "Bas. I will not listen any more to your excuses."

'Beautiful girls grow on trees for boys in America,' she continued, glancing at Romola who looked back at her expressionlessly. 'But good family and education are what we really value. Avi's father was a renowned professor, you know – he wrote three books. And I hear your Romola has an MA in English Literature.'

Romola smiled and inclined her head.

After Avinash's mother left, Romola said, 'I have to go lie down with an eau-de-cologne handkerchief on my forehead. That woman gave me a splitting headache with her non-stop bokbok.'

'Oh, but mothers are like that about only sons,' said her mother. 'Anyway, you are lucky. You won't even have to live with her. You'll just go to America with Avinash.'

By the standards of the time Avinash and Romola had a bit of a courtship. Avinash took Romola out for dinner once. He was a slight man with thinning hair and owlish glasses. He smelt faintly of some lemony aftershave. They did not have much in common. She knew nothing about economics; he had long forgotten his Wordsworth. They concentrated instead on the food and discussed the merits of the tandoori chicken. When they exhausted that topic, they ate in silence listening to the ebb and flow of conversation at the tables around them.

'What was he like?' asked her mother.

'All right, I suppose,' she answered.

At the time the only man, outside of cousins, she'd ever been out with was a young man she'd met through her friend Leela. He was a handsome man with a nose as straight as a knife-edge and thick waves of black hair. When she walked into a restaurant with him she noticed young women at nearby tables look at him out of the corners of their eyes. She had enjoyed that. But he wanted to be an actor and Romola knew that wasn't going anywhere. Her mother had tolerated him as a friend but she would never allow an actor as a son-in-law. Though she had not found much in common with

Avinash she had not found anything objectionable either. At least he did not wear those loud colourful shirts with big flowers that she had seen American tourists wear.

Only once she said, almost wistfully, 'You know I really wanted to go to England.'

Her uncle laughed and said, 'Romola, Wordsworth's England is long dead. In your grandfather's time people would go to England, for then England still had power and glory. Now it is truly becoming a nation of shopkeepers. And most of the shopkeepers are Indian anyway. You are lucky, you are going to the richest country in the world.'

'And such a brilliant husband,' added her mother.

'And so courteous and well-mannered,' chipped in her aunt. 'I hope my daughter is as lucky as you.'

Romola shrugged and said nothing. She was not sure if flowers like lavender and primrose grew in America. Perhaps, she thought, she'd have a small garden there and she could grow them.

At the wedding she glanced at Avinash as they went around the fire seven times. His gaze seemed far away, his brow furrowed in thought. She wondered what he was thinking. Was he imagining his life in America and worrying how she would fit in there? She realized they had talked about his interests and her interests but nothing about their lives together. She didn't know what kind of house he lived in. Did he even want to get married? What had he told his mother when he had come back from dinner? That she was 'all right' as well?

With the white topor on his head like an ornate dunce cap, little dots of sandalwood paste on his forehead, she thought he looked slightly ridiculous. She could see beads of sweat sparkling on his brow. She debated offering him the neatly folded handkerchief she had tucked into the fold of her red-and-gold sari, just in case her own make-up started to run. But in the end she did nothing at all, quietly walking around the fire, her eyes smarting from the crackling smoke, the priest's chants buzzing around her. When she lifted her head to allow him to put the garland around her neck, her aunts squealed with excitement.

This is supposed to be the most important moment in my life, thought Romola smelling the flowers, trying to imprint the scene in her memory. The smell of wet rajanigandha stayed with her all night, a sickly smudge of perfume still clinging to her long after they had removed the heavy garlands from around their necks.

'Now put that garland around your husband's neck,' said the priest in her ear. As Romola reached up, Avinash looked at her as if he was seeing her for the first time. He smiled slightly but the tinge of that smile dried up before it reached his eyes. He looks lost, thought Romola, suddenly feeling tender, an anxious, lost boy.

Later that night Romola saw herself reflected in a mirror on the bedroom wall and stopped, startled. She was married. The parting in her hair was filled with red sindoor, which Avinash ('my husband') had poured into her hair with unsteady hands. Specks of the red powder had landed on her nose and cheeks, dusting them, soft as pollen. Their bed was decorated with a curtain of white rajanigandha and velvety red roses. She pushed the strands aside to sit down, still in the heavy wedding sari. There were rose petals scattered on the new white sheets – like specks of blood. 'You must be tired,' said Avinash without really looking at her. 'Tonight let's just sleep.' Romola was a little relieved. She was tired and nervousness knotted her stomach. As she lay down she worried about how she would be able to sleep listening to him breathing beside her. Did he snore? she fretted right before she fell asleep.

The week after the wedding was a blur of dinners and relatives. Romola spent most of her time at her mother's, getting ready to leave for America while Avinash stayed at his. Romola was amazed at how easily she left India behind. Her mother and aunt wept copiously at the airport while her uncle kept offering everyone cups of tea. But Romola was calm as if she was an actor in someone else's script.

As the airplane left the airport she looked out of the window at the lights of Calcutta growing smaller and smaller. She had a sense of her past, her ties, her home all falling away behind her like an unravelling sari. Perhaps, she thought, sipping her Coca-Cola, I was not meant to be Indian at all. She glanced over at Avinash, seated next to her, absorbed in the latest issue of *Time*. This was really the first time she had been alone with him since the wedding night – if one could be alone in an airplane filled with strangers. Sometimes she hardly felt married at all. He glanced up at her and, finding himself caught in her gaze, looked away guiltily. Then he said quietly, 'How do you imagine America?'

'America – I don't know,' she said hesitantly. 'Big buildings, fast cars, movies.'

'Washing machines,' she added as an afterthought. 'Lawn-mowers, ovens.' Then she thought for a while and said with a smile, 'My aunt had a magazine about how to entertain in America. They had a recipe for a turkey. I always wondered what it might taste like. Have you ever eaten a turkey?'

'Yes, it's not that exciting,' he replied. Then he added, 'You never thought of America as freedom?'

'Freedom?' she was perplexed. 'No, not really.' Then she smiled slightly and said, 'Maybe it was for you when you went there as a student. But I am going there as your wife.'

'That's true,' he replied.

'Are you afraid that now that I am going with you, you will lose your freedom?' she asked half-teasingly.

'Who is really free anyway?' he answered without looking at her and returned to the magazine. She opened her mouth to speak but he seemed to have drawn curtains around himself.

Romola hated America from the moment she stepped off that plane. At the immigration counter, she couldn't understand a thing the man in the uniform said. She knew it was English but the words seemed foreign, tangled together like a ball of wool. The accents were jarring – they had none of the clean crispness of the BBC World Service programmes she so loved and listened to on her father's prized short-wave radio. She stared at the man, baffled, and then looked to Avinash for help.

'It's okay,' said Avinash to the man. 'This is my wife's first time in the US. She is still getting used to things. We just got married.' He was suddenly in charge, thought Romola. The nervous lost boy in the wedding dhoti was gone, sloughed off in Calcutta.

'Congratulations,' said the immigration man, his teeth white against his bristly black moustache. 'Welcome to America.'

Romola thought she should say something. But instead she just nodded and quickly looked away.

Avinash's house was nothing like the quaint cottages with their filigree of honeysuckle she remembered from the biscuit tins. He lived in a non-descript one-bedroom apartment in a squat blue-grey concrete block of identical buildings each with a stubbly patch of green lawn in front. For some reason it was called Nile Apartments though Romola could detect nothing Egyptian about it. There was a child's bicycle lying on the lawn in front of his apartment and old newspapers near the front door, the newsprint discoloured into a brittle yellow. As they walked up the stairs she could hear the television in the apartment below going at full blast. She could smell something cooking, something fried. For a moment she felt a twinge of hunger and wondered what they would eat for dinner. Would he expect her to cook? Did he have things like rice and cumin and coriander in his kitchen?

When Avinash turned the key in the lock and pushed the door open her heart sank. The apartment smelled of trapped air and stale food. 'I should have left a window open,' he said apologetically. Romola said nothing. On a dining table she could see an old overripe banana in a fruit basket, its yellow skin blotched with black leopard spots. She could almost taste that banana from the door – its rich and cloying smell pooling around her stickily. She suddenly lost her appetite. 'Let's get some pizza,' said Avinash. 'Would you like that?' She just nodded.

That night, as they lay in bed jet-lagged and trying to sleep, Avinash turned to her and tentatively stroked her arm. When he raised his face to kiss her, Romola could smell the bath soap on him. Lime, she thought. He smelled cool. He kissed her on the lips, his eyes closed. Her heart thudded wildly. For a moment she longed to be back in her bedroom in Calcutta. She wanted the hum of traffic around her, the sudden blare of horns, the voices of people walking on the street at all hours of the day, snatches of conversation trailing through the air, the yapping dogs, the cheerfully noisy night. Here the night felt almost naked in its silence, filling the room with just the harsh sound of his breath and the drumbeat of her heart. She heard him curse softly as he fumbled with the drawstring of his pyjamas. She felt his hands pulling at the pale blue nightdress her aunt had bought her from New Market a week before the wedding.

Her friend Leela who had got married two years before had told her the first time would hurt. But she hadn't realized it would be so short. Avinash climbed on top of her, still wearing his nightshirt, though she could feel the bare skin of his legs on her. His fingers digging into her arms, he tried to position himself between her legs. When he finally managed to get

33

inside her she gasped at the sudden tearing pain, biting her tongue, tasting the salt of her blood, afraid that any sound would carry through the silent night, startling the neighbours. But almost before she could get used to the feeling of Avinash inside her, he was done. She realized that his eyes had been shut throughout. She wondered if she should have closed her eyes as well. He lay on her limply as if all the air had drained out of him and then patted her gently on the cheek. 'Sorry,' he mumbled. 'Are you okay?' It was the first thing he had said in bed.

'I am okay,' she said. 'But I need to clean up.'

In the bathroom she stood at the sink and gingerly lifted up her nightdress to touch herself between her legs. She didn't want to look. She just wanted to stand under the shower and let everything wash away.

When she came back he was already asleep. She stood at the window staring out at the patches of grass outside. The child's bicycle still lay on its side, like a capsized ship. Across the lawn one of the apartments still had the light on. She could see the blue-grey flicker of a television set. She wanted to throw open the window and lean out into the night and breathe deeply. What kind of flowers bloomed here at night? What did an American night smell of, she wondered. But she was afraid she'd wake Avinash. He slept curled up on one side of the bed, his arm sprawled across the pillow where she had been. She looked at his face splashed with the moonlight and thought to herself, 'He is quite pleasant-looking, really. Tomorrow it will be better. Desire will come. Desire will grow.'

She wondered what time it was in India. Lunchtime, probably. She closed her eyes and imagined her mother serving lunch. She could almost smell the rice. She carefully clutched that smell to her, like an amulet, as she crept back into bed.

By the time she woke in the morning he was already up

and she could hear the hiss of the shower. 'Good morning,' he said with a smile when he came out towelling his hair. 'Welcome to America.'

But Romola never quite felt welcome. The freeways with their whizzing cars and many lanes terrified her. She could not imagine ever being able to drive on them. Yet Avinash had told her that if you did not know how to drive here you were a prisoner. She was confused by all the machines she needed to handle and all the buttons she had to press to do anything. The first time she took the laundry down to the basement of their building she just turned around and left, unable to decipher the hieroglyphics of all those settings on the washing machine. But most of all she missed having people to talk to.

Two days after they came to America, Avinash returned to school. Research was busy he told her. He had lots of catching up to do. 'Don't wait for me,' he said when he left in the morning. Soon he spent long hours at school, sometimes coming home after she had gone to bed. She would lie in the dark hearing the purr of the microwave as he warmed his dinner. As a little girl she remembered her mother always waited for her father to come home before she ate. But Romola invariably got a headache if she let herself go hungry too long. She would leave his dinner on the table in front of the jar of mango pickles she had found in the international section of the grocery store. She would lie in bed and try and figure out what he was eating.

'He must be finished with the dal, he is probably on the chicken now.' She would hear him open the refrigerator as he took out some Coke. They needed to get more Coke and detergent and something else. She knitted her brows and tried to remember what. Soon she knew she would hear the tap running as he rinsed the dishes and then the clank as he loaded them into the old green dishwasher. That was when she closed her eyes and turned on her side, away from his half of the bed. She wanted him to reach out to her, to apologize, to kiss her, to make her turn around and face him. But he did not seem to mind that she had gone to bed. She would feel the bed sag as he climbed on to it. Then the sharp minty smell of toothpaste. In a little while she would hear his gentle easy breathing and she would lie awake angry, making grocery lists in her head.

Within one month she felt she had been in America for ever, the routine of their lives already engraved. All week he worked late. On Saturdays they would go grocery shopping. Sometimes they would go to a film at the theatre near the university. Afterwards they would stop at an Italian place near campus. He would drink one beer. She would have a Coke with her pasta. Sometimes upon his encouragement she'd try a glass of wine even though she did not much like the taste. When they came home they would have sex. Now she shut her eyes as well. Once, the face of the actor she had once gone out with slipped into her head as Avinash panted over her. It was so vivid she opened her eyes with a start almost convinced Avinash could see it too, that it hung between them like a picture projected on her face. But Avinash's eyes were still closed.

She thought once of writing to her mother, asking her whether she needed to do something. Who was supposed to tell her these things? But instead she wrote long letters about the weather, about meals she was cooking, about how the international store didn't stock any panchphoran spices though it had most of everything else she needed.

Soon Romola too had her own rituals. After Avinash left for school she washed the cereal bowls. She examined the refrigerator and made a grocery list. She made lunch for herself always making a little extra in case Avinash stopped by unexpectedly to eat.

Around two o'clock every day she ran down to check the

mail. She had even come to know the postman. He always said, 'Hi, how's it going?' But usually all she got were catalogues from department stores and letters addressed to Current Resident. She would spend the afternoon reading about furniture sales and instalment plans to buy home entertainment systems. Apart from that all they seemed to get were bills and coupons from pizza joints.

She had written two letters home but had not got anything back. Letters from India could take three weeks, sometimes longer, Avinash told her, if they didn't get lost.

It was over a month after they had arrived when she got her first letter from India. It had been raining all day – a fine dispiriting drizzle. It was a Saturday but Avinash had needed to go to school to grade papers. She had wanted to walk down to the library but was stuck indoors, since Avinash had taken their umbrella to his office. Frustrated, she had spent the whole day rearranging her spices. She had poured them into individual little spice jars and then labelled the jars in her best handwriting. For a while she debated whether to write the Bengali names or the English ones – *holud*, *jeerey* and *dhoney* or turmeric, cumin, coriander? She finally decided on 'Turmeric' 'Cumin' 'Coriander'. But she did not know the word for *methi* so she left it blank. She smelled her hands – and suddenly remembered her mother cooking and then wiping her hands on her sari. Her old saris always had turmeric stains.

Seeing the little postal truck pull out of the driveway Romola wiped her hands on a paper towel and ran downstairs to get the mail. And there it was, a neat rectangular envelope with a whole line of crookedly stuck postage stamps on it – her first bona fide letter from India. The familiar bald head of Gandhi and the smudged postmark made her heart twist. She didn't wait to recognize the handwriting and there was no return address on the envelope. She raced up to the apartment two steps at a time, smiling, tossed the rest of the mail on the dining table, pulled out the Kashmiri letter-cutter her friend Leena had given her and slit open the envelope. There were two sheets in there – ruled sheets torn from a writing pad.

Dear Avinash,

Oh, she thought, it's for him. Maybe it's his mother. But she kept reading, greedy for news from home.

Your wedding invitation came in the mail the other day. Not even a handwritten note with it. I guess I should say congratulations and send you felicitations for a long and happy married life as they do in those wedding telegrams. But pardon me if I am unable to do that. I wonder though why you never bothered to call or let me know. After all, after everything we shared, didn't you owe me at least that much?

My mother said your father passed away suddenly. My condolences. Perhaps it was all too much for you. I don't know. I was hoping somehow that you would be waiting for me in America. Remember we told each other that all we needed to do was find our own way there and then no one could stop us from doing what we wanted.

I wanted to surprise you by telling you I had finally secured admission to graduate school in the United States. I guess the surprise ended up being mine, getting your wedding invitation. I was hoping that once we were there away from the prying eyes of families we'd be able to live the life we dreamed about during those evenings in Calcutta.

Now it tastes like dust in my mouth. I feel betrayed that you couldn't be stronger. Couldn't you have waited longer? Or did you feel, since whatever we had was a secret anyway, we could just carry on as before? Hadn't we promised to be together, the world be damned? Did you think it was just a phase we'd outgrow like children do with their clothes?

I never asked you to tell the world. I just hoped you might wait for me. I wrote and rewrote this letter three times wondering whether I'd ever send it. I don't really expect you to reply.

Yours
Sumit

Sumit, she read the name over and over again. What kind of name was that? No one had ever mentioned a Sumit to her. That's a man's name, she told herself. Sumita, maybe it was meant to be Sumita. But what kind of letter was this? Who was this Sumit? What was he talking about? It's some kind of silly mistake, she thought. It's some kind of joke. Avinash will explain it all.

Outside the rain had stopped. The sun was finally breaking through. Romola sat at the dining table feeling her heart slowly turn cold inside her. She held the letter up to her nose as if trying to breathe in the Calcutta air trapped inside it, as if she could unread the words. In her head she retraced her steps down the stairs, down to the mailbox. In her mind's eye, she saw herself again open the mailbox, look at the pizza coupons, leaf through the furniture sale catalogues and come upon the letter from India. This time she didn't open the letter. This time she saw Avinash's name on it and she just laid it down on his pile of mail. If only she didn't open it, everything could stay the same. Today was Saturday. Today they would have pizza and watch a film. Avinash had said *Breakfast at Tiffany's* was playing. She had wanted to see that. She really had.

She put the letter down with shaking hands. Then she picked up the pages and turned them around as if she could rearrange the words to say something else. Four times she lifted the receiver to call Avinash. Four times she put it down.

'You are lucky,' her mother had told her the night before she got married. 'You don't have to worry about making your mother-in-law happy, like we did. You can just honeymoon with your husband like a modern couple. You can do what you want – there's no one looking over your shoulder.'

Romola wondered if she was in India what she would have done. Would she have gone home and talked to her mother? Would she have called her cousins? Would they know what to do? Could they fix him? Could they teach her how? Her thoughts rattled inside her head like a window shutter banging in a storm. 'I need to be calm,' she told herself. 'I need to think.'

She had wanted things. She had wanted to travel in America with her husband. She had wanted an album of photographs – of her in front of the Statue of Liberty or the Golden Gate Bridge.

She sat and stared at the neatly arranged spices and tried to remember the English for methi. Maybe she should just write 'Methi'. She wondered what would happen to her now. How much did a one-way fare to India cost? She sat and watched one television programme after another, letting the images drip meaninglessly in front of her. When Avinash came home she was already in bed.

'It's only seven-thirty,' he said. 'Are you angry? I am sorry, I got stuck. We can still make the late show.'

She didn't answer him. Her eyes were wide open memorizing the wall beside the bed, tracing every crack, every bubble in the paint, etching it into her head – a relief map of her American life. She didn't trust herself to speak.

'Are you all right?' Avinash asked anxiously.

She lay curled up on her side, her fists clenched in her mouth to prevent herself from screaming. She buried her face in the pillow and tried to summon up the old familiar smells of home.

'Turmeric, coriander, cumin,' she whispered fiercely as if in exorcism.

But all she could smell was the happy lemon-lime spring-fresh smell of freshly laundered sheets. She buried her face deeper, trying desperately to go home.

She felt him approaching the bed.

Mustard, poppyseed, *methi*. She was drawing a ring of spices to protect herself.

She felt his hand on her forehead – cold and clammy. She flinched, shrinking away from his touch. 'I'm sorry,' he mumbled, his voice low. 'What's wrong? Can I get you something?'

Turmeric, coriander, *methi*.

Avinash's hand was still stroking her forehead. Her nails dug into her palms as she tried to stop herself from swatting his hand away like a fly, a fly on a rotting ripe banana. Flies, yes, flies buzzing around her head.

Turmeric, coriander, *methi*.

Her mother in the kitchen...

Her father reading the newspaper...

Old Sushila chopping the fish...

Turmeric, dhoney, methi...

Holud, dhoney, methi...

III

The Games Boys Play

'DO YOU want sugar with your tea?' asked Sumit's mother from the kitchen.

'Of course I do, Ma,' said Sumit, looking up from the newspaper. 'I always take two teaspoons of sugar with my tea. Have you forgotten everything?'

'Well, who knows what eight years in America have done to you. From what I read, over there everything is low-this, low-that, no sugar, no fat. You look skinnier than ever, anyway. Does the food there have any taste at all?' She emerged from the kitchen with a cup of tea and set it down in front of him. 'Tell me,' she ruffled his hair. 'Does it feel good to be back?'

He smiled and said, 'Of course it does. It feels good to see you and all my aunts and uncles and friends.'

'Speaking of friends, have you called Avinash yet?'

'No.'

'Aren't you going to?'

'Ma, I just got here last night. I'll call him, I'll call him. I am here to see you. Are you already shipping me off to do the rounds?'

'No need to get upset. Before he went to America the two of you practically spent twenty-four hours together. And his mother tells me after you went to America you hardly ever wrote.'

'I never was much of a letter writer.'

'Still – at least you could have written something when I told you that he'd had a son.'

'I meant to buy a card.'

'Hmmph. Card. As if a card with your name scribbled hurriedly underneath can say anything except you are too lazy to write a letter. Anyway, why don't you go to his house today?'

'Today?' he said uncertainly, stirring his tea.

'Why not? It will be a big surprise for him.'

'Ma, let me settle down. I am going to be here for one month. There is plenty of time. I haven't even unpacked. I'm not ready.'

'Ready? What nonsense. What's to be ready? Well, actually, I met his mother in the market and I said you'd go over. And she said she wouldn't tell Avinash and it would be a great surprise. Besides, he's going away on tour on Wednesday.'

Sumit put down his cup, looked at his mother and said, 'So you've already planned it all for me, anyway.'

'Well if I didn't, you'd be meeting him for two minutes on your way to the airport.'

Sumit seemed about to say something but thought better of it. Putting down the newspaper he said resignedly, 'And what time have you told Avinash's mother I would be there for this surprise visit?'

'Oh, around six, six-thirty. I have to go to my Ladies' Circle then. And I thought I could drop you off on the way there. The driver will be here at five-thirty. Now drink your tea before it gets cold. What do you want to have for dinner?'

'Ma, I'm not even finished with breakfast,' laughed Sumit.

Avinash's house still looked the same except that it had been a dirty cream the last time he had seen it. Now it was yellow, its sun-bleached green shutters streaked with chalky white crow droppings. The wizened old neem tree in front of the house was still there, gasping for breath, as the shops all around seemed to crowd in on it. Sumit threaded past the gossiping maids and a loitering cow and rang the doorbell. A dog napping on the front step cocked its head and regarded him solemnly. There was no answer. One of the maids sitting on the porch, in a flowery synthetic sari, stopped in mid-story to inspect him. He pressed the doorbell again. Hard. He heard shuffling feet and an old grumbling voice.

'Oof-oh. Coming, coming, I'm not deaf. Can't you wait a minute? What is it now? Ringing the bell like the world is on fire.'

The door opened an inch and a wrinkled face peered out suspiciously.

'What is it? Whom do you want?' it demanded.

'Oh, Mangala-di – how are you?' answered Sumit.

Mangala adjusted her thick glasses and stared at Sumit. Then her jaw dropped. 'Oh my goodness. If it is not our little Sumit. After all these years. I thought this old woman would never see you again. Bouma, look who's here.' With that she started sniffling. By the time Avinash's mother emerged, Mangala's eyes were streaming with tears as she stroked Sumit's arm while the gaggle of maid-servants on the porch gaped at them, the thread of their gossip lost in the far more intriguing drama unfolding before them. Sumit knew that soon after he left Calcutta, Avinash's father had suddenly died of a heart attack. Even so, seeing his friend's mother in a widow's plain white sari made him start. Like his own mother, her hair was more silver than black and she seemed to have physically shrunk. He had once been a little scared of her, the way she had ruled the household with an iron ladle. Now she seemed small, an old woman, faded and crumpled, crumbling into the old house itself. She smiled at him. A couple of teeth were missing.

'If it is not Mr America-returned,' said Avinash's mother. 'Do you still remember us ordinary people?'

'Oh, what are you saying, Mashi?' an embarrassed Sumit reached out to touch her feet in a sign of respect. 'How could I forget you? You are like my own family.'

'Let it be, let it be. You are just back from America. No more of these old-fashioned customs.' But she did not quite stop him.

'How tall he has grown,' sighed Mangala, wiping her eyes. 'Like a tree.'

'Mangala-di,' protested Sumit, 'I was an adult when I left. I don't think I grew any taller.'

'No, you can't fool your old Mangala-di. Then you were a boy. Now you are a man.'

'So, where is the wedding invitation?' Avinash's mother stretched out her hand.

'Wedding invitation?'

'Oh my goodness, don't you think it's about time? What are you waiting for – till my last few teeth fall out? And think of your poor mother.'

Sumit smiled sheepishly and changed the subject. 'Where is Avinash?'

'He just got back from the office and is changing. Come and sit down in the living room. Mangala, go tell Avinash to come down. But don't tell him who is here. And ask him to bring Amit too.'

Time seemed to have stopped in the living room. The old cuckoo clock that Avinash's father had brought back from a trip to Europe was still there. The sofas still had the hideous bottle-green vinyl-like covering, now a bit shinier and balder with age. In the corner stood the dark wooden display case jammed with Avinash's trophies and medals and little costume dolls from all over the world, most of them still cocooned in plastic wraps to protect them from the dust – diminutive Swedish Heidis with stiff flaxen pigtails crammed next to Rajasthani maidens with armfuls of silver bangles and swirling red skirts, their plastic bubbles turning grimy with age. A vase with plastic pink flowers tried to brighten up one corner of the room next to the telephone, with a burst of artificial cheer. Little half curtains with hand-embroidered flowers hung on the shuttered windows. Those were new. Sumit wondered if Avinash's wife had made them. There was a side table with copies of *India Today* magazines, and the room had a new coat of paint – a rather bilious salmon. The only other thing that was new in the room was a big portrait of Avinash's father looking very stern and professorial on the wall next to the cuckoo clock. It had a garland around it, the white flowers slightly wilting, the petals browning at the edges.

Noticing him glance at it, Avinash's mother said, 'It was so sudden. He had just come back from college. I was in the kitchen getting dinner ready. He said, "I'm not feeling so well. I think I'll go and lie down for a bit." And the next thing I knew Mangala was screaming, "Bouma, Dada-babu has fallen down."' She sighed and then said, 'Massive heart attack' with the air of a judge handing down a sentence. 'Two days in intensive care but it was no use.' She flung open a window and repeated, 'Massive heart attack' with an air of grim satisfaction. Turning back to Sumit, she said, 'We had the best cardiac specialist, Dr Biren Chandra. People even come from America to see him. We did all we could, no expense spared.'

'Of course,' Sumit said uneasily, not knowing quite what to say. Just then a little boy came hurtling into the room, took one look at him and promptly ran behind the old lady. 'Who is that, Thama?' he asked suspiciously.

'It's an uncle,' she answered. 'An uncle from far away who knew your father when he was not much older than you are now. Where is your father?'

'Here,' answered Avinash, walking into the room. Sumit turned around. Avinash's mouth fell open. 'You?' he said incredulously.

'Me,' smiled Sumit. Avinash was showing his years – mostly around the middle. His hair had started to recede and he looked astonishingly like his father. In the old days he used to affect a beard (he called it his Leftist look). But now he just had a very corporate trimmed moustache. He somehow seemed shorter. Perhaps he was just stouter. Sumit wondered what he looked like to Avinash after all these years. He stepped forward unsure whether he should hug him. They paused awkwardly as if they had both bumped up against a wall neither had seen and then Avinash shook his hand formally.

'My God – when did you get to India? I didn't even know you were coming.'

'Who is this uncle, Baba? Thama says he is from far away,' said the little boy inching out from behind his grandmother.

'This is your Uncle Sumit from America,' answered his father. 'I haven't seen him in many years but we were best friends from when we were young boys.'

'My friend Mintu says Mickey Mouse lives in America. Is that true?'

'That's right,' answered Sumit. 'And see what I got you from there.' He held out a packet of Mickey Mouse colouring pens. The boy stepped forward. 'Oh no – first you have to tell me your name.'

'Amit Mitra,' answered the boy.

'And how old are you, Mr Amit Mitra?'

'I am six years old,' the boy said, holding up six fingers as additional proof.

'And which school do you go to, Mr Amit Mitra?'

'St John's School for Boys.'

'Like father, like son,' said Sumit looking at Avinash.

'Oh, he was lucky he got in. You can't imagine what it is like to get a boy into school these days. I had to take three days off work. They interviewed both Romola and me. I tell you, it was tougher than landing a job.'

'Are any of the old teachers still there?'

'A few. Father Rozario, though he's not quite the old terror he used to be.'

'Yes, I can imagine. He must be quite old now.'

'Anyway, sit, sit,' said Avinash, 'and tell me, how is America? Where are you now? Boston?'

'No, I moved to California two years ago.'

'San Francisco or Los Angeles?'

'Well, about thirty miles from San Francisco.'

'Hmmm,' said Avinash. 'And how's the job?'

Sumit smiled. 'It's all right. Busy. And yours?'

'Getting by. Getting by.'

'Avinash got a promotion last month,' his mother piped in. 'He is now a manager.'

'Oh, Ma,' said Avinash flushing. 'Sumit earns millions of dollars. Don't bore him with all this manager nonsense.'

Sumit smiled and said, 'Hardly millions.' The conversation slid to a halt. Seeing both Avinash and his mother look at him expectantly, he tried to pick up the threads. 'So how are our friends – Madhu and Subir and . . .' his voice trailed off.

'I've kind of lost touch with most people,' said Avinash quickly. 'Work keeps me so busy and I have to constantly go on tour. And when I am at home there's Amit's homework. You can't believe the amount of homework they give six-year-olds these days.'

'I see,' said Sumit. He didn't know what to say any more. He didn't know anything about being an executive in a pharmaceutical company and even less about homework for six-year-olds. Then he tried again. 'Speaking of friends, I met Abhijit's brother once. He said Abhijit had died in an accident. I was thinking of visiting his mother.'

As soon as he said it Avinash went still.

'Accident?' Avinash said dully, his voice so low it was almost a whisper.

'That's what his brother said,' replied Sumit. 'Something about falling off the roof.'

Avinash just continued to stare at him.

'Abhijit committed S-U-I-C-I-D-E,' said his mother leaning forward, spelling out the word in a hushed tone, glancing at her grandson. 'Of course his family had to say it was an accident. But everyone knows the truth. It was terrible. That poor young wife. They had been married less than a month. Thank God, girls these days get educated. I hear she is teaching at some girls' school. But what a tragedy. His mother almost went mad with grief. Avinash here did a lot for them. He was distraught too. Only natural. After all, you had all gone to college together. People said he had a love affair. I tell you these are modern times. He could have just told his parents. I mean how bad could it be – maybe she was older than him or of a different religion or something like that. Eventually his family would have adjusted.' She shook her head.

'Oh,' said Sumit. 'I had no idea.'

'You used to know him fairly well – didn't you work with him on that college magazine of yours? You were quite a little group,' Avinash's mother pressed on. 'Did he have some secret romance? Was he depressed?'

'Ma,' said Avinash hurriedly, 'let it be. It's over now. Why dredge it up again?'

'I'm just saying,' said his mother. 'You all were so close then. I remember how you'd say we won't ever get married. We'll look after each other like some kind of a boys' club. Such boyish silliness.'

'No,' said Sumit, slowly looking at her. 'He never seemed that depressed when we knew him. No more than the rest of us, at least.'

He turned to look at Avinash who dropped his eyes and fiddled with the magazine lying on the side table. 'I'd lost touch with him,' Avinash said almost defensively. 'You know, marriage and then Amit. Things just got so hectic. It was hard to keep in touch. How is your mother, by the way?'

'She is well, just getting older. Her blood sugar is a little high.'

'I keep meaning to go see her. So how long are you here for?'

'A month.'

'Good, good. You must come over for dinner soon. Romola is a wonderful cook. Amit, can you go and see if your mother is finished with her phone call? Tell her to come down.'

'I don't want to go,' pouted Amit, who was trying out his new pens. 'I want to sit here with Mickey Mouse Uncle.'

'Mickey Mouse Uncle won't go anywhere,' said Avinash smiling. 'Now hurry up and call your mother.'

The boy ran off, hollering for his mother.

'It changes everything, having a child,' smiled Avinash. 'Tell me, are you going to live in America for good?'

'Oh no, no,' exclaimed his mother. 'How can you say that? Who will look after your mother? No, no, you must come back and marry a nice girl. You have stayed there long enough. Enough of dollars and cars. We are not getting any younger. We need our sons near us.'

'I don't know,' said Sumit uncomfortably. 'I haven't made up my mind.'

'So who is this Mickey Mouse Uncle?' said a young woman as she was dragged into the room by Amit. Sumit stood up, his hands folded in greeting. She was dressed in a plain blue cotton sari, her hair loosely knotted in a bun.

'My wife, Romola,' said Avinash rather stiffly. 'This is Sumit, my old and very dear friend.'

'Oh,' said Romola, her eyes suddenly sharp and questioning. But then she folded her hands in greeting and smiled and said, 'The notorious Sumit from America?'

'Notorious?'

'Well, when we came back from America, your friend was so distraught that you had moved there. I think we just missed each other.'

'But I did . . .' began Sumit but Romola interrupted him. 'Anyway, do sit down. Let me get you some tea and sweets.'

'Oh, don't bother with sweets.'

'No, no, no,' Avinash's mother would hear none of it. 'Coming here after all these years – you must have something sweet. I will not take no for an answer. Romola, see what we have, otherwise send Mangala to the store. See if they have that lemon sandesh – Sumit used to love those.'

Romola left the room ignoring Sumit's protestations.

'Oh,' said Avinash. 'You never said no to sweets before. Are you on some diet? I hear everyone in America is on a diet. Actually, you look quite slim.'

'Well, you have to take care of yourself, you know,' replied Sumit. 'As we keep saying, we aren't getting any younger.'

Avinash's mother laughed. 'He has to keep trim because he is not married yet. Once you get married and taste your wife's cooking all that exercise business ends. Look at Avinash here – he used to do yoga and morning walks when you knew him. Now the only exercise he gets is climbing up the stairs and maybe a walk in the park at night.'

'Really? What park?' asked Sumit.

'Oh just . . .' Avinash suddenly turned to his son and said, 'Amit, go see if your mother is done with the tea. So tell me Sumit, you must have a car. What kind do you drive?'

They spoke of cars and jobs and whether Sumit had learned to cook in America. By now Sumit knew all these conversations as if by heart. He had had them so many times with so many relatives he could almost predict the next question. He looked at Avinash, mystified that that was all they had left between them. But Avinash's eyes were opaque. He just kept talking as if anything was better than silence. And when he paused, his mother jumped in, the swirls of conversation eddying around them, dragging them into ever safer waters. Sumit suddenly craved a cigarette though he had given up smoking three years ago.

Romola came back bearing a tray with a teapot and four cups. They were part of a matching set – white with a pattern of pink peonies. Sumit had never seen peonies till he went to America. He had actually never been one to notice much about gardens anyway. Now he had a little kitchen garden. He was growing herbs there – basil, mint, rosemary. On summer afternoons he liked to sit around in his kitchen garden with friends. He remembered the smell of freshly cut grass, the tang of fresh lemonade with crushed mint leaves from his garden and Russell making martinis with a flourish. It all seemed so far away. Russell? What was he doing now? He wondered if all that had really existed or if this was reality, this man in front of him, his son's homework and the mother sipping tea in a living room that kept time at bay, where life as they had known it was carefully preserved under a dust-cover.

Romola placed a cup in front of him and said, 'Have some biscuits.' She held out a little plate with a matching peony pattern in front of Sumit and a glass of water. 'I'm afraid we have only Horlicks biscuits. If you'd only let us know a little in advance. But Mangala has gone to get some sweets.'

'Really,' protested Sumit, 'you shouldn't fuss so much over me.' He put the glass of water down. He didn't know how to ask whether it was boiled or not. Instead he mumbled, 'I'll just have tea.'

'Oh man,' said Avinash. 'You can't drink the water here any more? Don't tell me you've become so delicate in America.'

'It's not that,' Sumit said feebly. 'I've been sick. Stomach problems, you know. I don't want to get sick here again.'

'So,' Romola sat down across from him. 'Tell us about

America. Doesn't it get lonely there? No wife, no children, no family. I can't imagine how you can live so far away by yourself. I was there for only a year or so after our marriage and I told your friend, "Better starve in India among friends and family than live here all alone like a vagabond."'

'Well, one gets used to it,' Sumit said a little defensively. 'You make friends. There are things to do – films, theatre. But it was lonely at first when I didn't know anyone. I would wonder what it would have been like if you, I mean both of you, had still been there.'

'Well,' said Avinash, his voice suddenly sharp, 'you never wrote to me. I thought you were just too busy enjoying being Mr American.'

'I did too,' replied Sumit. 'I never heard back and . . .'

'Oh the mail,' exclaimed Romola with a laugh. 'Can anyone rely on it for anything? Do you know I still haven't got my cousin's wedding invitation they mailed ten days ago? And they live just across town.'

'So do you still write poetry?' Sumit asked Avinash.

'Poetry?' laughed Romola, looking at her husband incredulously. 'When did you write poetry? You never told me that. Did I miss all the romance? My, my, I wonder what other hidden talents you have.'

Avinash flushed and said, 'It was just a stupid childish hobby. You grow out of these things.'

'No, no,' protested Sumit looking at Romola. He felt as if he was being challenged in a game whose rules he didn't quite get. 'He used to be pretty good. I don't know if he ever took you to Manali. I still have some of the poems he wrote there.'

'Oh Manali,' said Romola, her lips curling in a smile though its light didn't reach her eyes. 'Isn't that the most beautiful place on earth? I went there with my parents once and I thought to myself I must come back here with my husband someday. And walk under the pine trees down to the river. And those beautiful mountains and cherry orchards. I wanted to go there for our honeymoon but your friend here said, "No, I've been there already with Sumit. I don't want to go there again." My goodness – I thought at that time if this man doesn't realize the difference between going to Manali with his friend and going there with his new wife, there is no hope for him.'

'So where did you go?'

'Oh, Agra, but only after we moved back from America,' she said. 'And that's very nice, but I mean the Taj Mahal is so clichéd.'

'I want to go to Agra,' said Amit who was sitting on the floor drawing with his new pens.

'Do you know what's in Agra?' Sumit smiled, glad for the distraction.

'Yes,' he said, 'I have a picture of the Taj Mahal on my lunchbox. A king called Shah Jahan built it.'

'My goodness,' said Sumit, 'you know a lot for a six-year-old. Surely they are not teaching history to six-year-olds these days? How do you know about Shah Jahan?'

'Because sometimes my Ma calls me Shah Jahan. She says I was made in Agra.'

'Made in Agra?' Sumit looked perplexed, and then noticed Romola was blushing furiously and casting desperate glances at Avinash, who was looking steadfastly at his tea.

'Yes,' continued the boy undeterred. 'My mother said Baba and she made me in Agra and so I am her little Shah Jahan.'

'Oh,' said Sumit as the light dawned on him.

Romola glanced quickly at her mother-in-law and then hastily averted her gaze.

'That's enough, Amit.' Avinash tried to regain control of the situation. 'Why don't you show this uncle your drawing book?'

There was an awkward pause as the boy left the room.

'Very bright boy,' said Sumit trying to conceal his smile.

'Precocious,' said Avinash's mother sharply. 'Too precocious. That's what you get for being an only child. I keep telling Romola that she should have another one. For Amit's sake, if nothing else. It's not healthy for a child to grow up among adults and maid-servants.'

'Well, Ma,' protested Romola, with a sudden edge to her voice, 'it's not enough just to tell me. I would love to have another baby, maybe a little girl. But your son here thinks one is enough. He says look at all the trouble we went through to get this one into school.'

'Oh, Ma,' said Avinash a touch testily, 'you have a grandson to carry on the family name and all that. What more do you want?'

Sumit tensed up realizing he had not just indavertently wandered into well-worn battlefields, but had also tripped over some mines.

'So,' said Avinash turning to Sumit, 'tell me about your work.'

As they talked about computers Amit returned with his drawing book under his arm. He clambered up on to the sofa and settled down beside Sumit. 'Look,' he said, opening his book with a flourish. There were pictures of lions and tigers and mountains and a village scene complete with a pond and palm trees.

Then he turned the page. There was a picture of a wedding – a man with a moustache and a woman in a bright red sari sitting side by side.

'Who are these?' said Sumit.

'Ma and Baba getting married.'

'How would you know?' teased Sumit. 'Did you go to their wedding?'

'But I've seen pictures,' protested the boy.

'That's not me,' said his mother. 'That doesn't look like me. Am I so beautiful and is my skin so golden?'

'That's you,' protested the boy. 'You are beautiful.'

Romola laughed and stroked his head and for the first time since Sumit had met her, her face softened as she let down her guard. Sumit's gaze caught Avinash's who looked away as if embarrassed. Romola was not really beautiful but she had a certain easy grace. Her hair was knotted loosely in a bun and Sumit suddenly had a vision of it unravelling around her face like the black monsoon clouds that Tagore sang about in his songs. He wondered suddenly if Avinash still sang Tagore songs. Like he used to on summer nights when they were up on the roof. Sometimes there would be a power cut and everything would be dark – the houses black shapes cut out of an inky sky. Downstairs Mangala would have lit an oil lamp and he remembered the dim smoky light creeping up the stairway. From where he lay, smoking a cigarette, he could see the shadows of people downstairs – elongated and distorted like grotesque puppets. How hot and still it used to be on those nights – and lying there looking up he could very well believe that the stars were made of fire. Burning fiercely in the sky, scarcely bigger than the glowing end of his cigarette. From a nearby house he would hear a woman laugh – the noise jaggedly clear like a glass breaking. And the hum of the city – the noises all melted together in the heat – a yapping street dog, the clangour of a bicycle bell as the rider weaved through the lane between pedestrians and rickshaw-pullers. And then Avinash would start to sing, softly at first, as if he was singing only to himself. Then his voice would get bolder and stronger.

'Je raatey mor duarguli bhanglo jhorey . . .' On the night that my doors were broken by the storm . . .

He would lie there contentedly, watching Avinash singing with his eyes closed. About storms, and rain, and unrequited

56

love. During the day they would often laugh at Tagore's songs. Sumit always argued that they were too sickly and sentimental. But at night he was just content to lie there and let the melodies wash over him and imagine that there was really a storm brewing in the corner where the neem tree stood. A storm that would break down the doors. And maybe the woman who was laughing in the flat next door had fallen silent listening to Avinash sing. He imagined her standing quietly at the window behind the curtain with the pattern of little flowers. Perhaps in one hand she still held the oil lamp she had been about to light. And he would fall asleep on the crook of Avinash's arm and be woken up by Avinash stubbing out his burning cigarette.

'Silly,' Avinash would say gently mussing Sumit's hair. 'Do you want to set the world on fire?'

'Let's go into our club room,' Sumit would reply, stretching, his fingers touching the stubble on Avinash's chin in the darkness. In the dingy storage room on the roof where as young boys they'd once had secret clubs they would reach for each other, the darkness guiding their hands. Later that night as he rode his bicycle home through the shadowy sleeping streets, he'd lift his hand to his face and smell Avinash still clinging to him, his fingers, his lips, his neck, and he would start to sing as well. He couldn't hold a tune but it didn't matter as he wobbled down the streets, scraps of song trailing behind him.

'Penny for your thoughts,' said Romola brightly.

Startled, Sumit shook his head and smiled.

'We learned that in school from our English teacher,' she laughed. 'We thought it was such a fashionable thing to say because Miss Cole had actually been to England.'

'It's just this house. It brings back so many memories,' said Sumit. Then turning to Avinash, he said, 'Is the old room up on the roof still there? The one we called the club room?'

Avinash replied, 'Yes, where would it go?'

'I would love to see it again.'

'There's nothing to see – just old junk and stuff.'

'Still.'

'No, really,' said Avinash with a touch of irritation. 'It's all dusty and no one's opened it in ages. I don't even know if the light still works. And I'd have to look for the key.'

'But I know where it is, Baba,' piped up Amit. 'It's next to Ma's powder case. I'll take Mickey Mouse Uncle up to the roof.'

'Now Amit – you have to do your homework.'

'Oh, let him go up,' said Romola with a glimmer of a smile. 'It'll only take a minute. Why are you getting so worked up?' There was a slight tone of mocking in her voice that made Sumit glance at her. But he couldn't tell if it was directed at him or at Avinash.

'I am not worked up,' shrugged Avinash. 'It's just that there's nothing there.'

The little room was almost exactly as Sumit remembered it. The door cracked with the streaky green paint faded by sun and rain. Amit opened the door. It creaked on rusty hinges as if it had indeed not been opened in years. Sumit reached around and turned on the light, a naked light bulb dangling from a wire. The room was full of junk as Avinash had warned. There were trunks and suitcases and old half-broken file cabinets all covered with dust. Piles of yellowing newspapers and torn mattresses and dented utensils. Something scampered away behind one of the piles making Amit jump.

'Did you and Baba play here?' asked Amit.

'Yes.'

'What games did you play?'

'Oh, just games.'

'Fun games?'

'They seemed fun then,' smiled Sumit, ruffling the boy's hair.

'And why did you stop playing?'

'I don't know.'

'Because we grew up,' said Avinash appearing behind them at the doorway. 'Your mother is calling you, Amit.'

Amit shuffled reluctantly down the stairs.

The two men stood there watching the hustle-bustle of the neighbourhood. They could hear the impatient honks of passing buses and the cries of vendors. The television next door was blaring and the radio was on full blast at the corner store.

'How little seems to have changed,' said Sumit. 'You are lucky. It is easy to keep time still here.'

Avinash lit a cigarette and leaned his elbows on the parapet. Abruptly he turned and looked Sumit full in the face and said, 'I had no choice.'

'I wasn't blaming you,' Sumit said touching Avinash's elbow.

Avinash jerked his hand away as if Sumit's hand was burning hot. 'After Baba died all of a sudden, there was never any choice for me. My grandmother was still alive and completely distraught. Ma said I had to come back and get married and settle down. And then after I took Romola to America, Ma started writing letters asking me to come home – she was beside herself. And Romola was so unhappy in America almost from day one. I had to come back.'

'I'm not blaming you.'

'You don't have to – it's there in your face. I couldn't help it, Sumit. You don't know what it's like. You got away. I got married. That's just the way it is. It's just something that happened.'

'I understand, Avinash.'

'How is it there?' said Avinash. 'Are you happy? Do you have someone? Was it all you hoped it would be?'

'It's . . . it's different. Yes, I think I am freer. But sometimes

I look at you and feel perhaps you were not wrong. You seem so much, so much safer. Are you happy?'

Avinash looked at him for a minute. Then he looked away and replied, 'I have a good job. My mother is happy. She has a grandson. Romola takes good care of her. And I adore Amit.'

'But are you happy?'

Avinash didn't answer at once. He blew the smoke out and then said, 'I don't think too much about that any more. I'm contented, I guess. That's good enough.'

'Don't you ever want to get out, away from all this like we used to plan up on this roof? Do you ever imagine what might have happened if you and I, together, could have . . .'

'I told you Sumit, I'm at peace,' Avinash cut him short as if stubbing out a cigarette. 'Why should I torment myself needlessly about things I might have done? I get up. I go to work. I come home. Watch TV or—'

'Go for a walk in the park maybe,' said Sumit quietly. 'Which park do you go to, Avinash? The one where men like you come out to stroll at night?'

'You have no right,' said Avinash fiercely. 'You have no right. Just let me be, Sumit. Why did you come back? No letters. No messages. Nothing. After all these years. What do you want from me now?'

'I did write but you never replied. Forget that. But you are right,' said Sumit slowly. 'I lost my right a long time ago, Vino.'

Avinash flushed. No one had called him Vino since Sumit had left. That was his name for him and it was as if someone had stepped up to a long-forgotten door and knocked on it.

'I know you were upset at me for getting married but to disappear from my life like that,' Avinash flicked the ashes from his cigarette. 'And now you just walk in like this.'

'I needed to see you,' said Sumit. 'I put it off and I put it off. And if my mother hadn't pushed me maybe I wouldn't have been able to do it this time either. But I needed to see you.'

'Why? To flaunt your San Francisco in my face. To pity me?'

Sumit turned away from him looking across the street. The first stars of the evening were appearing encrusted like diamonds in the pink-flushed sky. He could hear the calls of the birds settling down for the night in the tree across the street. He could see the evening market setting up, the potato seller with the dusty gold mounds of potatoes and onions next to the woman selling eggs. All this used to be his too. Once he had belonged to it as effortlessly as that white cat on the roof next door, sitting there flicking its tail watching the world amble past. Now it was sand through his fingers.

'No,' he said. 'I just wanted to know why you never replied.'

He slowly turned back to look at Avinash who just stared at him as if he had been changed in to stone.

Avinash opened his mouth as if about to say something.

But just then a voice behind them said, 'There you are.'

Turning around they saw Romola had come upstairs. Sumit wondered how much she had heard. But she just smiled cheerfully and turned to Sumit. 'You must stay for dinner. It won't be anything fancy since I didn't get any warning. Just simple chicken and rice. My mother-in-law insists.'

'Oh no, some other time,' said Sumit. 'I promised Ma I'd be home. You know how it is when you come back after so long. There's a special meal planned for every night.'

'Oh, you can call home, can't you?' Romola turned to Avinash and said, 'Ask him to stay, why don't you? After all, he is your long-lost friend.'

But Avinash did not say anything.

The two men went down in silence. As Sumit walked down the street he glanced up. Avinash was still standing at the door. Romola was still standing on the roof, holding Amit close to

61

her, watching him leave. A southern evening breeze was picking up, ruffling her hair. He could smell rain in the air.

He raised his hand in goodbye. Amit waved energetically. Romola just watched him, her hand resting on the little boy's shoulder.

IV

The Discipline of Haircuts

A VINASH HATED haircut Sundays with a passion. When he was a little boy, Nripati-babu, the ancient neighbourhood barber, would come to the house on the last Sunday of the month carrying his beat-up black box with a set of scissors, a strop razor and a discoloured powder puff that had once been blue and was now mottled. Without fail, on haircut Sundays Avinash would throw a tantrum but to no avail. He would be deposited on a rickety stool in the courtyard, his face dark with mutiny. His mother would yank a newspaper down over him and his head would pop out like a jack-in-the-box. Nripati-babu would adjust the newspaper to his satisfaction, wipe the scissors on his old white shirt and then, without a word, start chopping. Avinash would stare at the thickets of grey hair growing out of Nripati-babu's ears and see his own black hair tumbling down over the black newsprint as if the letters themselves were being uprooted. Sometimes he would look up and see his friend Indrani, from the house next door, peeking at him through their kitchen window. When that happened his humiliation would be complete.

'Why, why, why must I get my hair cut? You don't,' Avinash once said accusingly to his mother.

'You are a boy and boys have short hair.'

'Why?'

'Because boys are one way and girls are another. And if you have long hair people will think you are a girl.'

'So what?'

'Well, then you don't need to study at St John's School for Boys. Look, I have a hundred things to do. I can't sit here and argue with you all day. If you don't want a haircut, don't. We will put a ribbon in it and enrol you in St Teresa's like Indrani next door.'

When Avinash turned seven his exasperated mother announced he was old enough to go and get his hair cut, just as his father did, at the New Modern Saloon for Gents (Air-Conditioned). She thought it would make him feel grown-up and that his passionate hatred for the ritual might dissipate. But it did not help. The New Modern Saloon was neither new nor modern but it was indeed air-conditioned. In fact, before B.C. Sen and Sons Fine Jewellers installed an air conditioner, New Modern Saloon was the only shop in the neighbourhood that boasted of one. More often than not, though, the air conditioner was turned off. 'Electricity bill too high,' explained Harish-babu, the head barber.

Harish-babu, as head barber, reserved his cutting talents for the more exalted customers, like Avinash's father, a professor and thus automatically held in high regard. Avinash had to be content with Lakshman-babu who was probably ten years younger but seemed ancient anyway. They were an odd pair. Harish-babu was tall and thin with wire-rimmed spectacles and white hair that matched his spotless white shirt and dhoti. On bright summer days he glowed like a detergent advertisement. Lakshman-babu was plump and dark, with caterpillar eyebrows. On hot afternoons Avinash could see the beads of sweat gather like hungry flies on his big bald domed forehead. Avinash would stare at them fascinated, trying to will the drops to grow bigger and heavier and heavier until unable to stop themselves they would roll down his forehead. Lakshman-babu always smiled unctuously at Avinash and said, 'Well, if it's not the little sahib. Already time for another haircut, eh?'

Then he placed two cushions on the chair so that Avinash's head would come up to the level of his scissors.

'My, my, you are growing. Soon you'll be needing only one cushion. Ha ha ha.'

Scowling fiercely, Avinash would clamber on to the foot-stool and then on to the chair and plant himself on the cushions. The chair was big and wide and Avinash always felt he was being swallowed whole.

'Very good, very good,' Lakshman-babu chortled as he wrapped a starched white sheet around him and knotted it tightly behind Avinash's neck. He made a few practice swipes with his scissors. Then his big shiny moon-head loomed over his ear.

'Hold still now, my little gentleman,' he said, the fingers of his left hand brutally digging into Avinash's neck and jamming his head in place. 'We don't want to cut off a bit of our ears now, do we?'

Avinash bet he did. Avinash bet he kept the ears of young boys in jars. He had once seen a whole baby with three legs in a big jar at the museum. Avinash imagined his ear floating in a jar like that.

By the end of the haircut Avinash had hair all over him and inside his shirt and it tickled and scratched. But the torture was not over yet. One final ritual was left. Lakshman-babu opened his shiny blue powder case, dabbed the pale pink worn-out powder puff vigorously in the cheap talcum powder and then daubed it liberally on Avinash's neck raising puffy white clouds. Finally satisfied with Avinash's parted, powdered and tamed look, he pushed the stool forward so Avinash could clamber down to freedom.

Over time the stepping stool went away and then one by one the cushions too but Avinash's hatred for Lakshman-babu and his haircuts remained undiminished. His stalling attempts at rebellion, however, always came to nothing, thanks to Father Rozario.

Father Rozario was the school prefect. Every now and then, with no warning, he would announce hair-check days. All the boys would wait trembling as he strode into the classroom swinging his slim cane. They would have to turn around and face the wall. Avinash would smell the nicotine on his breath as he came closer and closer, his cane measuring the gap between his hairline and his collar with geometric precision.

'So what have we here?' Avinash could feel the cane on the nape of his neck – a gentle tap, almost a loving caress. 'Is someone trying to be a Hindi film star?'

Little nervous titters.

'Silence!' The room fell quiet. 'Turn around, turn around so I can look at your face.'

Avinash turned around slowly quaking in his shiny black school shoes.

'What's your name, boy?'

'Avinash.'

'Avinash. Avinash, what?'

'Mitra, Father.'

'So, Mr Avinash Mitra, can you touch your neck for me? Yes, right there where the collar is.'

Avinash touched his collar.

'And what can you feel there?'

Avinash knew the answer because he'd heard the question so many times before. 'Hair, father.'

'Hair,' Father Rozario paused as if Avinash had presented him with a curious new piece of evidence that needed to be mulled over. 'And Mr Avinash Mitra – do your parents pay your fees so you can attend a reputable school for young men of good families or—' here he paused for dramatic effect and then his voice took on Biblical thunderousness. 'Or do you think you are one of those no-good loafer boys who have nothing to do all day except smoke cigarettes and style their hair like good-for-nothing Hindi movie stars?'

Without waiting for an answer, he roared on, seeming to grow larger and larger as if he would crush Avinash under his big toe. 'We want you to become decent law-abiding citizens. Short hair is a sign of discipline and one thing that St John's is known for is discipline. I will not let this school turn into a Bombay film studio. You are not here to become movie stars. Your parents don't pay their good money to see you all grow into louts who can't hold a job for two days. Do you know why they can't?'

He jabbed the cane at Avinash and said, 'Because they have no discipline. And discipline begins with a proper haircut.' He glared around to see if there were any objections to his theory. Seeing none, he turned back to Avinash. 'So, Mr Avinash Mitra, put out your hands, palms up.'

Avinash put them out, shaking.

'Steady, hold them steady!' Father Rozario barked.

Gritting his teeth, Avinash willed his hands to stop shaking. The cane came whistling down and struck his hand with a sting. Avinash tried to squeeze the tears back. But then the cane came down again and left another smarting stripe.

'All right, boy, come to my office tomorrow and show me your haircut.'

Avinash nodded mutely. Beside him, Rajiv, whose turn it was next, had almost peed in his pants.

What filled Avinash with even more dread was the prospect of coming home and telling his mother everything. One week ago he was supposed to have had a haircut. But he had put up a bitter fight. He wanted to finish his book. He needed to do his homework. He had a stomach ache. He had to go to

Nitin's house. Nitin's hair was longer than his. His was not all that long. They had just had a hair-check. Finally, exasperated, his mother had given in. 'Fine, do whatever you want. You will find out soon enough whether your hair is too long or not.'

And now Avinash would have to tell her that he needed a haircut after all.

Then one day, soon after Avinash's fourteenth birthday, everything changed. He had gone to New Modern for his monthly ritual and found, to his surprise, a new face. He was much younger than any of the other barbers there. As soon as Avinash saw him he had a vision of Father Rozario's scowling face. This fellow looked just like the 'no-good loafer boys' they had all been warned about. His hair was long – way over his collar – and in the front it was pouffed exactly like a Hindi film star. What was even more shocking was that he had left not one, not two, but three buttons open on his dark blue shirt. In their school Arijit had been caned and given a C-grade for leaving two buttons open. Avinash could see the hair on the barber's chest and a thin golden chain nestling in it. Harish-babu said, 'This is Sultan. He is here because Lakshman-babu had to go to his home in Baharampur. His son was hit by a scooter.'

Avinash tried to look concerned but his eyes were hypno-tized by the golden chain.

He sat down on the chair.

When Avinash saw Harish-babu coming towards him with his scissors he almost cried out, 'No.' He didn't know why and he didn't know how to say it without making a com-plete fool of himself but he really wanted Sultan to cut his hair. Avinash imagined that there was a small stool on the floor which Harish-babu could not see. He imagined him stumbling over it, the scissors flying out of his hand and then Harish-babu himself falling, toppling over, his white dhoti unravelling as his foot caught in it. Avinash imagined all the clumps of hair on the floor rising up like a flurry of pigeons and then settling gently on his white shirt. And his glasses, yes, his glasses would go flying off and hit the little magazine stand with old dog-eared issues of *Reader's Digest* and *Nabakallol*. And one lens would just pop out and go spinning across the floor.

But there was no stool, and there was no escape. Avinash felt Harish-babu's coarse fingers tying the white sheet around his neck. In the mirror he saw Sultan and was it his imagination or was he looking at him with a knowing smile? Avinash dropped his eyes in confusion. He saw men like Sultan every day – loitering with cigarettes on street corners. Some days he would stand on the balcony and see them drinking endless cups of tea and smoking. Their loud carefree laughter and scraps of heated arguments would float up, peppered with 'bad' words. Acutely conscious of his mother standing beside him he'd pretend he hadn't heard. But the words would hang in the air obstinately. He would look away but would be inexorably pulled into their conversation, secretly thrilling to the swear words they tossed around with such casual bravado.

When Avinash walked home from school they would be there standing at the corner as if they owned it. The boy from the tea-stall opposite would come by with his kettle filling their cups with hot sweet milky tea. His heart always skipped a beat when he walked by them. In his clean white school uniform with his striped school tie, Avinash felt like a creature from another planet. He was a mother's boy without his mother to protect him. Avinash felt that they looked at him with the contempt that is reserved exclusively for mothers' boys. Every time Avinash walked by the corner he would brace himself for a taunt, an insult tossed his way as casually as a cigarette butt. He would swing his satchel on his shoulder and loosen his tie with what he hoped was casual style. Once he even unbuttoned the top two buttons on his shirt. But then Avinash saw Madhu's mother, who worked next door, returning from the ration shop and quickly buttoned up again. Then he would walk past the young men quietly, his eyes firmly on the road, not sure whether he was hoping they would not notice him or whether he was hoping deep inside him that they would.

Sultan had probably been there as well – laughing uproariously at some dirty joke. And now here he was barely three feet away from him cutting the hair of some fat man who was almost bald anyway. Avinash wanted him to cut his hair because he didn't know how else he could talk to him. Maybe he would ask him to have a cup of tea with him. But that was just fantasy. In real life Avinash knew he could say little to him other than 'No, shorter.'

'Can't we turn on the air conditioner, Harish-babu?' Sultan said, wiping his brow.

Harish-babu froze, scissors in mid-air. 'Air conditioner?' he said slowly enunciating each syllable.

'Yes,' said Sultan calmly. 'This is supposed to be air-conditioned, isn't it? Look, that's what it says.' He gestured towards the door. 'New Modern Saloon for Gents (Air-Conditioned).'

Harish-babu slowly lowered his scissors. In all his years at the saloon he had never encountered such insolence. And in front of the customers too.

'Well,' he said quietly, 'do you know how much it costs to run the air conditioner? Perhaps I should take it out of *your* salary. Perhaps then you'll understand that money doesn't just grow on trees.'

'Well, then you shouldn't say air-conditioned,' said Sultan evenly, pausing to admire his handiwork on the fat man's head. 'I mean, if you don't run the AC in the middle of summer, what's the point?'

70

Harish-babu put down his scissors. Avinash was afraid he might drop them on his head. Then he turned round to face Sultan who was still snipping the fat man's hair as if nothing had happened.

'The point is that we have an air conditioner,' said Harish-babu, his voice so tightly controlled it seemed to twitch. 'And it is *my* decision as to when we want to run it.'

'But don't you think it makes sense to run it on a hot afternoon like this?' said Sultan, cocking his head to inspect the fat man's pate. 'I'm sure your customers would agree, wouldn't you?' Now he looked straight at Avinash and raised one eyebrow questioningly. Trapped between them Avinash squirmed. He felt Harish-babu's lightly laid hand on his shoulder tighten its grip.

Sultan's eyes held his with easy familiarity.

Avinash flushed and swallowed.

'Well?' said Sultan smiling, 'Isn't it hot?'

'Yes,' Avinash replied. 'Yes, it is.' His words came out as a squeak. But with those words, Avinash had a feeling that he had just taken a huge hatchet and hacked away the ropes that tied his boat to the shore and he was now floating away, uncontrollably, into the ocean. Harish-babu's fingers clenched tighter.

'Yes,' chimed in the fat man. 'After all, you charge three rupees more than Prince Saloon across the street.'

Harish-babu let go of Avinash's shoulder and stalked over to the air conditioner. He turned it on and as it grumbled into life Avinash looked up into the mirror. He caught Sultan's eye as he bent over the fat man's head. There was a half-smile on his lips and when he saw him looking Sultan grinned and winked.

Avinash blushed and looked away. Harish-babu returned to his chair and said icily, 'I trust the little sahib is feeling cooler now.' Then he turned to Sultan and said, 'When you open your own saloon you can keep the air conditioner running eight hours a day if you like. But here I make the rules.'

'Of course I will,' said Sultan. 'Why eight? I'll run it twenty-four hours a day.'

Then he started humming a hit song from the latest Hindi film. Avinash looked at him several times excitedly, hoping he would accord him new respect as a fellow-rebel, a comrade-in-arms. But he seemed to have forgotten Avinash was there.

That night Sultan appeared in his dream. Avinash did not remember anything of it except that he woke in the morning with his image graven in his head and he knew he had been in his dream. He closed his eyes and tried to go back to the dream, to see what they had been doing together. But it was gone. But he knew whatever it was, it had been painfully pleasurable in a way that only truly secret secrets are.

The next time, Avinash went for his haircut with an eagerness that surprised his mother. She had wanted to take him to the fancy Ennis Ladies and Gents Saloon near his father's office because she wanted her hair trimmed as well. But Avinash insisted on going to New Modern.

'That boy just never ceases to amaze me,' she complained to her husband. 'For years he fusses about going to New Modern. And now when I offer to take him to Ennis he only wants to go to New Modern.'

'It's that age,' said his father soothingly. 'He just wants to be contrary. Why don't you start offering to make him tea? Maybe then he'll suddenly want his milk too.'

But the moment Avinash walked into the shop his heart sank. The air conditioner was turned off. Lakshman-babu was back. There was no sign of Sultan. Avinash didn't know how to find out where he'd gone. He didn't want to show that it mattered to him, that he even remembered that there had been another barber named Sultan. He sat down on the chair and let Lakshman-babu tie the sheet around him.

'So,' Avinash said redundantly, 'you are back.'

Lakshman-babu just knotted the sheet tight behind his neck.

'Hmmm, so what happened to the other barber?' Unable to stop himself, Avinash plunged on recklessly. 'Ummm, what was his name?'

'Sultan,' said Lakshman-babu shortly. 'He's gone.'

'Oh,' Avinash said. 'Was he from your village?' Avinash ventured.

'Of course not. We don't have smart-alecs like that in the village. Our village has honest hard-working men of the soil. He was a city boy, that Sultan. Too cocky for his own good. Will come to a bad end, mark my words.'

'Why do you say that?'

'No respect. Just shooting off his mouth like this was his own property. Harish-babu told me everything.' Lakshman-babu shook his head in dismay. Then he leaned forward so that his mouth was almost in Avinash's ear. 'Young people these days. No discipline. No discipline at all.'

'But,' Avinash said, undeterred, 'where did he go?'

'Hell, for all I care,' said Lakshman-babu. 'What would you want with the likes of him? You are a good, well-mannered boy. Your parents are bringing you up with so much care. You are so lucky. Not like that Sultan. If he was my son I'd have straightened him out long ago.'

Two days later, Avinash bumped into Sultan just like that. Avinash was out shopping with his mother when he saw him at the street corner with a group of other young men. A couple of them were from his neighbourhood. Sultan was smoking and talking animatedly. He was wearing a black shirt and and had the same thin gold chain around his neck. Avinash wanted to run up to him. Instead he just stood there unable to move. His mother was bargaining fiercely over the price of tomatoes. Avinash stood by her, clutching the bag of groceries, sneaking looks at Sultan. Avinash wondered if he would remember the air conditioner and how they had fought Harish-babu together.

He looked at the cigarette between Sultan's fingers and suddenly imagined him turning around and asking him if he wanted a drag. The image was so sudden and so vivid it shook him. Sultan looked up to hail the boy from the tea-shop across the street. For a moment their eyes met. Avinash opened his mouth to say something.

'Who are you gaping at?' said his mother. 'Put these tomatoes in the bag.'

'Look,' Avinash said. 'That's my barber.'

His mother glanced over and said with a frown, 'Him? I didn't know they had people like him at New Modern. How can he give a haircut? He doesn't look like he ever gets one!'

Sultan looked over. Avinash smiled uncertainly. And then, plucking up all the courage he had, he said what he already knew. 'You don't work at New Modern any more.' He meant it to be a question but it came out more as an accusation.

Sultan's friends turned around to look at him. His mother, who had been examining some green chillies, suddenly looked up with a frown. Avinash felt the whole street teeter and he felt hot with embarrassment.

Then Sultan laughed. 'Oh no – not with that old miser. Now I have my own place with my cousin Aziz. It's called Badshah, right on Lake Avenue across the street from the temple. It doesn't have air conditioning yet, though.'

'Let's go,' said his mother, abandoning the chillies.

As they went off Avinash looked back to see if Sultan was looking at him. He was not, but at least he had remembered. *It doesn't have air conditioning yet, though*. He remembered.

'Well, good for Harish-babu,' said his mother, marching down the street. 'Once you let people like that in, business goes downhill. You go in for a haircut, you'll come out looking like a two-paisa film star.'

Barely a week later, Avinash decided that his hair was too long and he needed a haircut.

He walked by the Badshah saloon three times to make sure that Aziz had a customer and Sultan was free. Then glancing around to see that no one was looking he walked in as nonchalantly as he could. Sultan was reading the newspaper and looked up as Avinash came in. If he was surprised to see him he didn't show it. He just put the paper down and said, 'Haircut?'

Avinash nodded, not quite trusting himself to speak.

Sultan was wearing a dark blue shirt and brown pants of some slightly shiny material. Avinash could see the blue straps of his sandals. The shirt was not tucked in and the first two buttons were, as usual, undone. Inside he wore a white vest. Avinash could see a few strands of chest hair peeping over the top of his vest and for some inexplicable reason that made his heart pound. Avinash had seen the hair on his father's chest many times but it had never made his heart go faster. He wondered if Sultan would notice that he too had left one button undone on his own shirt or that his pants were a little too tight. But Sultan did not say anything.

'Sit down,' he said pointing to a chair.

Avinash sat down and then said, 'Oh, I must not spoil the shirt with hair. Can I take it off?'

'Yes, but you'll get hair all over yourself then.'

'I know, but my mother will kill me if I get hair all over the shirt.'

Sultan shrugged and handed him a hanger.

Avinash started unbuttoning his shirt, sure that his ears were bright red. As he sat down on the chair again he saw in the mirror his scrawny body, the flat chest with all the ribs showing through his white banian and wished he'd kept his shirt on. But it was too late. Sultan was preparing to drape the big white sheet around him. Avinash felt Sultan's fingers knot

75

it behind his neck and then his hands patting the sheet down over his body. His heart was racing like an express train.

Sultan opened his drawer and took out his scissors and clippers.

'So how do you want it – short?'

Avinash wanted to say, 'Like yours.' Sultan's hair was brushed up in front and carefully styled at the back so it just curled over his collars. His sideburns were long and angled. But Avinash knew that was never going to work as long as there were hair-checks.

'Yes, short,' Avinash said, resigned.

Sultan started humming a song as he began to snip the hair on the back of his head. Avinash sat there watching him through the mirror as if memorizing him, – the packet of cigarettes that showed through his shirt pocket, the watch with its stainless steel band, the golden chain always around his neck. Avinash tilted his head slightly to get a better view of him.

'Hold still now,' Sultan said holding him in place. The touch of his hand was warm and rough, almost electric against his skin and Avinash suddenly had a vision of holding his hand to his nose. What would it smell of – tobacco and hair-cream? He was acutely aware of his bare body under the sheet. Though there was no air conditioner, Avinash could feel goosebumps on his arms.

'Sultan, I am going to get some tea,' Aziz said.

'Okay, can you get me a cup too?' Then he looked at Avinash and said, 'Do you want some?'

'I don't drink tea,' Avinash said without thinking and then instantly regretted it.

'Oh, are you still drinking milk?' said Aziz laughing. 'You are getting a moustache now – when will you start drinking tea?'

'Let him be,' Sultan said. 'Look how skinny he is. He needs milk.'

Now Avinash wished he had never taken off that shirt. He watched Aziz leave the shop, the swivel door swinging behind him. Sultan was standing beside him now his body turned towards him as he cut his hair. His chest was at the level of his eyes. Avinash could see every strand of black silky hair pushing past the confines of Sultan's vest. Avinash wondered what it would be like to touch them. Would he get hair on his chest too? His fingers itched to play with Sultan's chest hair. Avinash edged his hands forward so that his fingers were almost touching Sultan's leg.

Sultan moved forward and Avinash's clenched knuckles grazed his pants. Sultan made no attempt to move his leg away. His heart beating with some delectable fear, Avinash left his hand there. As Sultan leaned in to trim his hair his legs pressed against Avinash's knuckles. Avinash found himself wondering if his legs were hairy too. He felt he was sweating. And then he felt cold. Sultan raised his arm to hold his head firmly and Avinash could see the dark half moon of the shadow of his sweat in his armpit.

'Oh, you are very fidgety,' Sultan said.

Avinash looked up and he was smiling. His teeth had tobacco stains. Avinash smiled back. He was so very close to him. His hand pressed even more firmly against his trousers. Sultan smiled and his hands rested lightly on his shoulders. Very gently he started pressing Avinash's shoulders, kneading the muscles through the cloth.

Then Avinash felt him go behind him and his hands unknotted the white sheet. It drifted down his body and settled on his lap.

'Look at all the hair on your chest,' Sultan laughed. 'It's almost as hairy as mine.'

He was rubbing him with a towel now brushing away the hair.

'Oh, it's not as hairy as yours,' Avinash protested. 'How old were you when you got hair on your chest?'

'Oh, I don't know. Maybe seventeen or eighteen. But I don't have that much – you should see my father.'

'Really? It looks like a lot to me.'

'No – see,' Sultan said tugging his vest down with his finger.

'I can't see,' Avinash complained.

He unbuttoned the other buttons and pulled down his vest further, exposing his chest. He was right – his hair grew like a dark soft feathery fan in the middle of his chest. More than anything else Avinash wanted to touch that hair. He wanted to trace it like a river on an India map and follow it down his belly and then he wanted his finger to burrow under his pants and trace it all the way down. All the way. Avinash shut his eyes terrified about where this was leading.

'Touch it,' said Sultan, his voice as silky as his hair, his tone teasing, almost a dare. Avinash kept his eyes shut but his fingers reached out of their own accord. As they traced the silky roughness of Sultan's hair he felt the room grow stiflingly small, his own clothes uncomfortably tight. Sultan was no longer humming anything. Instead he moved closer to Avinash, his trousers rubbing up against his legs, at first casual and then insistently. Avinash realized his fingers were a hair's breadth away from the buckle on Sultan's belt. Avinash touched Sultan's crotch and jerked back as if he had touched something scalding because he knew that if he pulled that zipper down there was no going back.

Just then Sultan laughed and said, 'There, you are all done.' He opened his eyes and saw the sheet still around him. Sultan was holding a little mirror behind him so Avinash could look at the back of his head.

'Is that all right?' he asked.

Avinash nodded for his mouth was too dry and his tongue too thick and twisted to trust with words. Sultan took a small towel and vigorously rubbed him. The roughness of the old towel seemed to set off sparks on his skin. Then, too soon, he stopped and handed him his shirt. Avinash's fingers were all thumbs as he buttoned it.

As Avinash paid him, Sultan said 'Wait, you've buttoned the shirt all wrong.' Avinash just nodded and bolted from the store. 'Come back again,' Sultan called after him.

Avinash turned around. Sultan was standing at the door lighting a cigarette and looking at him. As their eyes met he smiled, and Avinash was not sure if he had imagined everything.

That night Avinash dreamt of him but he was in the old shop and then his mother was scolding him and Avinash woke up trembling with fear and guilt. But when he closed his eyes he saw him again standing at the door looking at him and smiling. And Avinash wondered what would happen if he just walked back, past the newspaper store, past the tea-stall, past the sleeping dog, up the two steps and Sultan shut the door behind him.

A few days later as Avinash was walking down the street he saw Sultan sitting on the steps in front of his shop. He was smoking a cigarette and chatting with the man who sold newspapers and magazines in the little stall down the road. Sultan saw him and grinned and waved, wispy tendrils of smoke curling up from his fingers. Caught in his grin, like an animal in the headlights of a car, Avinash suddenly knew he could not walk past him without remembering his dream and the strange feeling in the pit of his stomach. He stopped short and pretended he had just remembered something on the other side of the road. He turned and ran across the road almost knocking over a boy on a bicycle going the wrong way. The boy teetered down the street, a few choice curses wafting in his wake like Sultan's cigarette smoke.

Once safely on the other side, Avinash looked across the street to see if Sultan had noticed his flight, if he was looking to see where Avinash had run off to. But he had gone back to his conversation. Avinash saw him toss his head back and laugh, his teeth white against his tan. He ran his fingers through his hair and Avinash shivered uncontrollably. He stood there for a couple of minutes trying to will him to turn and seek him out. But he carried on unconcerned, as if he had forgotten how their paths had almost intersected, before Avinash ran away. Then he finished his cigarette and stubbed it out with his sandal, stood up, stretched and wandered back inside his shop.

Avinash never went back to get his hair cut at Sultan's again. One day he noticed the Badshah saloon had gone out of business. When Avinash got married and had a son, Amit got into St John's School as well. 'Like father, like son,' Avinash's mother said with a proud smile. Father Rozario was still there, as were hair-check days, but these were different times and no one got caned for long hair any more. Instead, they were fined.

Unlike Badshah, the New Modern Saloon for Gents (Air-Conditioned) survived. But Avinash refused to take Amit there for his haircuts. Harish-babu had died and Lakshman-babu was now in charge. Avinash took Amit to a far more expensive saloon even though it was much further away, something the boy's grandmother thought of as a ridiculous indulgence bound to spoil the child. Sometimes on lazy holiday afternoons she would tell her grandson the story of how his father hated having his hair cut. The story was part of family lore now, worn into familiarity by its telling, rendered perfectly harmless, even slightly boring.

V

Great-Grandmother's Mango Chutney

TWO WEEKS after Amit was dumped by his first serious American girlfriend, he was suddenly stricken by an urge for homemade mango chutney. The memory, sweet and tart at the same time, tugged at him so insistently that he got into his run-down old Honda hatchback, drove down to Valencia Street, past the taquerias with their mariachi bands, the second-hand bookstores and the newly sprung chic tapas restaurants, until he found the only Indian grocery store in the neighbourhood. As he stood in the store deliberating over the bottles of Pataks and Priyas while a tinny song from the latest Bollywood blockbuster wafted through the aisles, he noticed a battered can next to the pickles. The blue paper on the can had faded in the sun and the yellow fruit pictured on it was bleached to a pale ivory. Amit looked at the expiry date – it was about four months ago. But there it was: canned jackfruit. It was a far cry from the jackfruits he would see in India – hacked open, their golden yellow pulp voluptuously spilling out on to the street, the buzzing shiny black-blue flies hovering over them as eager as wedding guests. But for a moment, in the aisle of that grocery store in San Francisco, over the sharp whiffs of fresh cumin and stale samosas, Amit could smell that cloying sweet jackfruit odour that clung thickly to everything it touched. And he heard his mother as if she was standing in the next aisle.

'I will not have it,' said Romola. 'Not in this house, while I am alive. I have told her once, I have told her a thousand times – I will not have jackfruit in my house. The smell makes me want to throw up.'

'But did you find any?' asked his father, Avinash, trying to be rational.

'Find any? You think she was born yesterday? She has eaten every last bit. She and that old maid of hers. But the smell – my whole refrigerator smells like it was bathed in it.'

'Well, it's done now,' said Avinash placatingly, unwilling to forsake his newspaper and step into the fight.

But Romola was not to be appeased. 'You think it's just for me? What about her? At her age, eating so much ripe jackfruit.'

She looked at her mother-in-law for support. But Amit's grandmother had told Romola a long time ago that she did not want to handle the old lady's demands any more. Now that Romola was around, her duty as daughter-in-law was done and she was going to spend more time volunteering with her Rotary Club Ladies Circle.

So Romola looked at Avinash and muttered, 'If tomorrow she has an upset stomach, you clean up – she is your precious grandmother, after all.'

Amit's Boroma, his great-grandmother, was ninety-four. She still had her own teeth – with a few missing here and there. When it suited her she was blind. When she did not want to hear something she was deaf. At other times she would prop the thick black-framed glasses with their almost cloudy yellowish lenses on her hooked nose and peer at the newspaper with great concentration. Her favourite section was the obituaries, which she read with ghoulish relish.

'Harihar Shastri died,' she would announce, looking at Romola chopping vegetables for lunch. 'He used to come to study under your grandfather-in-law. He was a full twelve years younger than me.'

But today Great-Grandmother was in her helpless, sightless mode, as if her very spine had crumpled inside her. She sat on her bed, her plain white sari falling off her wrinkled shoulders, and peered up at Avinash.

'Jackfruit, blackfruit,' she bleated mournfully. 'When your grandfather still had the house in the village we had jackfruits the size of bolsters growing in our own courtyard. And all the mangos we could ever want. Do you remember?'

'Ma, you make it sound like a zamindari plantation,' said Amit's grandmother. 'I just remember a couple of mango trees. You really do exaggerate.'

But Great-Grandmother carried on undeterred. 'We had fresh mangos, mango chutney, mango pickles, mango squash, even homemade mango ice cream. Where will I get that any more? Have I legs that I'll go walking? Have I my own money that I'll buy myself anything?'

As Avinash awkwardly patted his grandmother on her shoulder and fixed her sari, Romola standing near the doorway muttered darkly, 'No legs? That woman has eight legs.'

Amit imagined Great-Grandmother as an ancient toothless spider crawling from room to room and giggled. Hearing him, Romola said, 'Come here. I feel a white hair growing. Pluck it out carefully. Mind it, don't go pulling out all my black hairs too.' Romola often complained that her hair was turning white from looking after all of them – Amit and his father and his grandmother and his great-grandmother. 'Your school ends at three, your office ends at six,' she would tell Amit and his father in exasperation. 'My duties never end.'

Great-Grandmother survived the jackfruit without any

stomach upset. 'She could digest iron,' said Romola with grudging admiration.

'It's all that unadulterated milk she drank in her day,' Amit's grandmother added.

Great-Grandmother one, Mother zero, Amit tallied in his head as if it was a football match. He wondered sometimes why his great-grandmother and mother always seemed to be butting heads. 'Does Ma hate Boroma?' he asked his father once.

'No, no of course not,' laughed his father. 'They both think they are the boss of the house. But they both love you very much.'

That Amit knew. When Great-Grandmother sent the old maid Mangala out to get thick slices of batter-fried aubergine from Dasu's tea-stall down the street, she'd always sneak Amit a slice. He wasn't supposed to eat street food but Great-Grandmother said that was all nonsense.

'You have to build the boy's immunity,' she would tell Romola. 'You can't just shelter him. Why, when I was a child—'

'Yes, yes, grandmother, when you were a child the world was ruled by the British and the cooking oil was pure,' said Romola shortly. 'Amit has school tomorrow. He can't afford to have a tummy upset.'

But the next day when she picked Amit up from kindergarten, she bought him a chocolate pastry from the bakery on their way back. 'There,' said Romola. 'Isn't this much better than some oily gutter-fried aubergine?'

As he licked the chocolate icing Amit thought contentedly that if he played his cards right he could have both.

He almost did, except the next time Mangala tried to sneak the fried aubergine into the house, she bumped into Romola. Mangala immediately hid her hands behind her back but to no avail.

'What do you have there?' demanded Romola.

'Nothing,' Mangala lied.

'Nothing – I'll teach you nothing. Show me at once.'

The offending article was revealed – thick slices of aubergine fried in hot golden-brown batter, the oil seeping through the newspaper cone they came in.

'Oh! From Dasu's tea-stall,' Amit's grandmother said accusingly, looking at Romola to pick up the fight.

'Filth and rubbish!' exclaimed Romola on cue. 'Cooking in the open on the street next to that gutter. God knows what oil he uses. Here I am spending your master's hard-earned money to buy good oil on the black market and you want to poison her with this garbage?'

'Oh, but they were for me,' said Mangala in a last-ditch effort to save Great-Grandmother.

Hearing the noise Great-Grandmother herself had now shuffled out. She stood there leaning on her little stool with wheels, which Avinash had designed for her after her knees started giving way.

'What is it?' she demanded. 'Can an old woman not shut her eyes in peace in this house?'

'Mangala was just telling me that she bought some fried aubergine to have with her tea,' said Romola with a sly smile.

'She'll have a stomach upset, no doubt' said Great-Grandmother sourly, eyeing the oil-stained paper cone.

They stood there watching Mangala eat five pieces of fried aubergine one by one.

When the last crumb was gone Romola turned to Great-Grandmother and asked sweetly, 'And what would you like for dinner?'

Mother one, Boroma zero, thought Amit.

Great-Grandmother sighed heavily and said, 'Whatever you give me. I am an old woman, a burden on you. I won't bother you too much longer. Legs gone, eyes gone, ears gone

. . . how long before I am gone as well? Husband, brother, sisters – everyone is gone. Even my own son taken before his time. I ask God every day how long must I wait for you to take me.'

'Old woman, my foot. She'll outlive us all,' muttered Romola under her breath.

But Amit knew Great-Grandmother wasn't really indestructible. He could see the little cracks, as fine as the veins on her hand. Like the time she suddenly looked at him and called him Gopal. She had been dozing in bed after telling him one of her fairy tales about brave princes and Bengoma-Bengomi, the talking birds, when she said groggily 'Gopal, come to your mother.'

'Gopal?' Amit, who was making a house with her playing cards on her giant four-poster bed, giggled. 'I am not Gopal.' He knew who Gopal was. His father's father, his great-grandmother's son. Grandfather's photograph hung in the front room – a bald man with round glasses and a big belly.

'Yes, you are my little Gopal.' Great-Grandmother's eyes fluttered open like shutters on a window. 'Don't tease me.'

'I am Amit,' he protested. But Great-Grandmother leaned forward. Her gums were bluish. Her eyes had turned unseeingly opaque. Like a witch from one of her own fairy tales, her claw-like hand fastened around Amit's neck.

'Don't tease me,' she repeated, her voice steely, her papery hands rough on Amit's neck. 'Gopal, little Gopal.'

Amit wriggled, calling her urgently, trying to break the spell. As he pushed her hands away her white sari fell away and to his horror he saw her breasts, wrinkled and flapping like washing on the line. As he gasped and twisted, Great-Grandmother abruptly let go of him. The milky darkness left her eyes as suddenly as it had come, a passing storm that had veered off course.

Amit scrambled off the bed. 'Where are you going, Amit love?' she said. 'I didn't finish the story, did I?'

'Tell me tomorrow, Boroma.' Amit gathered up his books. 'I have to show Mother my drawings.'

He wondered if he should tell his parents but decided not to. The last time he had told them about Great-Grandmother's cold, his mother forbade him from going into her room for three days. 'You can't be too careful,' she said.

Amit tried to tell her that Great-Grandmother's bed was his favourite place in the house but she just shushed him. Great-Grandmother allowed him to arrange her pillows into mountains and oceans, which he would then defend against run-of-the-mill pirates and fantastic demons with heads of buffaloes and tongues of fire. And she would sit there playing endless games of patience while spinning her stories full of gods and monsters.

That was why Amit loved the third Thursday of every month. That was when his mother went to visit her best friend across town. His grandmother went to her Ladies Circle monthly meeting and bingo game. Thursdays were Amit's day off from school. Romola would deposit him in Great-Grandmother's room and say, 'Now you two look after each other. And don't get into any mischief.' That was meant as much for Great-Grandmother as it was for Amit.

'I will just tell him stories about gods and goddesses,' said Great-Grandmother meekly. 'Tell me, my little darling, what does the Goddess Durga ride?'

'A lion,' Amit shouted.

'Very good. Now draw your old Boroma a picture of the Goddess Durga.'

Scarcely had Romola left than the house erupted into frenzied activity. The coal stove had to be fired up, vegetables cut, fruits chopped.

'This is the end,' grumbled old Mangala as she poked at

the coals. 'If Bouma finds out this time I'll lose my job for sure.'

'We'll fry our own aubergines today,' said Great-Grandmother gleefully 'And make some mango chutney.'

Amit helped her stir the batter while Mangala sliced the aubergines. He watched Great-Grandmother supervise the mango chutney – the bubbly golden orange syrup like thick winter afternoon sunshine with a hint of roasted red chilli, the fat slices of mango floating in it, all poured into round-bellied glass jars with glass lids. She would let him help her pour, and then he'd lick his fingers and taste the sweet sunny syrup. Sometimes little red ants would drown in the syrup. 'Don't worry,' Great-Grandmother would reassure him. 'If you eat the chutney with the dead ants in it you'll learn to swim.' Amit's father said that made no sense because the ants had drowned, but Great-Grandmother paid him no attention.

Great-Grandmother would stash most of the mango chutney somewhere in her room. 'So if I wake up in the middle of the night and want some I'll have it right there. Now don't tell your mother – she'll say mango chutney is not good for you in the middle of the night.' Then she would add with unassailable logic, 'What does she know? Your mother was not even born when I started making pickles and chutneys.'

Amit would lie on his stomach on Great-Grandmother's bed drawing pictures, while she told him stories about how Calcutta used to be covered with forests with jackals and even the occasional tiger and Great-Grandfather had been a police officer chasing robbers. If occasionally Great-Grandmother added a few extra details that hadn't been there the last time (five robbers attacking Great-Grandfather instead of two) Amit didn't mind. He'd lie on the bed smelling the clean sheets and Great-Grandmother's hair oil, watching the after-noon shadows trailing across the foot of the bed. Soon the doves in the window eaves would start gurgling, lulling him to sleep, a little boat on the gently rolling tides of her stories.

By the time Romola came home all traces of cooking were gone. The pots and pans were washed. The chutneys stashed away. The aubergine eaten. Amit had even finished his drawing of the Goddess Durga and her four children. Great-Grandmother was asleep, snoring gently, her pack of cards beside her.

Of course it never fooled Romola. She'd take one look at the storeroom and announce, 'The sugar jar was three-quarters full yesterday morning. Now it's three-fourths empty.'

Great-Grandmother looked up from her game of patience and said loudly to no one in particular, 'Servants. Thieves all. Can't trust anyone these days.'

Stung, old Mangala, who was pottering around the storage room, muttered under her breath, 'That's right. Call me a thief. My hair is going white, working, working for you.' Amit would giggle and Romola would look at him and say darkly, 'And if you tell me you're not hungry when it's dinner time, you are in big trouble, mister.' But a smile twitched at the corners of her mouth as if they were all playing a game together.

Once in six months when she got her son's car and driver, Great-Grandfather's youngest sister Renu Thakurma came visiting. Renu Thakurma was a pious old lady and always had sandalwood paste smeared on her forehead. She was a good fifteen years younger than Great-Grandmother but had been widowed much earlier. Now she followed every religious rule she could find with fanatical fervour. Renu Thakurma had her own kitchen separate from the family kitchen. In her kitchen even the word 'Meat' was forbidden.

One Sunday she came visiting when Great-Grandmother was having lunch. After Great-Grandfather died at the age of ninety-five, Great-Grandmother cropped her hair and gave up her coloured saris. But she loved fish too much to give that up. She had been raised along the rivers of what was now Bangladesh. She would recite the names of fish like a nursery rhyme – ilish, pabda, leta, boal...

When Renu Thakurma spied her eating fish, she was scandalized.

'Why, Boudi,' she exclaimed. 'You still eat fish?'

Caught red-handed, Great-Grandmother fumbled for a reply. 'Well, only once a day. Besides, fish is almost a vegetable. Fruit of the river, my mother-in-law would say.'

'Oh those are just excuses. When my husband died I turned my back on onions, garlic *and* fish and have not touched them since. It is written – those things excite our senses. You think I have not wanted a piece of ilish drenched in mustard gravy? But I told myself, "Renu, your husband could feed you ilish twice a day when he was alive. What is the use of lusting after fish now that he himself is gone?"'

Great-Grandmother stared guiltily at the fish head she had been about to crunch and put it down. Amit wanted to jump up and tell Renu Thakurma something. He didn't know what but he felt like he had to do something. Renu Thakurma peered at the plate and said, 'Oh my, tangra! How my poor dead brother loved a good tangra curry.' With that she wiped the corners of her eyes. Great-Grandmother looked stricken. Amit glanced at his father, who was sitting there with his newspaper, not saying anything.

'Well, um, you know these days things are different. Change you know,' Amit's grandmother said hesitantly, attempting to steer the conversation away. 'But Renu-pishi, tell me, how is your son's job?'

But Romola, who was standing by, turned to Renu Thakurma and cut her short. 'The doctor has said she needs to have fish,' she said bluntly. 'He said she must have fish at least once a day.'

Amit gaped at his mother. He had never heard her lie so blatantly.

'The doctor?' asked Renu Thakurma sceptically.

'What's more, he said if she did not like fish she could have chicken stew instead.'

'Chicken stew?' exclaimed Renu Thakurma clutching her breast.

'But if she has fish every day it should be enough.' Then Romola turned to Great-Grandmother and said, 'Eat up the fish head, Thakurma. Don't you remember the doctor said especially to eat the head? It has the good vitamins that you need.'

As Great-Grandmother chewed the fish head Amit saw beads of sweat on Renu Thakurma's forehead. Romola and Great-Grandmother exchanged triumphant looks.

'Standing in my house telling my grandmother-in-law what she can and cannot eat, hmmph,' muttered Romola to Avinash after seeing Renu Thakurma out. Great-Grandmother didn't say anything but quietly sat on her bed while Mangala brushed her hair. When Amit dragged his feet as usual about taking an afternoon nap, she looked up and said, 'Go now, little one. Listen to your mother.'

But the truce was short-lived. The next day Romola discovered that Great-Grandmother had been coaxing the fruit-seller into giving her mangos on credit.

'Am I dead? Is your grandson dead?' she screamed. 'Begging mangos from that Mohanlal. Have you no self-respect? Today when I said he was asking for too much for his Himsagar mangos do you know what that good-for-nothing said? He said, "What about all those free mangos I feed the old woman?" Just like that in front of everyone in the market. As if I was starving my own grandmother-in-law. I was so mortified I wanted the ground to open up and swallow me. Go eat mangos four times a day. See if I care – I'll even buy them for you. Just don't ask me to call the doctor. You are ninety-four years old. Haven't you eaten enough mangos?'

Great-Grandmother quietly went on playing her game of patience. After Romola had gone upstairs in a huff she told Amit, 'This Thursday we'll make puffed-rice mowas. Go, run and check in the storage – see how much jaggery we have.'

But that afternoon when Amit was sitting on her bed with his crayons, Great-Grandmother looked listless. She pulled up her blanket around her and complained it was cold.

'It's not cold, Boroma,' said Amit. 'It's only September.'

But Great-Grandmother pulled her blanket closer and said, 'My bones are old.'

'Are you sick?' said Amit putting his hand on her forehead like his mother did when he had a temperature.

'Maybe a little fever,' said Great-Grandmother. 'But don't tell your mother. She'll just say don't eat this, don't eat that. As if at my age anything matters.'

'Okay,' said Amit. He had no intention of telling his mother. He didn't want to be banished from Great-Grandmother's room.

'Bring me that jar from the top of the shelf,' said Great-Grandmother. She carefully extracted a mowa, the grains of puffed rice glued together with sweet brown jaggery. 'Eat it up before you go upstairs to your mother. We'll make more on Thursday.'

Amit sat on the bed eating the mowa. He waited for Great-Grandmother to say, 'Don't drop crumbs everywhere. Otherwise the ants will come and eat up this old woman.' But she didn't say a word. When he looked at her, her eyes were closed and her head was lolling, her mouth slightly open. Amit touched her on the shoulder as he clambered off the bed.

'Where are you going, little Gopal?' she mumbled her eyes still shut.

'You've come upstairs early,' said Romola as he walked into her room. 'Is anything wrong?'

'No,' said Amit quickly. 'I just came up. Just like that.' He hoped by the time he woke up, Great-Grandmother's fever would have gone away as well.

But the fever just hung on. Soon she was coughing every time she tried to talk. At first Great-Grandmother wouldn't let Mangala tell anyone she was sick. She made her eat her food instead. It took two days for Amit's grandmother to realize that her mother-in-law was really ill.

'Do you think we should call the doctor?' said Romola. 'I gave her the cough medicine but it doesn't seem to be doing much.'

'Well, maybe she will pull through,' said Avinash. 'It's only been two days. I'll give the doctor a call from my office.' Amit wondered if he should tell them how long Great-Grandmother had been sick. But it was too late to say anything. He was afraid they'd scold him if they knew he hadn't told them before. Even worse, they would scold Great-Grandmother. So Amit just kept quiet.

But the next day she was drifting in and out of consciousness. Romola called the doctor. It was just age, he said. She was so old that all the pieces that held her together were falling apart as if they were rusty.

'But her heart still keeps pumping,' he said to Avinash. 'She is a tough one.'

'Call Renu-pishi,' Amit's grandmother said to his father. 'I think we should start informing people.'

The next day and the day after Amit watched his relatives parade through the house. They talked in low voices and stood near the door to Great-Grandmother's room drinking endless cups of tea. Romola had made Mangala change the old faded curtains. Amit thought that was funny since Great-Grandmother didn't really notice anything. Thursday came and went. Only Amit remembered the puffed-rice mowas Great-Grandmother had wanted to make. Instead, her bedside table was piled up with foil-wrapped sheets of tablets and bottles of pink and white liquids that Mangala had to give her every hour, on the hour.

On Saturday his mother called Amit down to Great-Grandmother's room. The shades had been pulled down and the room was full of shadows and smelled of medicine and disinfectant. The dirty old fan whirred listlessly overhead. Great-Grandmother lay on the bed, breathing through her mouth in loud choking gasps. Mangala was pressing her feet and sniffling loudly. The room was full of relatives who huddled around the bed, their murmurs buzzing like flies. Amit's grandmother sat at the foot of the bed though she had nothing to do.

'Come in, dear,' said Romola seeing Amit hesitating near the door. She seemed tired. Amit could even see some white hairs near the front of her head that she had not plucked out.

She took a little brass pitcher and said, 'This has holy water from the Ganga. Put a few drops in your Boroma's mouth.'

Amit shrank back because he did not want to go near Great-Grandmother. She smelled funny, ripe and musty at the same time, and her loud wheezing scared him. The room smelled stale and old. He couldn't hear the doves any more.

'Go on,' said his grandmother. 'It's your duty. Your Boroma will find peace in heaven if you give her some Ganga water now.'

Amit stood near Great-Grandmother, one hand clutching his mother's sari while with the other he gingerly poured a few drops between her parched old lips. Her eyes were closed. Her lips were dry and cracked. She smelled as if she was rotting, though he had heard his mother tell Mangala to give her a sponge bath that very day. He could see the straggly white hairs on her chin. They were almost longer than the cropped hair on her head.

As the drops of water dribbled into her mouth and ran down her wrinkled chin, he wished he was giving her mango chutney instead – thick orange-red mango chutney, great sticky drops of it.

Late that night Mangala came and banged on his parents' bedroom door long after all the shops on the street had shut down and the only sounds were the yapping street dogs fighting over the garbage. Lying curled up in his bed Amit could hear nothing except the taut urgency in their voices. He heard his father going downstairs while his mother started dialling the telephone. Soon she went downstairs as well. He heard his grandmother talking to someone on the telephone. Amit saw the lights come on and wondered if they would ever come to get him.

When he finally heard his mother at his door, he quickly shut his eyes as if he had been asleep all along.

When they took Great-Grandmother away, no one wept – not his grandmother, not his father nor his mother. Only Mangala cried piteously. Romola just seemed drained and tired. 'Don't cry,' she kept telling Amit even though he was not crying. 'She had a long life and lived to see her great-grandchildren.'

The next day they stripped her bed. When they pulled up the mattress, they found to their surprise little bottles of mango chutney stashed under it. Fat slices of mango swimming sluggishly in pools of hot-sweet red-gold syrup. Great-Grandmother had been hiding away her precious mango chutney, for a time she might be totally bed-ridden.

On seeing that Romola burst into tears.

Trying to console her Amit said, 'But look Ma, they are still full. She did not eat any.'

But that did not stop her tears at all.

*   *   *

Amit looked at the jars of mango and lime pickles and chutneys standing at attention next to each other on the shelf. And he wondered if any of them would taste like his Great-Grandmother's mango chutney. He felt a lump in his throat.

'Foolish,' he told himself. 'Crying about old Boroma, dead almost twenty-five years now.' He remembered Mangala – now dead as well. Dasu's tea-stall was long gone – swallowed up by the parking compound for a new mall. He wished he had told his girlfriend the story about his Great-Grandmother's mango chutney. But it was foolish to even try to summon up the thick, sweet taste from oceans away and decades ago. The girl was gone and he had let her go just as he had let old Great-Grandmother slip away. And now here he was, thought Amit, a twenty-nine-year old good boy, single again, programming in Microsoft Windows, with no idea what to do with his life. Or even what he was going to have for dinner.

He wondered if he should tell the store owner about the expired can of jackfruit. Instead he hid the old dented can behind the pickle jars. Then he walked out of the store without buying anything.

VI

Father's Blessing

ROMOLA KNEW something was going to happen that day. Ma did not pack her lunchbox. Instead, Dipti-mashi from next door did. She put her sandwiches in just like that, not knowing that her mother usually wrapped them in foil first. When it was time to eat them at school she found that some of the cucumber slices had fallen out and gotten all mixed up with the sweet sandesh. The sandesh was shaped like a conch shell and very crumbly. It was quite strange – sweet cucumber. She could never think of that day again without evoking the ghost of that peculiar combination – pale green cucumber with sweet white sandesh crumbs sticking to it like little pieces of lint.

When she woke up in the morning Ma was not even there to make breakfast. The sun was out, seeping in through the pale blue curtains on her bedroom window, and she could hear the bustle of the market setting up on the street and the loud voices of the vegetable sellers. That was the time she would hear her mother humming in the kitchen, the kettle starting to boil with a loud whistle. But that morning everything was quiet inside the house.

'Where is Ma?' she asked Bela-di. Bela-di was the old family maid. She had been working for them since before Romola was born. Even before Romola's father got married.

'She is busy downstairs with your father,' Bela-di said.

Ma was in the sick room. That's what they called the room where Baba was ever since he got sick. Romola did not quite know what kind of sick it was but he had become very thin. Doctor Uncle came every few days and talked to Ma in a low voice. Once, seeing Romola hiding behind the curtain, he said in a jolly Santa Claus voice, 'Well what ho, Miss Romola Dutt? Tell me the capital of Yugoslavia.'

'Belgrade,' replied Romola twisting her skirt in her hand. Though she had been outside Calcutta only once, when she had taken the train with her parents to the seaside in Puri, Romola knew her world capitals.

'So that school of yours does teach you something after all. Keep it up, keep it up. How old are you now?' He ruffled Romola's hair.

'Ten, almost eleven,' replied Romola.

'Excellent.' Doctor Uncle beamed as if she had won a prize in a spelling competition.

But Romola knew his cheerfulness was all fake, from her mother's tired, distracted smile and the dark smudges under her eyes.

That morning Ma did not even have that smile on her face.

'Won't Ma make my breakfast?' Romola asked Bela-di.

'You are a big girl and don't need your Ma to make you breakfast any more. Here, I made you some toast.' Bela-di put a plate with two pieces of toast in front of her. Romola inspected the toast and sulked. Bela-di didn't trust the toaster that Romola's aunt Ila had brought from England and always toasted the bread over the gas stove. The toast was soft in parts, while other parts were burned, the black sooty splotches like charred maps of small countries.

'What's the matter now?' said Bela-di noticing her not eating. 'Come on; eat up your toast quickly. You will be late for school otherwise.'

'It's burnt.' Romola scowled at the two charred pieces of bread.

'Oh ho,' said Bela-di. 'Do I have time for all this huss-fuss? I have so much work to do. Now be a good girl and eat it quickly. Here, have it with some jelly.' She plonked a jar of guava jelly in front of her and bustled away.

At that moment, her mother came up the stairs and said, 'Did Bela make you your breakfast?' Romola was surprised to see her mother was still wearing the same striped sari she had worn to bed last night. Usually the first thing she did was change into a fresh sari as soon as she got up.

'Yes, but she burned the toast,' said Romola pointing to her plate.

'Well, just be a good girl and eat it up.' But her mother was not even really looking.

'Ma, why are you still wearing the same sari?' she asked.

But her mother merely said, 'Bela, when you get a minute could you take Romola's lunchbox next door? Dipti will make her her lunch today. Just give her the box. She said she would send Mohan over with it when it was ready.' Mohan worked for Dipti-mashi. He was about thirteen, maybe fourteen, a lanky boy with shiny dark skin and tousled hair. Sometimes he played with Romola and her friends though he would call them babies. What he really liked to do was hang out with the drivers in the neighbourhood and tinker with cars.

'Why not keep her at home today?' Bela-di wiped her hands on her sari. 'Don't you think she should stay?'

'She is too young, Bela,' said Ma. 'She will just be in the way and get scared. It's better if she goes to school like normal. And we don't know how long this will go on.'

Everyone spoke around her as if she wasn't there. Romola wanted to say that she would much rather stay home. She had her geography class test that day and didn't want to take it. But her tongue felt tied up in knots. So she just quietly ate the middle of the bread where it was not so burned while the conversation circled around her.

'Oh my,' said Bela-di. 'Look at how she has eaten. She just gouged out a piece in the centre and left all the sides.'

Normally that would have resulted in an argument and a lecture. But Ma just said, 'Let her eat whatever she wants. I don't have time for all this. She needs to get ready. I have to go downstairs. I think Doctor Mallick should be here.' Romola looked triumphantly at Bela-di and spitefully arranged the sides of the pieces of toast so it looked like a house with a big hole in the middle as if a thunderstorm had knocked it out. Then she wondered what else she could get away with.

Romola felt very grown-up as she dressed herself that day. She took her shower and dried herself carefully. She powdered herself under her arms and around her neck just like her Ma did when she got her ready. Then she even combed her hair, though Bela-di had to fix her plaits in her red school ribbon. She made sure she wore clean panties and socks and checked to see her grey school skirt had no ink stains.

Soon Bela-di came bustling up to check on her. She put her lunchbox in her school bag and went downstairs with it. Romola followed swinging her water bottle. On any other day Ma would have scolded her and said, 'Stop swinging the bottle. All the water will fall out.' But today she had a feeling she could get away with it. And she was right; Ma did not even notice.

Her mother came out of the sick room, gave her a kiss and said, 'Be careful. I hope you don't make too many spelling mistakes in your test. Check everything twice. Don't rush. Did you sharpen your pencil?'

'Yes,' she replied.

Just then Doctor Uncle came out from inside the room and said, 'Well, well, if it isn't the little scholar. So tell me, what is the capital of Austria?'

'Canberra,' she said but Doctor Uncle did not seem to care. Perhaps, thought Romola, her geography test would be like this too. She could just write whatever she wanted and no one would care. As she walked towards the door, she saw Doctor Uncle glance at her and tell Ma, 'What do you think . . . ?'

'I don't know,' Ma's voice sounded worried and as frayed as her old kitchen towel. 'All this will just make her anxious and scared. And she has an exam today. Maybe when she comes home she can sit with him for a while if his condition has stabilized a bit.'

Romola was secretly relieved. The sick room with its smell of medicines and decay scared her. Sometimes her father's eyes seemed glassy with pain, sometimes he was dozing and barely able to recognize her. When she was younger Romola wished her father would pay more attention to her. But all he liked to do on weekends was put on his cricketing whites and organize the neighbourhood boys into cricket teams. He even bought Mohan a cricket bat. Romola had once asked her father if he would teach her about off-spin and googlies but he'd just laughed and said, 'But you're a girl.' Now his booming laugh was gone, his voice a cracked whisper. Sometimes she would see Mohan walking down the street with the bat and a little knot of anger would coil in her stomach.

When Romola went outside, Tublu from three houses down was standing outside reading the newspaper. Romola's father had helped get him a job. Tublu looked up and asked Bela-di quietly, 'How is Ramen-babu?'

Bela-di did not answer. But out of the corner of her eye Romola saw her shake her head. Tublu sighed, then he smiled at Romola. 'So, off to school, eh?'

By then Romola had learned to recognize false smiles. At first it had made her feel shut out, as if she was the outsider in a conspiracy. Now she was used to it and knew that it also meant she was free from their attention. She looked back at the house, swung her water bottle extra hard as she and Bela-di started walking down the street. Ma was standing at the door. But instead of waving to her, she was talking intently with Tublu.

'Aren't we taking the car?' asked Romola.

'No,' said Bela-di. 'Your mother might need it today. We are going to take a taxi.'

Romola decided to see how much she could push things on this most unusual day. 'Can I get a little money to buy some peppermints? I forgot to ask Ma.'

'Okay, I will give you some when I get change from the taxi driver,' Bela-di said. 'Now come along. We have to hurry or we'll be late.'

Romola turned again to see if her mother was looking at her. This time she was. Ma raised her hand to wave. The sari slipped down and she saw her bangles glint in the morning sun. That was the last time Romola remembered her mother wearing those bangles. It was as if inside her head something clicked and took a photograph of her mother knowing she might never look quite the same again. The sari with the thin blue stripes and the blue fishes on its border. Her hair still loosely knotted near her neck like it had been when she had gone to sleep. And those red and white bangles. Then her mother turned and went back into the house.

'Watch where you're going.' Bela-di grabbed her elbow crossly. 'You almost stepped into that puddle.'

'Okay, okay,' Romola said, stepping around it. 'But tell me you won't forget to give me the peppermint money.'

'I said I'd give it to you, didn't I?' Bela-di said sharply. 'Now walk nicely and give me your bag. You are swinging it so much your lunch will be one big mess.' She meekly handed her the bag but as she would discover later – it was too late. The sandesh was already all over the cucumber.

When school ended that day she saw to her surprise that

neither her mother nor Bela-di had come to get her. Instead it was Dipti-mashi from next door with Mohan. Mohan was wearing a blue shirt that Dipti-mashi had given him last year as a gift for the Pujas. But he had grown a bit since then and now the shirt was tight under the arms. But since that was his newest shirt he always wore it, especially when he went shopping at big stores.

'There you are, Romola,' Dipti-mashi said, coming forward and taking her bag and giving it to Mohan to carry.

'Where is Ma? Or Bela-di?' she asked frowning.

'They were busy. And I had some shopping to do at New Market so I just said I would pick you up.'

She wished grown-ups would not lie like that. Dipti-mashi went shopping at New Market all the time. She had never picked her up before.

'How was school?' she said.

'All right,' Romola replied, kicking a stone. She had mixed up Narmada and Tapti rivers again on the map but she figured Dipti-mashi did not need to know. After all, she probably had no idea she had had a geography test.

'How was tiffin?'

'The cucumbers were all mixed up with the sandesh and they tasted funny,' she said grumpily.

'That's because you swing your bag so much,' she replied.

'Ma always puts them in foil,' Romola retorted.

'Well, she did not tell me,' said Dipti-mashi, 'but I'll do that for you next time.'

'Are you going to make tiffin for me tomorrow again?'

'Oh I don't know. I might, if your Ma is too busy.'

'Why would she be too busy?' she asked.

'Oh, you know,' she said vaguely.

To Romola's surprise, they did not go home. Instead they went to Abha-mashi's house. Abha-mashi was actually not Romola's aunt. She was Dipti-mashi's sister. But they called her aunt anyway. She lived about two streets away from them so she was always over at her sister's. Sometimes Abha-mashi would give Romola a Cadbury chocolate bar.

'Come on,' said Dipti-mashi opening the car door.

'What, here?' she said in surprise. 'Why?'

'Oh, we need to stay here for a little while,' she said.

'But what about my bath? What about Ma?' she said, puzzled.

'Oh, your Ma already knows. We will go over soon. We can leave your school bag in the car if you like.' But Romola carried it with her anyway.

Abha-mashi did not seem surprised at all to see her. 'Go upstairs. I'll send Mohan up with a snack and some lemon squash in a minute,' she said.

'Mohan, go tell the cook to make some squash for Dipti and Romola,' Abha-mashi said. 'And then go to the roof and play with Romola for a bit.'

'Go on,' she said, giving Romola a little push. 'Go upstairs. Mohan will be up in a minute.'

But he doesn't want to play with me, Romola thought to herself. However, she said nothing and slowly climbed up the stairs dragging her school bag behind her. It went bump-bump on the steps. She looked back once and saw Dipti-mashi and Abha-mashi still standing at the foot of the stairs talking in hushed voices. Abha-mashi was looking at her as she said something to her sister. Seeing Romola watching her, she smiled and said, 'Go on. Make yourself at home.'

But I can't eat without having a bath first, Romola thought.

Romola went into the study where Abha-mashi kept all her books. She saw a comic book lying on the table. She started leafing through it when she heard Mohan coming in.

'What are you reading?' he said putting a glass of lemonade down in front of her.

'It's not for you,' Romola said, without looking at him. 'You won't understand it.'

'It's only pictures anyway,' he shrugged. Out of the window Romola could see the street. Dipti-mashi's driver was leaning on the bonnet of the car talking to Abha-mashi's driver, the smoke from their cigarettes wafting in the air around them lazily in the late afternoon sun. 'What are we doing here, anyway?' she asked Mohan.

Mohan pulled a face but did not say anything. But after she had finished the drink he turned to Romola and said, 'Well, do you want to go to the terrace or not?'

Romola shrugged and followed him out and up the stairs. Romola had come to Abha-mashi's house once before. She remembered they had all played hide-and-seek on the roof. Their roof was a good place to play hide-and-seek. It had little rooms with the water cistern and concrete posts that were good places to hide in.

But today there was no one except Mohan and her. The sky was still blue and cloudless but it was no longer as hot as it had been all day.

'What shall we play?' she said kicking a pebble.

'I don't know,' Mohan curled his lip. Then he said, 'I'll just sit here and watch you.'

'You can't do that,' said Romola. 'Dipti-mashi told you to play with me. You must play.'

Mohan did not answer her.

Undeterred, Romola said, 'Let's play school-school.' Then she added quickly, 'I'll be teacher. You can be the student.'

'What rubbish,' said Mohan. 'You're just a baby. How can you be the teacher?'

'I can too,' said Romola. 'And you are only a few years older than me. I am not a baby.'

'You are too, silly,' he said.

'That's not true,' Romola's voice was sharp with agitation.

'Now I am going to give you a spelling test. No, no an arithmetic test. Can you do short division in your head?'

Mohan rolled his eyes and said, 'This is a stupid game. You don't know anything.'

'I do too,' said Romola. 'Now if you don't play with me I'll tell Dipti-mashi.'

'Big baby,' he scoffed.

'I am not,' she protested.

'Yes, you are.'

'No, I'm not.' By now she was close to tears.

'Yes you are, a hundred times. Anyway, the only reason I am playing with you is because you are a baby and your Dipti-mashi doesn't want to tell you your father is dead because you'll just start to cry and—' he clapped his hand over his mouth and stopped.

'What did you say?' said Romola squinting at Mohan.

'Nothing.' But Mohan would not meet her eyes.

'I heard you,' she said but she couldn't feel anything. His words kept ringing as if her mother's old gramophone needle had got stuck in her brain. Mohan had become quiet, looking around nervously as if to see who might have been listening to them. Romola looked away from him across the roofs of houses. In the late afternoon sun, rooftop after empty rooftop stretched before her. She could see the washing hung out to dry. Emerald green sari, white petticoat, small boy's checked shirt, dark blue shorts, another sari, this one yellow with little red flowers, another petticoat. She counted them in her head.

After a minute Mohan sat down hesitantly near her and touched her shoulder.

'Romola,' he said. 'I'll play school-school, if that's what you want.'

She did not say anything. She felt she was supposed to cry now but all she could do was count the clothes hung out to dry. She wondered if she would have to go to school tomorrow. Then she worried it was wrong to have thoughts like that.

'You can even give me an arithmetic test,' Mohan said with a touch of desperation.

She looked at him thoughtfully and said, 'I can?'

He nodded.

She said, 'Okay, and then I'll give you a spelling test too. And if you get more than two wrong you don't get any tiffin. Mohan, is Dipti-mashi going to make my tiffin tomorrow too?'

'I don't know,' he said.

'Tell her to put the sandwiches in a separate bag or something. They got all mixed up and yucky with my sandesh.'

He nodded.

'Here,' said Romola. 'Let's pretend this comic book is my text book.' She scribbled some figures on the ground with a piece of chalk and said, 'Okay, do some sums.'

As he crouched on the ground, she walked over and stood near him. She could see the traces of talcum powder around his neck, chalky smudges on his skin as dark as her grandfather's old teak furniture. His hair was slick with oil and plastered to his scalp as if with thick black paint. She could see the furrows his comb made in his hair. She was so close she could smell the coconut oil he massaged into it. She stared at the back of his neck and sat down next to him. Then she said, 'I am not a baby, you know.'

'I know.' But he did not look at her.

'I know things,' she said, twirling a piece of string around in her fingers.

'Like what?'

'Things,' she said mysteriously. 'Like do you know that guy who lives across the street from us? The one who goes to college? He smokes. I saw him one day when he thought no one was looking.'

'Who cares about that?' he said.

'Well, I know other things too,' she said, slightly deflated. 'Like how babies are made.'

Mohan burst into giggles, finally meeting her gaze. 'No, you don't.'

'Yes, I do,' she said indignantly. 'I can show you.'

He looked at her eyes wide with disbelief.

'But first you have to show me yours,' said Romola.

'What?' he said. 'You must be crazy.'

'Show me,' said Romola. 'I won't tell anyone.'

'Don't be silly.'

'No one can see us here.'

'I don't want to show you anything.'

'You have to,' said Romola.

'I have to?'

'If you don't show it to me, I'll tell Dipti-mashi you told me.'

'You little—' he said reaching out to grab her.

Romola jumped out of his way and sang, 'Show me, show me.'

Mohan looked at her baffled.

'Or I'll tell,' she said. 'And then Dipti-mashi will give you two tight slaps. Maybe fire you too. Once Ma and Baba had a fight and Basanti-di who worked for us went and told Dipti-mashi all about it. And Dipti-mashi told Ma and Basanti-di was fired.'

'You are just a silly girl,' said Mohan but his tone lacked conviction.

'Try me,' Romola pretended to head towards the door. But she knew she had won for the fight had drained out of Mohan's face. His head was drooping slightly, his eyes darting nervously to the door.

'Look here, near the water tank,' said Romola. 'No one can see you except the kites.'

He stood near the tank and said grudgingly, 'Only for a minute then. And if you tell anyone I will tell everyone you made me do it.'

'Yes, yes,' said Romola.

Mohan unbuttoned his shorts, glanced around and then pulled them down. For a moment, he looked at her and hesitated and then, dropping his eyes, quickly pulled down his cotton underpants to his knees. Romola stared at him. All her bravado had trickled out of her. She stared at the dark brown of his thin legs held together by the well-washed, yellowish-white strip of his underpants. She dragged her eyes up from his dark knobbly knees to his thighs. Her view was partially obscured by his shirt dangling in front of him.

'Eeesh,' she said in a small voice. 'You have hair there.' She could see the hair – little strands around his penis that hung limply like a shrunken wrinkled finger. It reminded her of a tamarind pod, the kind Bela-di dried in the sun to make sour pickles.

'You will too, one day,' he said.

She looked at him shocked but did not say anything.

'I can't see it properly,' she said trying to move his shirt out of the way. He smacked her hand away but held his shirt up so she could see.

'It looks silly,' she said. She tried to remember what Ranjana from Class Six had told her about how this thing went into a woman's secret place to make babies. But it seemed too far-fetched an idea. She realized she had not shown Mohan her secret place. But he did not seem to care.

Just then an airplane passed by. Startled, Mohan dropped his shirt as if the passengers flying overhead could see him. He turned his back to her and pulled up his underpants. When he turned around his lips were pinched tight. Right at that moment Dipti-mashi called out, 'Mohan, Romola, are you up there? Come down now.'

Silently he headed towards the door. He did not look back to see if Romola was following him. But she was right behind him. As she came down the stairs, Romola could see Dipti-mashi there.

'Romola,' she said slowly as if she was spelling the words out in case she did not understand. 'We need to go home now. Your mother called. Romola, my dear, I have something to tell you. But you must be a brave girl because your mother needs you.' Romola glanced at Mohan. He was standing at the bottom of the stairs looking at her. He smoothed down his shirt and touched the front of his pants to make sure it was all buttoned.

Romola did not cry when she saw her father laid out on the bed. The last time she had come to the sick room, her mother had said, 'Ogo, look, it's Romola. Open your eyes.' And he did slowly as if it hurt to open them.

Romola had perched herself warily at the edge of the bed. Her father had put his hand on Romola's hair and, with a great deal of effort, tousled it. Then he took her hand in his and closed his eyes again as if the strain had worn him out. Romola looked at the vein on her father's forehead. It was throbbing and seemed the only thing about him that was alive. After a minute she glanced at her mother. She nodded and Romola gently extricated her hand and scuttled out of the room.

But today the smell of medicine and Phenol disinfectant was gone. The pile of dark bottles and shiny silvery foil strips of tablets had been removed. His stainless steel tumbler of water covered with a coaster that always stood on the little table by his bed was missing. Instead the room only smelled of flowers – her father was covered with wreaths of bluish-white rajanigandha and gladioli, his eyes closed, his skin pale as if he had been powdered and dressed up. She could see some of the dark wet green leaves had come off from the wreaths and were lying on the floor being stepped on by all the people milling around. She had never seen so many of her relatives together before. There was a pile of their slippers outside the room. Even Dahlia-pishi who lived all the way out near the train station, and whom they perhaps saw once a year, was there. Her mother was sitting at the foot of the bed. She stood up as she saw Romola. Then she opened her arms out and Romola ran straight into them and hid her face against the folds of her sari. She could feel the cold metal of her bunch of keys against her cheek and it felt indescribably comforting. She peeked out – her father seemed asleep, his eyes shut. He was wearing a crisp white cotton kurta with fine white embroidery – Ma had given that to him for his birthday that year but he had not had a chance to wear it.

'Romola,' said her aunt. 'Touch your father's feet and ask him for his blessings.' Still clutching her mother's hand, she did as she was told but she didn't actually touch the feet. The toes sticking out from under the thin sheet covering him scared her.

'Such a brave girl,' she heard Dipti-mashi say in a low voice to another woman. 'I had to tell her. And she took it so bravely. No tears. Just said, "I want to go to Ma."'

The lady nodded and wiped her eyes with her sari and said, 'So, will she, I mean, do the last rites?'

'Oh no,' Dipti-mashi said. 'She's too young. I think Ramen-babu's younger brother will do them.'

When they took her father away Romola gripped her mother's hands. That was when she noticed her wrists were bare, the red and white bangles gone. She watched wordlessly as six men lifted her father on their shoulders. The women started to weep. Dahlia-pishi began ordering everybody around.

'*Hari bol, balo Hari*,' chanted the men. Romola shrank back, afraid her father would roll off their shoulders and fall to the ground. But he didn't and soon the men had borne him out of the house and turned the corner and they were gone scattering handfuls of puffed rice behind them to keep away the bad spirits.

'Keep that oil lamp burning till they come back from the cremation ground,' instructed Dahlia-pishi. Romola's mother did not say anything, her eyes still fixed blankly on the corner of the street where the men had turned with her husband's body. So Romola nodded instead.

That night Romola's mother said, 'Do you want to sleep in my room, Romola?'

Ever since she had turned four, she had to sleep in her own room in her own bed. Only on special treat nights Ma and Baba let her sleep in their big double bed. Romola would pretend some nights to be scared of shadowy monsters and try and crawl into their bed but soon they would shoo her back. After Baba got sick and started sleeping in the sick room, Ma would sleep alone in the big bed.

The bed felt so big, like an empty playground, as Romola crawled into it with her own blanket and bolster. She lay there looking up at the ceiling. There was a little crack near one corner. She remembered Baba talking about needing to fix that before it got bigger. She wondered if anyone would fix it now. She glanced over at her mother to see if she had fallen asleep.

'Ma,' she said softly. 'When did Baba, you know, die?'

'Around one-thirty in the afternoon,' her mother replied, gently stroking her hair.

She lay quietly for a while and then said, 'Ma?'

'Hmmm?' she said sleepily.

'Ma, Dipti-mashi said that Baba can see me from heaven. Do you think that's true?'

'Yes, dear. I hope so. Now try to sleep.'

Romola looked out of the window. Through the leaves of

the neem tree outside she could see a patch of the night sky above the serrated edges of apartment buildings below. She could see a couple of stars twinkling faintly. She thought of her father looking down at them from the sky and felt her heart grow cold. She wondered if it took some time for a soul to go to heaven or if they went right away. If father died at 1.30 would he have been able to see her at 3.30? She felt sick to her stomach.

'Even when I am at school? Or at Dipti-mashi's house?'

'When you are what at Dipti's house?'

'You know, can he see me when I am at Dipti-mashi's?' But without waiting for an answer, she started to cry, great hot tears welling up from her stomach and trickling down her face.

'Shh, shh,' said Ma wiping her eyes. 'There's a good girl. Don't cry, my love. Your father can always see you – he will always watch over you wherever you are.'

VII

The Gifts of Summer

WHEN AMIT came back from school and rang the door-bell, instead of Mangala's usual shuffle, he heard the sound of running feet. A young girl's voice shouted, 'I'll get it, Dida.' He heard the door unlatch and saw a girl standing there. He had never seen her before. She was skinny, wearing a yellow frock with little blue flowers, the sooty darkness of her skin making the frock almost glow. The dress was too small for her, thought Amit. It seemed tight around her arm-pits and her bony knees showed. Her jet-black hair glistened with oil. It had been tied into a tight braid with a red ribbon. Amit noticed she had a tiny silver nose stud.

She stood staring at him with her hands on her hips.

'Who are you?' Amit asked.

She stared a few seconds more and then grinned, her teeth flashing against her skin.

'Why, I am Durga, of course,' she said. 'You are Amit. I remember seeing you when you were very young. Grand-mother used to have to clean your bottom after you did potty.'

Amit flushed but she seemed to find the memory hilarious.

'Who are you jabbering with?' said Mangala, coming into the room and wiping her wet hands on the edge of her old cotton sari. 'Oh, Amit's back from school. Remember my

114

granddaughter Durga?' Then she turned to the girl and said, 'Go on, take Amit's school bag upstairs and tell his mother he's home. I'll go warm his milk.'

Amit remembered then that his mother had said that Mangala's granddaughter Durga was coming to spend the summer in Calcutta with her. Amit's aunt Meena was also supposed to visit at the same time from Boston. 'We must make Meena feel at home,' his father had announced. 'We practically grew up as brother and sister till they moved to America. When I first landed in America, her parents looked after me like their own son.' Since Amit's mother was looking for an extra pair of hands around the house, Mangala had suggested that perhaps Durga could help out.

Durga grabbed Amit's bag and water bottle and sped off upstairs. 'That girl is a hooligan,' said Mangala, shaking her head. 'Why don't you teach her some reading and writing during your summer holidays? Maybe something will stick in her head.'

'Me, teach her?' asked Amit alarmed. 'How can I teach her? She is older than me, isn't she? How old is she?'

'Fourteen or fifteen,' said Mangala.

'But I am only nine,' said Amit. 'What class is she in? Doesn't she go to school?'

'That school in the village is no good. It's not like your school,' sighed Mangala. 'And her father thinks there's no point teaching her much more, because she'll probably end up in someone's house sweeping the floors or cleaning dishes. Like me. But who knows – maybe you can teach her something.'

Meena-pishi came a few weeks later. Amit stayed at home while his parents went to the airport. For hours he tried to stay awake, fiercely rubbing sleep from his eyes. But by the time the car pulled up he had fallen asleep in front of the television. The sound of his mother's voice woke him. The evening news was over and the transmission had ended for the night leaving only a crackle. He turned off the television and walked out to the head of the stairs and peered down.

His mother cried, 'Durga, come get the bags.' Looking up, she saw Amit. 'Amit, you're still up? It's past midnight. Come down then and say hello to your aunt.'

Meena-pishi looked different from the old photographs in the family album. She was both fairer and plumper now. Her hair was cut fashionably short, unlike his mother's. She wore a synthetic sari with a pattern of large magenta and yellow flowers. Amit noticed she used a lot more make-up than his mother. She smelled different as well – more fruity and expensive. She beamed at him and held her arms out.

'Oh my,' she said in English. 'What a handsome young fellow.' Even her English sounded different, the words smudged with an American accent. Then looking at Durga she turned to his mother and said, still in English, 'Who's this? A new maid? She's very young, isn't she?'

'Oh not really,' said his father. 'Remember our old cook Mangala? This is her granddaughter. She was in the village all this time. She wanted to spend the summer in the city. So we let her stay in our house. In return she does a little house-work.'

'Very little,' interjected his mother. 'But Mangala has worked for us for so many years. We could not refuse her. Durga, what are you doing standing there gaping? Go on, help with the bags. Be careful. Don't scrape them against anything.'

Meena-pishi had matching bags all as red as her lipstick. They looked brand new. 'Doctor Basu bought them for me before this trip,' she said proudly. Doctor Basu was what she called her husband.

'Too bad he decided not to come this time,' said Romola.

'He's so busy with his practice,' said Meena-pishi. 'And he's just opened a new chamber. Right downtown, you know.'

Amit didn't know. He had never met Doctor Basu and he had no idea what downtown even meant. But he nodded anyway.

Durga hoisted the big carry-all over her shoulder and started going upstairs. 'Now go up, all of you. Amit, back to bed at once,' said Romola. 'Meena, you must be so tired after that long flight. Did they feed you on the plane? Are you hungry?'

But Meena-pishi just stood there looking around the house as if breathing it in. Amit found it hard to imagine that once she and his father had been children in this house. Her mother and his grandmother had been sisters and all the cousins played together in this house. His father said they had once written a play together and acted it. Their mothers had made them costumes and everyone had to pay one rupee to watch it. Meena-pishi had been the princess. His father had played a magician. Then her father had moved to America and the visits had petered off. All this Amit had heard from his father.

'I remember right here we used to have your mother's prayer room with all her gods and over there was your father's library,' said Meena-pishi. 'Isn't that right, Avinash?'

'You remember,' replied his father with a chuckle. 'We couldn't touch anything as long as Grandmother was alive. After she died, we got rid of some stuff. Then, after Ma went soon after, Romola sold off everything to the bikriwala.'

'It's not like you ever touched those books,' protested Romola. 'They were just a breeding ground for termites. And Amit needed a place to study.'

'But those pictures? What happened to the pictures on the wall?' said Meena-pishi. 'I remember there were pictures of our parents on a holiday in the hills. And one of my grandmother on her wedding day.'

'And there was one of all of us in the park for a picnic. That's when my father had just got the new camera from England,' said Avinash excitedly.

Amit stared at him curiously. His father was a quiet man, rarely demonstrative with either affection or reprimand. He seemed to live in his own world. He had rarely seen him so alive and voluble.

'I am sure they are in the storeroom somewhere,' said Romola with a slight smile. 'You know, Meena, I can hardly get your brother to say five words when we are alone. And now look at him – just on a non-stop memory train ever since you stepped off that plane. Remember this, Meena, remember that? But we can't always live in the past, can we? We have to go on with our lives. Now, come along, let me show you your room. Otherwise you brother and sister will spend all night talking right here.'

The next afternoon after lunch his aunt called Amit to her room. Amit stood at the door transfixed. His mother sat on the bed next to his aunt. Her suitcase was open and the contents were spread out everywhere. Clothes, biscuits, soaps.

'Oh,' said his mother inhaling a box of soaps. 'You know, Meena, that's what I missed the most after I came back from America with your brother. The soaps. They smelled so divine. I remembered my aunt coming from England and all the lovely soaps she had brought. Foreign always meant soap to me.'

'Well, make sure you use them and don't just stash them away for a special occasion, I know how you Indians are,' teased Meena-pishi. 'I hope this shirt fits Avinash. I got it in Doctor Basu's size.'

'Look what your aunt got you,' said Romola holding out a box of Lego and a T-shirt.

Amit smiled and took them carefully from her hands. 'Thank you,' he said politely.

But there was more. Meena-pishi looked at him and said, 'Come here, Amit. Show me your hand.'

He held his hand out and she reached into her handbag and

brought out a watch. As she strapped it on Amit's eyes grew wider. It had a Mickey Mouse on the dial.

'Oh, how did you know? He is such a Mickey Mouse fan,' laughed his mother. 'When he was younger, his father's friend Sumit once got him a packet of Mickey Mouse colouring pens. My goodness, I could not get him to throw away that packet even after the ink had dried and nothing came out of those pens any more.'

'You know this Mickey's eyes move with the hours. And when it is dark Mickey glows green,' laughed Meena-pishi.

'Really?' said Amit. 'Can I try it?'

'Just wait till night,' said his mother.

But Amit was already crawling under the bed where it was dark.

'Oof oh, what are you doing among all the dust and spiders?' scolded Romola. His aunt was right: Mickey glowed like a ghostly mouse in the dark.

Above him he heard his aunt say, 'I didn't know Mangala's granddaughter was here. I didn't really bring anything for her. Should I give her some money?'

'That's okay,' said his mother. 'We'll give her one of these KitKat chocolates. She'll be happy enough.'

But when Meena-pishi gave Durga the chocolate she slipped in some money with it as well. 'Don't tell anyone,' she said conspiratorially. 'Buy yourself something nice.' When she saw Amit looking she winked at him as if it was their secret. 'Do you like your watch? You know your cousin in America had one like that as well. Except his was Goofy the dog. We gave it to him after he did very well in arithmetic.'

Amit, whose mathematics results were often poor, looked down a little guiltily at his watch as if it might vanish from his wrist.

That night when his father came home from work, Amit showed him his watch. His father said, 'But the time is wrong.'

'It's still American time,' said Amit sheepishly hiding his hand behind his back. 'Meena-pishi will show me how to change it soon.'

'Now remember,' said his father. 'This is your first real watch. You must look after it well. It's not a pen or a book that we can easily replace.'

In the morning when Amit woke the sun was already shining. He could see the motes of dust dancing in the bar of sunlight streaming through the window. Outside, the clamour of the day had begun. He could hear the crows cawing in the tree in front of his window and cars honking on the street. Someone was shouting for a cup of tea; somewhere a clock struck eight. Amit reached under his pillow and felt for his watch. There was a little knob to press to change the time. He started jabbing at the knob with great concentration and did not notice Durga come into the room.

'What are you doing?' she asked.

He looked up. 'Fixing my watch,' he replied.

'Why? Is it broken?' she asked.

'No, of course not,' he said. 'But where it came from in America, it's a different time than here.'

'What time is it over there?' she asked

'Yesterday evening,' he answered.

She stared at him for a moment and then grinned showing her crooked front teeth. 'How silly,' she said, shaking her head 'Now go and have your breakfast. Your eggs are getting cold. Your mother sent me to ask you to get up and brush your teeth.'

After lunch his mother and aunt settled down in the big bed that had belonged to his great-grandmother. His mother was reading a Bengali women's magazine. She chewed paan as she read, her mouth moving slowly and methodically. Periodically she reached out to push her glasses up her nose.

Meena-pishi sighed and stretched. 'I tell you, Romola,' she

120

said. 'It is quite a luxury to have some rice for lunch and lie here quietly under the fan and take a nap. Over there – you eat some sandwiches or some leftovers and then you have to run to something or the other. Either the supermarket or soccer game or clarinet practice. There is always something. And Doctor Basu has so many social engagements especially after he became president of that cardiologists' association.'

'And it's not the same, is it,' said his mother, 'taking a nap by yourself?'

'So true,' agreed his aunt.

Amit watched his mother place the magazine on her breast and shut her eyes and settle down, one arm over her head. A little strand of greying hair trailed over her forehead. She raised her hand to push it back, smudging the red of the bindi. It left a streak but she did not bother to fix it.

'Tell me, Meena,' said his mother. 'Does it feel very different coming back?'

'Some things are still the same. Just older and shabbier. The city seems dirtier. That garbage dump from the market next door seems to be twice as big. It's a health hazard, if you ask me.'

'We complain and complain to the authorities. But nothing changes,' sighed his mother.

'I miss Calcutta terribly but I don't know if I can live here any more,' Meena-pishi continued. 'That garbage dump, the pollution. Nothing seems to work at all. It's getting too much.' His aunt closed her eyes. 'And the heat. I guess I am becoming American.'

'What will I do now, Ma?' asked Amit.

'What do you mean – what will you do now? It's the middle of the afternoon. There is nothing to do. Take a nap.'

'But I'm not sleepy.'

'Just close your eyes and lie still.'

'But Ma,' protested Amit.

His mother said, 'Read a magazine or something.'

Amit lay quietly for a minute watching the fan blades go round and round.

'Ma,' he said.

'What now?' grumbled his mother sleepily.

'I am not sleepy.'

'Try harder,' she retorted.

His aunt smiled and said, 'Amit, when you grow up, do you want to come to America?'

'I don't know,' he said.

'Do you ever wish you had stayed on after Avinash's PhD?' his aunt asked looking at his mother.

Romola didn't respond for a minute. Amit could see the vein twitch on his mother's forehead.

'That's so long ago. At that time we needed to come back,' said his mother. 'We had to take care of his mother and grandmother. If Amit studies hard maybe he will go on his own some day.'

'I still remember the day Avinash called to say you were going back. Romola doesn't like it here. Give her time, I said. She will settle down. Everyone is like that in the beginning. But your bags were already packed. You said you didn't want to stay one day after his PhD was done.'

'Why didn't you like it there, Ma?' asked Amit, curling up against his mother.

'It wasn't home. I thought if I had a child like you, he needed to grow up among his cousins and grandparents,' said his mother stroking his hair.

'That's all very well,' said Meena-pishi. 'But you could have tried to adjust a little, no? I mean Avinash could have done so much more research. He was always so academically inclined. And he would have been earning in dollars.'

'Well, we are getting by fine here, Meena,' replied his mother stiffly.

'Of course, of course. I didn't mean it that way,' Meena-pishi said hurriedly. 'I just mean it would have been nice to have you all in America as well. Maybe we would see each other more than once in seven years.'

Romola pursed her lips but didn't say anything. She turned to Amit instead. 'Why don't you go downstairs and see what Durga is doing? But don't play up on the roof. The afternoon sun will burn you to a crisp.'

Durga was sitting under the stairs eating rice. Her grand-mother was washing the kitchen floor. As Amit came down the stairs he heard her call out to Durga, 'Come and put away these dishes when you are done eating. Then I can sit down and get a bite.'

Durga did not answer. She was busy pouring dal on her plate. Amit watched it pool amid the snowy mountain of rice that she had piled high on her plate. Rice mounded so high a cat cannot jump over it, his mother was prone to grumble. She looked up at him with a frown, her hand poised midway. He could see the little dal-smeared grains of rice clinging to her fingers.

'What's the matter now?' she asked.

'Nothing. Mother said I could come down and play with you instead of sleeping.'

Durga put some rice in her mouth and chewed it reflect-ively. Still chewing, she said, 'Well, I'm not done eating.'

'After you finish eating then,' said Amit settling down on the last step.

'After that I have to wash the kitchen floor and do the dishes,' she said. Then she stopped, looked at him and cried out to her grandmother.

'What is it?' said Mangala peeping out from the kitchen.

'I need to take care of Amit. His mother said so. I can't wash your kitchen for you,' Durga announced triumphantly.

'What?' said Mangala stepping out, her hands still wet from washing dishes.

'See,' said Durga gesturing at Amit. 'There he is.'

'But—' said Mangala and then stopped. 'Well, hurry up and eat then and my goodness leave some rice for me. What an appetite this girl has – like a monster.'

'Monster,' grinned Amit. 'You're a monster.'

Durga stuck out her tongue at him.

Amit grew to love the afternoons best of all. Upstairs his mother and aunt would lie in bed, reading magazines, their conversations slowly losing steam and trickling away into nothingness as they fell asleep. All over the house the windows would be shut against the heat. Skinny drips of sunlight would leak in through cracks in the shutters and puddle on the floor.

Mangala would unroll her mat and lie down, her greying hair still wet from her bath. She would tell Durga, 'Now play quietly. If you wake me up, I'll wring your neck.' Then she would turn on her little tinny radio and listen to film songs till she too fell asleep.

Durga and Amit would go and sit in the cool dark living room and play ludo or snakes and ladders. Sometimes she would want to play dress-up but that bored him. She had a small worn-down crimson lipstick. When she got tired of painting her own lips, she would, much to his horror, want to colour his. Then he would try and distract her with his watch.

'Let me wear it,' she said once.

'No,' he replied instantly.

'Why not?' she said pouting.

'Because you might break it and my father won't give me a new one,' he replied.

'I'll be careful,' she promised. 'I am not going anywhere with it. I just want to see how it looks on my wrist. I have never had a watch.'

So he gave it to her. He watched her put it on. He had

never seen it on anyone else's wrist but his own. It looked funny on her.

'That's enough. Give it back,' he said stretching out his hand.

She laughed and shook her hand. 'What? I just barely put it on.'

'No, give it back. It's mine,' he said, reaching out.

She laughed and stood up holding her hand above his head. 'Get it,' she taunted.

'Give it,' he said, trying to yank her hand down.

'Careful, it will break,' she said, slipping out of his grasp.

'Don't break it,' he cried agitatedly.

'Stop pulling my hand then,' she said, waving her hand at him and grinning.

Just then Mangala walked into the room and said, 'What is all this noise?'

'Mangala-di,' complained Amit, whirling around, 'Durga won't give my watch back.'

'What? Give it back at once,' said Mangala.

Durga hesitated. Seeing her hesitation, her grandmother stepped forward and cuffed her on the head. 'Give it back, I said. Why are you playing with other people's things? Haven't I told you a hundred times to stay out of trouble?'

Durga scowled and pulled the watch off and handed it to Amit. Amit hurriedly put it on. Mangala looked at him for a moment and then told Durga sharply, 'If you have nothing better to do than create trouble you can go wash the dishes. And send Amit upstairs to sleep.' With that she turned around and left.

Amit and Durga stood there looking at each other. Finally Durga said, 'I have to go' and started walking towards the door.

'Wait,' said Amit.

She turned around.

'I didn't mean to get you into trouble,' he said quietly. She said nothing.

'Look,' he replied, 'you can wear my watch for a little while longer. I won't mind.'

'I don't want your stupid watch,' she said. But she didn't leave.

'We can play dress-up if you like,' Amit pleaded.

Durga said nothing.

'Meena-pishi has lots of old lipsticks. I'll get you one,' said Amit.

She shrugged. But she stayed.

One afternoon after lunch Amit was going downstairs with his colouring book in search of Durga when his mother stopped him. 'Amit, Amit where are you off to?'

'To find Durga,' he replied. 'We are going to draw.'

'Oh,' said Romola. 'I forgot to tell you. Durga can't play with you today. I want her to help me make fish chops. Your father really likes them and I thought it would be a treat for your aunt as well.'

'What treat is that?' asked his aunt coming out of her room.

'Fish chops. I was telling Amit not to bother Durga. I need her to help me make the filling.'

'Oh, I didn't know you needed Durga. I should have checked with you. I needed to get my blouses picked up. The tailoring shop said they would be done today. And my shawl that I gave in for dry-cleaning as well. I had asked Durga if she could get them for me.'

At that moment Durga came up the stairs dressed in one of her two going-out frocks.

'Durga,' said Romola. 'Did you completely forget about my fish chops?'

Durga said, 'But Meena-didi asked me to . . .'

'I had already told you about the chops yesterday.' Romola frowned. 'Why didn't you tell Meena-didi that?'

Durga stood stricken looking from one woman to the other.

'Can your brother pick them up tomorrow?' Romola asked Meena placatingly. 'Or the day after tomorrow I want to go shopping at New Market. Maybe I can pick them up then.'

'No no, the tailor is going away. Don't you remember? I told you that. That's all right. I'll just go myself. I am sorry, I had no idea you needed Durga now.'

Durga looked at Romola silently.

'No, no. It's not important,' said Romola though she looked annoyed. 'I'll manage. Durga, you go do what Meena-didi needs.'

'Here, Durga, let me give you something for your bus fare and a little extra.' Meena-pishi opened her handbag and pulled out several notes.

'There's no need for that. I'll give her bus fare,' Romola said a little sharply putting her hand on Meena-pishi's arm.

'I insist,' said Meena-pishi with a smile. Durga stood frozen between the two. Eventually Romola just dropped her hand. Durga took the money and walked out of the room.

'Maybe we can make the chops together, the two of us,' said Meena-pishi brightly after Durga had left the room. 'I can teach you my mother's recipe. It was Avinash's favourite.'

'Of course,' said Romola politely. 'But I had wanted to treat you to my recipe, the way my mother used to make them.'

Amit knew someone would notice it sooner or later. He was actually surprised it took as long as it did. He was sitting near the window drawing in his sketchbook when his aunt came in from her bath. Towelling her hair vigorously she said, 'Amit, what time is it?'

'I don't know,' shrugged Amit without looking up from his drawing book.

'What do you mean?' said his aunt, still rubbing her head

with the towel. 'Where is that watch of yours? It was like a second skin.'

Amit did not say anything.

'Huh?' said his aunt. 'Don't tell me you've gone and lost it.'

'Umm, I don't know,' he said looking up.

'Really, Amit, you had better find it and find it soon. Otherwise you know how upset your mother is going to be.'

'I know,' said Amit miserably.

'Where could it go? It can't just fly away. When did you see it last?'

'I don't know,' stammered Amit. 'Maybe yesterday. Or the day before.'

'Day before yesterday?' cried his aunt. 'And you haven't said a word about it. Have you looked for it even? Does your mother know?'

'I looked,' Amit said defensively.

'Have you searched under the bed? Maybe it fell there. Did you ask Durga or Mangala if they found anything while sweeping the floor?'

Amit shook his head and said, 'No, but they would tell me if they found it.'

'But have you even told them you can't find it? I have seen how that Durga sweeps. A little jab here and a little jab there. The dust just stays right where it is.'

Amit said, 'Well, I'll ask her to look for it. Properly. She likes that watch a lot too.'

'Does she?' said his aunt. 'I hope you find it. Otherwise you know you will be in big trouble.'

When Amit came back from the park that evening he knew the cat was out of the bag. His mother came downstairs with a pinched expression on her face. She saw him, frowned and said, 'Amit, why didn't you tell me your watch was missing?'

'What?' said Amit.

'Yes, yes,' said Romola sharply 'I overheard your aunt telling Doctor Basu on the phone. This is my house, after all. I need to know if something is missing. I cannot have thieves and robbers living under my roof eating my rice.'

'Oh, Romola,' said his aunt appearing on the landing behind his mother. 'I would have told you. It's not such a big deal.'

'I am sure it is not for you,' said his mother turning around. 'But that is not the point. You practically grew up in this house. I can't have you thinking it's turned into a den of thieves now that your aunt is gone.'

'I never said that, Romola,' his aunt replied, sounding tired.

'I know what you said. You said this would have never happened in your aunt's time. I am not my mother-in-law. But I can discipline the servants too.' She came down the stairs rapidly and shouted, 'Mangala, Mangala, where are you?'

Mangala emerged from the kitchen, saying, 'What is the matter?'

'Where is that granddaughter of yours?' said Romola.

'Now what has she done?' said Mangala wearily.

'We will soon know,' said Romola, her tone grim. 'Remember Amit's new watch – the American watch? I hear your grand-daughter took a fancy to it. Now it's gone. Gone for two days, apparently. But no one bothers to tell me. Something disappears in my own house and I'm the last to know.'

'What are you saying, Bouma?' said Mangala, aghast. 'My Durga might be a little hot-headed but she is no thief. Why, the other day while sweeping she found a coin and picked it up and gave it to you.'

'This is no coin,' said Romola. 'This is an American watch. More expensive than six months' pay.'

'Well, I am sure there is some other explanation.'

'I hope so. And I will get it out of that girl.'

'Ma,' said Amit feebly, 'I think I might have lost it some-where.'

'It cannot just fall off your wrist,' said his mother. 'And I tell you – if you can't take care of expensive things, you shouldn't wear them.'

'Romola,' protested his aunt. 'Let's not get too carried away.'

'Really, Meena, perhaps things like that are fine in your Boston,' his mother shot back. 'Why give it to boys here so that others can die of envy?'

'But—' said Amit.

His mother cut him short. 'Come upstairs, Amit, and wash your hands.'

The she turned to Mangala and said, 'As soon as that girl gets home send her to me.'

'I will, I will,' grumbled Mangala. 'We are poor. But never have I taken a ten paisa that was not mine.'

As soon as Durga came home, Amit wanted to run to her. But his mother got to her first. He could hear her raised voice, sharp as a knife, cutting through the summer air.

'Meena-pishi,' he said fearfully looking at his aunt as she sat reading the newspaper.

His aunt just shook her head and said, 'I told you to take more care of that watch.'

Amit hung his head.

Just then he heard his mother at the foot of the stairs. 'Come down, Amit. I want you to see for yourself.'

He glanced at his aunt. She said, 'Go on' and nodded towards the door. He opened it slowly and looked down the stairs. His mother was standing downstairs, gripping Durga by the elbow. Durga's face was dark with anger. Or was it fear? Mangala stood behind them with her hand on her head.

Amit started down the stairs though he felt his feet were made of lead. He could see the cracks on the steps. Each looked big enough to swallow him. He saw a big black ant crawling up. It disappeared into a crack. He glanced up and saw Durga looking at him baffled and sullen.

His mother took Durga to the little room at the bottom of the stairs. She pushed the old green door open and shoved the girl inside. He could see the rolled-up mattreses where Durga and Mangala slept. There was a little pitcher of water in the corner and a small picture of the goddess after whom the girl was named. On an old rack on the side hung some of Mangala's white saris and a couple of dresses. In one corner were Durga's favourite red-and-gold slippers. The gold was fading but it was still the brightest splash of colour in the room. At the other end of the room was a battered suitcase.

'That,' said his mother pointing at the suitcase. 'Open that.'

'Why?' said Durga sharply. 'Those are my things.'

'Your things?' retorted his mother. 'I will show you your things. Living off my charity and a big mouth too. Open it at once.'

'This is too much,' protested Mangala.

'Mangala, this girl will come to no good because you don't discipline her enough. I hear people speak about how she's been talking to the next-door driver in the alleyway. And I think – it's not my daughter, not my business. But now it is my business: open that suitcase.'

Durga flashed a look at her and slowly walked over to the suitcase. She snapped it open and held it out. 'See,' she said.

There was not much in it – old containers of cold cream. Some bangles and hair clips. A little locket. Some small boxes and cans, their labels long faded away.

'Look at all those cosmetics,' said Romola trying to snatch the suitcase out of Durga's grasp. Durga jerked her hand away. The suitcase fell – the contents tumbling on to the floor. Little containers rolled under the rack. A necklace tore as it fell, the beads scattering on the floor like fat grains of rice. One of the plastic containers popped open and its contents rolled across the floor towards Romola.

Durga lunged after it but Romola grabbed it first.

'What's this?' she said, picking it up. 'Lipstick. Just a girl and make-up already!' She held it up to the light and said, 'Oh my goodness, this is a Revlon. Isn't this yours, Meena?' Amit stared at the lipstick as his mother unscrewed it – it was almost all gone. The coral tip poked out of the coppery container like a stubby crayon.

Meena-pishi who had been watching the unfolding drama silently was suddenly galvanized as if she had received an electric shock.

'Oh, it is mine,' she said. 'Though it was almost finished. I was about to throw it out anyway. But how did she get it?' Now she too started looking through Durga's possessions. 'And my old Maybelline eyebrow pencil,' she said picking it up from the floor. 'Have you been rummaging through my things?'

'I didn't take them,' protested Durga looking at Amit.

'Then how did they come here? Did they grow wings?' demanded Meena-pishi.

'But it's not the watch,' said Mangala.

'She's probably sold it on the black market. What else have you taken?' demanded Romola.

'I swear I didn't steal anything,' said Durga. Much of her defiance had drained away from her by now. 'I thought you were done with those cosmetics. I was just playing with them. I thought Meena-didi had thrown them away.'

'That's my business – what I throw, when I throw. Who are you to decide for me?' said Meena-pishi.

'Do you know how much one of these lipsticks costs? And now you embarrass me more by taking Amit's watch,' said Romola.

'I did not steal his watch,' Durga was close to tears. 'Tell her, Amit, I didn't steal anything.'

But Amit just stood there, unable to utter a single word.

Romola's voice rose higher and higher. 'I trusted you with the house. I trusted you with my keys. I trusted you with this boy.'

'But, Bouma,' pleaded Mangala, 'I swear my Durga did not take the watch. She would not do such a thing.'

Romola was unmoved. 'Today a lipstick, tomorrow a watch. I knew that all that money Meena kept giving her for every little thing would go to her head. Don't think I didn't know about the money.' Meena-pishi now went up to Durga and shook her by the arm. 'Tell me what else did you take?'

'I swear on God, nothing,' said Durga.

'Liar,' Meena-pishi cried, shaking her even harder.

Durga started to cry. Mangala came forward and said, 'Let her go.' She tried to pull Durga towards her. Meena raised her hand to slap Durga. But Mangala grabbed it saying 'No!'

Amit's aunt slowly dropped her hand looking stunned.

Mangala looked at Romola and said, 'I have worked here from before you came into this house as a bride. I've taken care of your grandmother-in-law like my own mother. I've emptied your mother-in-law's bed pan.' She turned to Meena and said tearfully, 'Tell her, have I ever taken a thing that was not mine? You can't slap my granddaughter. For a couple of old thrown-away lipsticks. Enough. We are leaving. Start packing your things,' she told Durga sharply. 'And make sure you show the mistress every little scrap you take.'

Romola looked thunderstruck. She clapped her hand over her mouth as if she wanted to throw up. Then abruptly she turned on her heel and left the room. Meena stood for a minute in the little room and then left as well. Amit stared back at the room – Durga was still standing near the bed, her face streaked with tears. Mangala glared at her and said, 'What are you standing there for? You good-for-nothing girl. What more misery do you have in store for me? Go pack – you will end up making us beggars on the street. Don't you know your place? Who told you to pick through their rubbish?'

Mangala left that very night. She went with that same battered suitcase that was in the room. She came to say goodbye before she left. Amit was sitting quietly next to his father trying to read an Enid Blyton adventure but the words seemed to float in front of him without any meaning. His mother had said she had a headache, turned down the lights and gone to bed. Meena-pishi had also said she did not want dinner and had retired early.

Avinash said, 'I am so sorry, Mangala. Look, I am sure your Bouma will calm down by the morning. You don't have to go. This is not your fault.'

Mangala shook her head. 'It is my fault. I did not keep that girl on a tight leash. I let her watch too much TV. It went to her head.'

Avinash opened his wallet and took out some money. 'Please take this, Mangala,' he said. 'You will need it.'

'No, no,' said Mangala backing away. 'I don't want any money. Bouma has given me my salary. I just wanted to say I don't think Durga would steal the boy's watch. She is a foolish girl – but she is not a thief.'

'I believe you,' said Avinash. 'But please take some money. Where will you go at this time of the night?'

'I'll stay with my brother tonight. Tomorrow we will see. But don't worry. Someone somewhere always needs a maid.' With that, Mangala touched Amit on the head and said, 'All right, little one, I'm leaving. You be a good boy.'

Amit shrank from her touch and pulled his knees up to his chin. He wanted to say something but not a word came out of him. He tried to say he would miss Durga. He tried to say, 'Don't go.' But instead he just stared at the floor. When he looked up Mangala was gone. Durga did not come to say goodbye.

The next morning Amit took his Lego container and ran up to the roof. He looked around to make sure no one saw him. Then he carefully reached inside and brought out the watch. Mickey's hands were stuck at 10.45, its face cracked. He knew he should not have worn it in the shower. But it had said 'Water Resistant'. And he just had to test it. How was he to know he was going to slip and fall? That the watch would go spinning out of his hand and land with a sharp crack on the wet floor? He remembered standing there, wet and naked, shaking the watch. But it was dead, stuck for ever at 10.45.

He picked it up and slowly walked to the edge of the roof. He looked around again to see if anybody was looking. Then he threw the watch as hard as he could. He watched it sail up into the air, higher and higher, and then curve down towards the street, past the old kadam tree, past the television antenna above the tea-shop, past the crows sitting on the windowsill of the red house next door and into the garbage dump. A crow sitting on the garbage heap jumped up cawing loudly. But in a minute it was back again pecking at the rubbish.

VIII
White Christmas

T HE FORECAST, said the weatherman, was 60 per cent chance of snow. 'My goodness,' said Amit's mother on a crackling phone line from Calcutta. 'You will have a white Christmas. We once had that when your father and I were in America. Oof, how cold it was. Over here it's still so warm. We haven't even had a chance to use the heavy quilts. Your father says it's global warming.'

'How is Baba?' said Amit cradling the phone with his shoulder as he tried to put on his socks. The heater was sputtering as usual filling his room with a musty mildewy smell. His feet felt cold in the early morning chill in spite of the carpet on the floor. The house was quiet. His roommate had gone home to Iowa for Christmas. Outside it was not snowing yet. But the sky was overcast and leaden, pressing down on the deserted little university town.

'Today morning,' continued his mother as if she had not heard him, 'I met Mrs Basu at Christmas lunch at the Club. And she said, "Mrs Mitra you sent your Amit to America. I think you should get him married quickly. Just the other day my sister-in-law's brother wrote from Texas saying he's getting married to some American girl. And such a fine boy too – never stood second in his life. First-class first in physics. And now his mother cries all day."'

Romola laughed nervously and paused. That was Amit's signal to reassure her that he would protect the family honour against evil, gum-chewing, cigarette-smoking, home-wrecking, disrespectful American women. He imagined them waiting at JFK airport in New York and LAX and O'Hare – hordes of buxom blondes in tight shorts and skimpy tops ready to snap up naive, god-fearing, rice-eating Indian boys as they stepped off the plane.

Unable to extract any reassurance, his mother went on. 'Why, look at your uncle Shobhan's son. He went to America just like you and then came back after four years and married that nice Radha.'

'Just like Baba came back to India to get married to you. I know, I know. But anyway, you always said Radha was fat and dark,' Amit quipped, rummaging in the pile of clothes at the foot of his bed for a sweater. 'At least if I married an American girl you would have nice, fair grandchildren. All pink with red cheeks, maybe blue eyes,' he said teasing her.

'Don't joke,' said his mother fiercely. 'It's not like I've not been to America. They are different. Very friendly, but different. These white people don't have the same sense of family that we do.'

'But who said that if I married an American she'd have to be white?' said Amit grinning into the telephone. 'She could be Chinese or Mexican or black too.'

'Black!' His mother was speechless for a second. Amit knew she was imagining grandchildren who looked like they had walked out of *The Color Purple* with braided hair. Then she abruptly swerved the course of the conversation. 'What are you going to do for Christmas?'

'I don't know,' shrugged Amit. 'Everyone's gone. Campus is pretty quiet. Everything seems closed.'

'I wish you could have afforded to come home. I worry about you all alone there in the cold. Be careful, remember to take a scarf with you. And wear a cap.'

When Amit had first reached Binghamton, it was still summer and everything was warm and green. Sometimes on a hot September afternoon, he would hear the little children across the street shrieking as their father sprayed them with a hosepipe. He could see their yard from his window. They had put up a plastic snowman in front of the house. Perhaps tonight, he thought, they'd have a real snowman with a carrot for a nose and an old black hat. He did not know them but their mother would smile and say, 'Hi, how's it going?' when they ran into each other on the street. But Amit had learned that they really didn't mean it.

'You just say "Doing good. How are you?" and keep walking,' Satish had told him. Satish was the president of the Indian Students' Union on campus and, having already been in Binghamton for over two years while he did his PhD in Electrical Engineering, he was Amit's authority on all things American, like health insurance, bars and race.

In Binghamton the highway neatly split the town. 'On the east side the rents are cheaper,' Satish had informed him days after he arrived in Binghamton, 'but that's also where most of the *kallus* – the blackies – live. So it's not too safe.' Amit, fierce opponent of apartheid and admirer of Dr Martin Luther King, meekly let the racist slur pass as he made his home on the west side of town.

He thought Satish was kind of a boor but in the early days, when bouts of homesickness would wash over him, Amit craved familiarity. He liked the way Satish's apartment smelled of frying onions and cumin and Basmati rice, his CDs of Hindi film songs. He suddenly wished Satish was around but almost everyone he knew had left town for Christmas.

It was after five and already getting dark when he finally stepped out of his apartment to look for some food. The cold was stinging and immediately made his nose water. Amit stuffed his hands into the pockets of his coat, hunched his shoulders and started walking towards the main street.

It was his first Christmas in America and the stillness was startling. It was as if aliens had swooped down and sucked all life out of the town leaving behind only empty houses trimmed with twinkling lights and lampposts festooned in red and white candy stripes.

A black lady, muffled up in a purple coat, was out walking her dog. The little terrier had on a festive red and green coat. The woman nodded to him as he passed by. 'Merry Christmas,' she said.

Amit nodded and said automatically, 'You too.' He remembered his conversation with his mother and grinned. He had once put up a poster of Tina Turner in his bedroom but to be honest he rarely found black women physically attractive. Sure, he enjoyed watching Janet Jackson and Whitney Houston on MTV but it was the brunette from *Friends* he really fancied.

Amit would have bristled if someone had called him a racist. After all, when he was fourteen, he had, in a voice quivering with emotion, recited Martin Luther King's 'I Had a Dream' at the school elocution contest. He remembered watching *The Color Purple* on television and weeping when the sisters finally went running across the field to each other like long-lost siblings from some Hindi movie. But physically black women did nothing for him. 'It's not about race,' he reassured himself. 'They are just not my type.'

Black men in Binghamton drove huge ramshackle gas-guzzling American cars blaring the most god-awful rap music. Amit didn't like the music, he didn't like the aggressive bristle of their flat-tops and he didn't like to look in their eyes. There was a guarded watchfulness in them that unnerved him. 'When you see a group of black guys hanging out in front of a liquor store or something, just cross the street and walk on the other side,' Satish had advised him. Amit muttered something about stereotypes but Satish cut him off. '*Arrey yaar*, screw stereotypes. When it's one in the morning and you're coming home from the lab and they've been standing around drinking, you don't want to take any chances.'

But on Christmas day even the little corner liquor store was closed. The sign still glowed, beckoning warmly in the gathering dark, but the store was locked. A handwritten sign was pasted on the door. 'Will open at 8 a.m. on Dec. 26. We wish our customers a Merry Christmas' it said in crooked blue letters. A Korean family owned the store. Amit wondered if they celebrated Christmas – if they were sitting around a warm apartment somewhere waiting for the turkey to finish roasting.

By the time he reached Main Street, he had not passed a single store that was open. Even the twenty-four-hour supermarket was closed, its massive parking lot desolate except for one rusty Chevrolet. Plastic shopping bags blew along the concrete like tumbleweed.

Amit realized he had no dinner at home. 'Shit,' he thought. 'I might have to just go home and make a peanut butter and jelly sandwich.' All week Main Street had been bustling, the store windows painted with wreaths and holly, Christmas sales signs everywhere. Sometimes Amit liked to sit at the cafe with his latte watching people shopping, their laughter echoing down the street. Though he had nowhere to go and no one to buy Christmas presents for, he didn't mind. He felt snug and comfortable, cocooned in the warmth of an approaching Christmas. Now it was all gone, packed away and out of sight. The stores were still lit up but nothing stirred anywhere. The twinkling lights and pine wreaths looked mournfully at him.

Just as he was about to turn back he noticed halfway down the block someone walk into a bar. The door swung open and for a minute he heard a burst of noise and laughter and loud music. He'd never been to a bar, really, except when Satish had taken all the Indian students to the beer garden one Friday night. But they had had to all watch their wallets and it was cheaper to just buy a crate of beer from the supermarket and drink at home with chicken curry and rice.

What the hell, thought Amit walking over, it's Christmas. The bar was called Bogey's. As he was about to go in he felt something wet on his nose. He brushed it away and stared up. The weatherman had been right after all. It was snowing. He smiled and tentatively stuck out his tongue. His first Christmas in America and it was really going to be white. He watched a snowflake land on his black coat. For a few seconds it clung there, tremulous and white, and then it was gone.

Amit pushed open the door and the warmth enveloped him and sucked him in. The bar was cosy. In one corner a fire burned cheerily behind a grate, the wood spluttering, spitting orange sparks. Amit breathed deep – this was what he imagined Christmas smelled like. Black-and-white posters of stand-up comics Amit had never heard of lined the walls, some with a signature scrawled across them. In one corner a card said Have your fortune told with Cristina in Olde English script. A woman, presumably Cristina, sat on an overstuffed armchair underneath the sign, her horn-rimmed glasses catching the sparkle from the flames in the fireplace. Christmas decorations in red and green were draped from the ceiling and red stockings with the names of the bartenders – Jeff and Lynne and Victor – hung limply above the bar. A sign on the wall announced the specials – hot buttered rum and frozen drinks. Amit thought that was a strange combo.

As he stood at the bar studying the little bowls of peanuts, one of the bartenders walked over. 'What'll it be, hon?' she said. Amit looked up and fell headlong into the bluest eyes he'd ever seen. This was no ordinary paintbox blue but the deep clear blue of an Indian sky after the first thunderstorm of the season had passed.

Lynne, it had to be Lynne, since she was obviously was not Jeff or Victor, smiled at him expectantly.

When Amit was young, he had the stupid notion that eyes and hair were somehow bound together. Blond people had blue eyes, redheads had green eyes and brunettes had brown eyes. And here stood this coffee-coloured woman with tight curly black hair looking at him out of the bluest eyes he'd ever seen. Even the silly Santa hat she wore could not hide how pretty she was.

'Hi,' she said extending a hand, 'you must be new around here. I'm Lynne. Actually, Evelyn.'

'Hi, Amit,' he mumbled shaking her hand.

'Aw-mit,' she said slowly, 'so what will it be, Aw-mit?'

'A . . . a hot buttered rum,' he said just reading the first special off the sign.

Lynne chuckled. 'You *are* new around here, aren't you? Where you from, Aw-mit?'

He nodded too tongue-tied to say anything more.

'And you didn't go home?'

'It's too far. My family is in India.'

When she handed him the drink, she said 'Careful, it's hot.'

'How much is it?' he mumbled pulling out his wallet.

'Don't worry about it. It's on the house. Merry Christmas,' she replied touching him on the shoulder. Amit felt his heart skip a beat.

All evening he sat on the barstool sipping buttered rum listening to the ebb and flow of chatter around him. A man with a ponytail sitting next to him struck up a conversation with him. But even as he talked Amit kept his eye on Lynne, watching her laugh and kiss the customers on the cheek. He found himself daydreaming about what it would feel like if she kissed him.

142

At one point, she handed him another drink and pushed a little plate of pretzels towards him. Then she leaned towards him and said, 'What do you think of America?'

It was exactly the kind of question that confounded him. Seeing the perplexed frown on his face, she laughed and said, 'Well, Binghamton isn't exactly America. But you know I have this guy who comes here regularly. He's from Saudi Arabia, I think, and he says he loves to come to a bar any time he likes and get a drink. He says he loves the freedom.'

'Hmm,' said Amit. 'It's different in India. We have bars there.'

'I know you have bars in India,' she chuckled. 'I'm not that dumb an American.'

He flushed, embarrassed. She grinned at him, her eyes sparkling. 'You're cute when you blush like that,' she said causing him to turn even redder.

By the time last call was announced, Amit was feeling quite lightheaded. He gathered up his coat and went out of the door, turning to see where she was. She was talking to another bartender and didn't see him leave. He could have left right then but instead he just stood outside in the soft pile of fresh snow watching the last few cars crawl slowly through the icy streets.

If she wondered why he was standing outside in the snow after the bar closed she made no mention of it.

He had elaborate excuses ready to prove he was not waiting for her. But she didn't ask. Instead she just pulled her coat tight around her and said, 'You still here? Do you live near campus? Want to walk home with me?'

He must have been staring at her with a silly grin plastered across his face because she stopped and said, 'Are you okay? How much have you had to drink?'

'I don't know, three, four. I lost count. I really came out to get something to eat but couldn't find anything open.'

'Oh my goodness, you haven't had dinner,' she said shocked. 'And I've been plying you with alcohol. I feel bad.'

As they walked they talked about Christmas dinners. He told her in India they called it Bada Din or Big Day and he'd go to the Club with his parents and they'd eat ham and mini samosas with cilantro-and-tamarind chutney. She found that funny and said some of the turkey she'd eaten could do with a little chutney. As they walked through the snow they spoke about pecan pie and yams and vegetables he'd never heard of.

The night was hushed. The snow had covered all the cars parked on the street turning them into ghostly cartoon shapes, their sharp edges rounded and softened.

The streets were completely empty and the clouds had lifted. Everything was washed in a pale cold moonlight and the only sound was the soft crunch of their shoes on the snow and their voices rising and falling. He felt his breath still warm from buttered rum and the bar turning smoky in front of him. Listening to her talk about pies and roast turkey reminded him again how hungry he was. In the moonlight her blue eyes were now ink-stained. Royal Blue, he thought – the ink of his childhood.

Lynne walked confidently through the snow, her black leather coat swinging, a woollen scarf casually draped around her neck. Amit was less confident – he was new to snow and the alcohol made him unsteady. Every now and then she put her hand on his elbow to steady him and Amit smelled her perfume – it smelled of jasmine and reminded him of hot summer nights in Calcutta even as he could feel snowflakes slide off the overhanging branches of trees and land on his hair and eyelashes.

When she asked him if he wanted to come up and she'd heat up some leftovers, he felt a surge of nervous excitement. Was it finally happening to him? He'd only read about this in books. But there she was – her blue eyes bright and shining against the darkness of her skin, inviting him to his first American Christmas.

Evelyn's apartment was small. A tiny Christmas tree stood in a corner, little red and green lights sparkling. Books and magazines were strewn everywhere. It turned out she studied International Relations and she said she wanted to work for the UN. Amit was embarrassed – he had thought she was just a bartender.

She checked her answering machine.

Someone named Margaret wanted to meet for breakfast.

Ann was wondering if she could get a ride on Saturday.

'Would you like some tea as well?' she said rummaging in her kitchen cabinet.

'That would be lovely,' Amit replied. Any excuse to stay a little longer.

'Peppermint, chamomile or orange blossom?'

What Amit wanted was some good strong Indian tea boiled with lots of milk and sugar to clear the cigarette smoke and bad jukebox rhythms swirling in his head.

'Peppermint,' he said.

He stood there leafing through a book on the collapse of the Soviet Union while she fixed a plate of leftovers. He heard the microwave hum to life. Outside it was starting to snow again, tiny flakes drifting by the window as if one of his mother's quilts had been ripped open. He wanted to hold the little Christmas tree in the corner out of the window and watch the white flakes settle on the dark green bristles.

'You don't have to be so serious, Mr Computer Engineer,' she said with a smile, coming into the room.

'How do you know I'm a computer engineer?' he asked, surprised.

'Aren't all Indians?' she said laughing. 'How's that for a stereotype?' The microwave beeped and she went back into the kitchen. When she reappeared she had a plate in her hand with neat little piles of leftovers.

'Not quite the traditional family Christmas dinner. It's a store-bought ham with all the trimmings,' she said with a smile. 'But hey, Merry Christmas.'

Somewhere over the ham, they fell quiet. At some point, as he ate Brussels sprouts for the first time in his life, he looked up and saw her looking intently at him and blushed. When she handed him a piece of pecan pie with some melting vanilla ice cream, their fingers touched and Amit almost dropped the plate. His mind moved in furious circles trying to think up something witty to say – something witty with lots of room for backpedalling. Instead he followed her to the kitchen with his empty plate and stood there awkwardly next to her in front of the sink, unsure and unsteady, too nervous to move.

'Thanks for everything,' he finally said. 'It was good.'

She touched his face and said, 'You are sweet.'

All Amit could do was stare at the slope of her breasts and inhale the smell of jasmine, scarcely daring to breathe out in case the entire moment melted as surely as a snowflake on his tongue.

The tightness in his chest was nothing like what he felt when he and his schoolmates had pooled their money to buy their first second-hand *Hustler* magazine. Tentatively he touched her neck, all the time staring out of the window into the hushed white night.

Lynne didn't pull away as he might have feared. She leaned back against him and let out a little sigh. Then she gently whispered, 'I have a sort of boyfriend, you know. Back home, not here.'

Amit shrank away, stricken that he had committed some terrible blunder, crossed some invisible line on the old lino-leum of the kitchen floor. But she put her hand on his shoulder and stopped him. When he looked at her, all he could see was the luminescence of her eyes reflecting the entire kitchen, no, the world itself. And then he felt the soft sheen of her lips on his own and her long shellacked nails stealthily stealing into his shirt, between the buttons, a razor-thin stripe of desire against his pounding heart.

'Stay,' she said. 'It's Christmas, we are far away from home.'

For a moment Amit wondered what would happen if his mother called that night. But then he looked at Lynne, the little silver cross nestled in her cleavage, and wordlessly allowed her to lead him to the bedroom.

Afterwards she stroked his hair and said, 'Was it your first time?'

Amit flushed. 'Was it that obvious?'

Lynne chuckled and said, 'I was just testing out another stereotype.'

Amit lay there, his head nestled in Lynne's arms, watching blurred images flickering on the TV. At that moment he trusted her deeply and implicitly. He was not worrying about grades, calls from Ma, suspicious looks from Satish.

'Talk to me,' she said.

'About what?'

'Anything. Tell me a secret.'

For a moment he wondered if he would tell her about the conversation with his mother that morning. But he didn't know what to say. Instead he just said, 'Once you know it was my first time, what bigger secret can I share?'

She smiled and then she turned to him and asked, 'Now can I ask you something else?'

'Sure.'

'Why did you want to sleep with me?'

Amit wondered where to begin. He wanted to tell her that he had never found black women attractive. But that she was different. Special. Or he guessed he just hadn't learned to look

147

at them. Until he met her. And fell headfirst into her blue eyes. Amit wanted to ask her who in her family had blue eyes. Was she, perhaps, mixed?

'Turn off the lamp,' he said.

But before he could say anything more, she said, 'Hang on, I need to go to the bathroom.'

Lynne went into the bathroom and turned on the light. Amit lay in bed admiring the long fluid curves of her back. He watched her brush her teeth. She wiped her face on the towel and turned back to the mirror. Very carefully she reached into her eyes and plucked out the lenses. First the left, then the right. Even from the bed Amit knew they were both blue. He watched her put each one carefully in its little round case. She squeezed a few drops of soaking solution into each container.

When she turned off the light in the bathroom Amit turned off the lamp as well.

In bed she put her arm around him and said 'Well, what attracted you to me in the first place?'

Amit turned his face away because he could not meet her eyes.

But he needn't have worried. In the dark he could not see their colour at all.

IX

Requiem for a Star

ROMOLA WAS checking to see if the tea had steeped long enough when she heard the news. Breakfast was set on the table – toast, butter, the mixed fruit jam glowing a dark ruby-red in the early morning sunlight slanting in through the window. Avinash was reading the paper silently, a half-eaten slice of buttered toast in front of him.

Without looking up from the newspaper, he said, 'Subir Kumar is dead.'

'What?' Romola almost dropped the teapot. 'What do you mean he's dead?'

'It says right here.' Avinash gestured at the newspaper. 'Subir Kumar, superstar of Bengali cinema, dies of heart attack at fifty-two.'

'Let me see,' said Romola snatching the newspaper from him. Avinash, startled, said, 'Oh ho, it's not going to run away. I was reading that.' But Romola had left the table, newspaper in her hand, and gone into the bedroom to look for her reading glasses.

Avinash looked at her with mild annoyance. He was a man of habit. Every morning after he brushed his teeth, he liked to sit down at the breakfast table with the newspaper. He would read it gravely, occasionally sharing a headline with Romola, who silently made tea and buttered his toast for him.

149

Avinash liked to read the newspaper first while it was still uncreased and neatly folded. Now he was afraid Romola would start reading the inside pages and soon the pages would all be out of sequence. He inspected his toast and said, a little more sharply than he intended, 'What happened to that tea?'

'It's right there.' Romola gestured absently towards the table. 'But check the sugar. I can't remember if I already added it or not.' She put the front page down and, just as Avinash had feared, started rummaging for the inside page where the story was continued.

'Fifty-two.' She shook her head. 'He could not be fifty-two. He must have been at least fifty-six.'

'If not older,' scoffed Avinash. 'He's a film star. Of course he lied about his age. They all do. Anyway, I don't get all this fuss about an actor. The reason this country cannot get ahead is because we are just obsessed with stupid, meaningless, escapist films. You know that cinema hall across the street from my office? I see scores of people queuing up to get into the noon show. Young people who should be at work or college or something. Anyway, can I have my paper back?'

Romola said sharply, 'What do you know about Subir Kumar? You haven't seen even one of his films.' But she handed him the newspaper.

'Romola, those bits I have seen on television have been more than enough.' Avinash had the patient tone he usually reserved for explaining investment strategies to her. 'I don't need to see one of Subir Kumar's films to know that it is just the same old emotional melodramatic nonsense.'

Romola looked at him but said nothing. All the while she eye kept glancing at the front page of the newspaper and the image of Subir Kumar. How handsome he looked, smiling out at her. It was an old picture, at least ten to fifteen years old. She could not believe he was dead and that she was sitting quietly drinking tea with her husband.

'Be calm,' she told herself. 'It will only be a few more minutes. He will finish his tea and then go for his bath.'

Avinash held up the newspaper in front of his face and took a sip from his teacup. 'Tch,' he exclaimed irritably, 'no sugar.'

'I told you,' said Romola. 'I couldn't remember if I'd put in any.'

'Well, you didn't,' he said irritably. 'Honestly, I don't know what gets into you sometimes.'

Romola opened her mouth to say something but decided against it. She quietly measured out one teaspoonful of sugar, put it in his tea and stirred it. She tore off a piece of toast with her fingers and then tore it in half again. A fly descended on the butter dish. She waved it away and stared out of the window. Over the cawing of crows in the neem tree outside, she could hear the neighbour's radio. They were playing a song from one of Subir Kumar's films. She tried to remember the name of the film but her mind was blank.

As soon as Avinash had stepped into the shower, she opened her cupboard and pulled out the old frayed diary tucked behind her carefully folded silk saris. It was coming apart at the seams, held together by a decaying rubber band, its pages yellowing, its red cover faded and discoloured, blotted with ink stains. In it she had listed in her careful, rounded handwriting, every single film Subir Kumar had been in, along with the name of the heroine and the year. She was, her friend Leela once joked, his 'Number One Fan.'

'I just like lists,' Romola had laughed, feeling embarrassed. She did like to make shopping lists, lists of books she had read, how much she spent every day on groceries and stationery supplies, ingredients for recipes she saw on cooking shows. Lists made her feel tethered, the long meticulously constructed columns of letters and numbers were a grid through which she was in control of her life. But Subir Kumar was different. He was her secret list. She couldn't remember when she first started it but knew that she had always hidden it away, tucked between the folds of the peacock blue Tanjore silk sari she never wore.

There it all was, from his first role as the hero's college-going younger brother to his flop from six months ago where he was unconvincingly paired with the new Miss India who was all of twenty-three. Oh, how out of breath he seemed, his paunch tucked into his white linen pants as he awkwardly romanced her by the sea. Like a beached whale, Leela had said uncharitably. Not a whale, Romola had replied loyally. Not yet. Not yet, snorted Leela, but getting there, thanks to all that drinking he does.

She remembered the first time she had gone to see him. It was decades ago but she could still conjure up the old Bharati cinema, the ramshackle seats with the stuffing coming out, the excited flocks of college girls. Every time there was a close-up of his face, Leela let out a sigh and clutched her hand tightly. Leela lived in Connecticut now, with her banker husband. Romola wondered if she knew about Subir Kumar yet. It probably wouldn't be in the newspapers there. She put the diary away and started laying out Avinash's shirt, his tie and socks.

As he put on his tie, Romola said, 'Will you be back at the usual time?'

He always was but she always asked him anyway. It was their little goodbye ritual before he went to work and she settled down to her day – going to the fish market, haggling with the vegetable seller, setting the menu, supervising the maid.

But today she had other plans.

As soon as Avinash left Romola took out the diary again. She sat on her bed and closed her eyes as if she was meditating. But in her head she could hear the swelling chorus of 'flashback music'. She felt the buzz of the city's cheerful chatter outside slowly fall away. The bedroom, with her colourful Rajasthani bedspread embedded with little mirrors, her cluttered dressing table, all dissolved, taking with them her grey hair and her plain, everyday sari with the turmeric stain that just wouldn't come off. And there she was, seventeen and radiant at that party at Leela's. As she stood there talking to her, she heard someone say, 'What a lovely vision – fancy seeing two princesses in one evening.'

She turned around and saw a handsome man in a dark suit, not too tall, his hair perfectly combed. She remembered exactly what she was wearing – a light pink tissue patola sari which made her complexion glow. Pink and silver – she had saved a piece of that sari for years – long after the rest of it had fallen to shreds.

Leela smiled broadly and said, 'Oh, you're such a flatterer. Do you know my friend Romola?'

'No.' The man graciously bowed his head. His hair was thick and glossy. 'I have not had the pleasure. Bel flowers, aren't they? Heavenly. Your name should be Bela.'

Romola had worn flowers in her hair – a single strand of fragrant bel, pearl-white flowers, their petals clustered together like sisters with their arms strung around each other.

'Oh—' Romola had replied with a flustered smile. It was a cheesy line but no one, certainly no young man, had ever spoken to her like that before. 'Nice to meet you, Mr . . .'

'Lahiri, Subir Lahiri,' he replied. 'The pleasure is entirely mine.'

Later she had found out that Subir Lahiri worked in an advertising agency. But he was trying to break into the film industry. There were some rumours that he was linked to one of the ageing heroines of the day – Seema Devi reputedly had an eye for handsome, much younger men.

'Can you imagine?' said Leela. 'That scrumptious fellow paired with that old witch.'

Subir Lahiri didn't end up in any film with Seema Devi. Romola never asked him about it, though she would keep running into him at one party or another. He always asked how her studies were going. She found that he was interested in music, especially classical music. One day he asked her if she wanted to go to a sitar concert with him.

'I don't know,' she said hesitantly. 'I'd have to ask my mother.'

'Please do,' he replied. 'I'd love for you to come with me.'

'Subir Lahiri – he works in advertising,' she told her mother. She deliberately kept mum about the acting. 'I think you know of his father. Atanu Lahiri – he is the editor of the *Daily Gazette*.'

'I don't know about this,' muttered her mother. 'I don't trust these men who work in advertising. I hear they are ladies' men and they drink and smoke.'

'But Leela is also going to go, and her brother too,' Romola persisted.

To her surprise, it was her uncle, her mother's brother, who came to her rescue. 'I am sure Romola can take care of herself,' he said. 'We need to trust her. Mind you, you have to come back right after the concert. No going out to any restaurants afterwards.'

Subir Lahiri came to pick her up in a shiny green car. In their little alley, which rarely saw anything fancier than a rotund stolid Ambassador, his bottle-green Plymouth swept in like a mythical winged creature, glinting in the late afternoon sun. The neighbourhood kids playing cricket at the end of the street stopped their game and came running to inspect the car. Romola tried not to be impressed as she answered the door.

'Come in and meet my mother,' she said. 'I'm almost ready.'

'You look lovely,' he whispered. She smiled, glancing at the woman standing on the balcony of the house opposite staring at the car, her mouth agape. At the time, the car was the object of everyone's attention – no one knew Subir Lahiri.

When he became a famous actor, the neighbour couldn't remember that he had once come by their little street to pick up the girl next door. 'Oh, was that Subir Kumar?' she said. 'I can't remember his face. But I do remember that car.'

Later Subir admitted that the car was not his. He had borrowed it from a friend. That evening, he kept his word and brought Romola home after the concert. He did, however, insist on buying her and Leela some ice cream afterwards. Leela agreed, reasoning, that since they didn't actually have to go to a restaurant, it was well within the bounds of what was permissible.

Soon Subir took to dropping in. He started calling Romola's mother 'Mashima' and flattered her by saying no one brewed a cup of tea as perfectly as she did. Sometimes he would give Romola a ride to her dance class. But he didn't bring the green car any more. He'd take a taxi. Once they pretended to go to the library and he took her to a film set instead. He didn't have a role in the film but he had a friend who was playing the hero's best friend. Romola couldn't stop talking about it afterwards. She wondered if she would recognize the scene when the film was actually released. She told Leela that it was the most exciting day in her life.

'Careful,' said Leela with a laugh. 'Don't go falling for Subir. He's fun and all but he's an actor, you know. You never know whether they are serious or just putting it on.'

Once they went out for tea in a hotel overlooking the Esplanade. Romola was very nervous that they would run into someone they knew. But in the end she gave in and ordered chicken sandwiches. Subir was talking about his dreams. She didn't quite know whether to believe him or not. She had never known anyone who was an actor. An uncle on her father's side had once been a sound engineer in films – that was the closest Romola had come to the movies.

'I think I am going to be able to get a part in this new adaptation of Sarat-babu's story,' said Subir. 'They say I should change my name. What do you think?'

'That's silly,' said Romola. 'Subir is a nice name. Very serious.'

He laughed. 'But to be a hero, you need something a little more flashy. Serious is for character actors.'

'Well isn't your role going to be the hero's brother anyway?' asked Romola pouring out the tea carefully into the beautiful china cups with gold rims.

'But I won't be a hero's brother for ever,' said Subir. 'That's just how it starts.'

She smiled at him. It felt unreal to her. This man sitting opposite her eating a chicken sandwich in a bustling restaurant would be in a film soon.

Subir grinned. 'What are you thinking?'

'That one day I'll go to the Bharati cinema. It will be the middle of the day, the matinee show. Outside it will be hot and sunny and the trams will be running making such a racket. And inside it will be quiet and there you will be on a huge screen. My goodness, it gives me the shivers.'

'When the film opens will you come to the première with me?' asked Subir abruptly, placing his hand on hers.

Romola almost jumped. 'What will I do at the première?' she said. But she didn't pull her hand away.

'Wear your pink patola sari and bel flowers in your hair,' he said. Then looking more serious, he said, 'Enough about me. What do you want to do, Romola?'

Startled, she said, 'Me? What will I do? Finish college, I suppose.' He looked at her quizzically and she felt that she had disappointed him somehow with the paucity of her dreams. So she started talking about how good the chicken sandwiches were.

As they walked out of the restaurant, she suddenly turned to him and said, 'How about calling yourself Subir Kumar?' Kumar sounded dashing – it conjured up images of debonair men who might ride horses and save lovelorn women in the nick of time.

Romola never made it to the première. When her mother found out that Subir had actually landed a film, she threw a fit. Romola was amazed. This was her mother who religiously read every film weekly there was. She kept track of what films were releasing when and which film star was married to whom. She knew who was going to divorce whom long before it actually happened.

'That's exactly why,' her mother said angrily. 'I know what kind of dirtiness goes on in that world. And no daughter of mine is getting mixed up with that.'

'It's not like I am going to become an actress,' Romola protested. But this time her uncle sided with her mother. 'Concerts are one thing but really, Romola, we have to think about your future. You can't be seen around town with some film star.'

'It's a classic by Sarat Chandra,' she said feebly. 'We have the book as a text in college.' But she knew that even if she won this battle, the war was lost. When Subir called, she apologized. She had exams. She had a headache. Soon he called less and less. Leela told her he had asked her why Romola was avoiding him.

When the film released in theatres she went to see it with Leela at Bharati just as she had once imagined. As she watched his name appear on screen her lips curled up into a smile. There, written in big white letters, were the words 'Subir Kumar'. Later as the camera panned into a close-up Leela sighed, 'He is pretty dreamy. Did you ever kiss him? Too bad your mother won't let you go out with a film star.'

Romola didn't really blame her mother. If she had a

daughter she would have done the same. The film was nothing extraordinary. Subir looked handsome but his acting was a bit shaky. Nevertheless, Romola wished she could have gone to the première with him.

After she and Avinash were married and had moved to America she got a letter from her mother in which, buried amid the gossip about cousins and maid-servants, was the news that Subir had married his co-star after his jubilee hit *Darpan*. Then came the divorce and another marriage. A couple of years ago she was reading about him being linked to some television starlet. Her mother was long dead. But in her head Romola could hear her voice. 'See, what did I tell you? These film stars are just gadabouts with loose morals. Handsome to look at no doubt but from a distance.'

As Romola shook her head at the memory she heard a voice calling her. It was Bhola, the cook, wanting to find out what to make for lunch. But Romola could hardly focus. The everyday decisions that seemed so important – what kind of dal to cook, whether he should make paarshey if the fish-monger didn't have any decent tangra – all of this suddenly seemed so trivial.

'Here, you go do the shopping today. Get some rui and some paarshey.' Romola handed Bhola some money. 'I have some things to do.'

Bhola was taken aback. Ever since she discovered he had been skimming a little change here and a little change there while shopping, Romola had taken to buying the groceries herself. Sensing his surprise, she said sternly, 'And don't think I won't know if you keep some of that money for your cigarettes.'

As Bhola left, she called him back. 'And would you get me a string of bel flowers? Make sure they're fresh, not old and wilted, already turning brown.'

After Bhola had gone she stood for a while at the window tracing imaginary flowers in her palm. Would he have even remembered after all these years the bel flowers in her hair? They had only met once more after she got married. That was years later and she had no flowers in her hair then. Amit was ten years old. She had gone to pick him up from school. They had walked into the confectionery nearby to get some pastries.

Suddenly she had heard the doors open and the little shop fill with the smell of expensive cologne. She turned around and gasped. It was Subir Kumar. He'd put on weight but his hair was still as thick and glossy as ever. He seemed even fairer. Perhaps those arc lights bleach your skin, she thought.

He looked at her and stopped short. 'Oh my goodness, isn't it Romola?'

She nodded, unable to speak.

'What a surprise!' he said. 'You look lovely. How are you?'

They exchanged pleasantries, like old acquaintances do, about their children, their lives. He asked after her mother and expressed his condolences when he heard she had passed away. He looked at Amit and said, 'And who is this handsome young man?' When she told him he was her son and ten years old, he feigned shock. 'Ten? How can you have a ten-year-old?' Then he turned to Amit. 'I knew your mother long before you were born. Can you imagine that?'

Romola turned to her son. 'Say hello, Amit. Do you know who this is? It's Subir-uncle. Remember, you've seen him on television?'

'Romola, honestly, you look beautiful. You haven't aged at all.'

Amit, tongue-tied, stared at his toes and shifted from one foot to another.

Romola wondered if Amit, now in America, would remember any of this. Romola recalled the store clerks at the confectionery staring at her with newfound respect. Later, on the way home, she tried to tell Amit how she had once known the great Subir Kumar but he was much more interested in telling her about the goal he had scored in his inter-class football game at school.

In the end, Romola just fell silent. But she played and replayed Subir's words in her head all the way home. 'You look beautiful. You haven't aged at all.' She smiled, toying with the words, polishing them in her head. If her mother had been alive she would have dismissed it as typical movie-star flattery. But Romola knew she would stash them away somewhere safe in the recesses of her mind. Someday when she felt old and creased, when her sari was blotched with turmeric stains and her face flushed from the heat of the kitchen, she'd play with the memory again and again as if it were a handkerchief soaked in lavender water carrying a whiff of a long-forgotten party.

She had hoped when they got home, Amit would tell his father about their adventure with Subir Kumar. But the boy had forgotten about it by the time Avinash returned from the office, and Romola was too embarrassed to bring it up.

Sometimes, like the time she saw him receiving a best-actor award on TV, she wondered if he ever thought about her. 'And I would like to thank the person who gave me my name. Romola, wherever you are, this one is for you,' she imagined him saying.

Even now, just thinking about it made her smile. She flipped through the pages of her diary. The ink, once Royal Blue, was slowly changing colour over time, as if the words themselves were getting rusty. It occurred to her that she would have no more entries to add. Perhaps there was still some half-finished movie they'd quickly wrap up and cash in on as his 'last screen appearance'. But that was it. Her Subir Kumar diary was ending its run as well.

By the time Bhola came back from the market she had showered and was ready. She had chosen a cream sari with a blue border, something elegant but not ostentatious. She took the large brown handbag that Amit had brought her from America. She carefully placed the bel flowers still wrapped in a piece of wet palm leaf inside it, the fragrance making her catch her breath for an instant.

'Listen,' she told Bhola. 'I have to go do something. If anyone calls, tell them I'll be back soon.'

'But what about lunch?' said Bhola. 'How do you want me to cook the paarshey? And what vegetables should I make?'

'Really!' exclaimed Romola. 'Surely you can manage to cook on your own for one day. What if I dropped dead? Would all of you stop eating?'

Bhola looked at her, stunned for a moment, and then just shrugged.

'You'll manage.' Romola was a little embarrassed by her outburst. 'I shouldn't be that long. Just make a light curry with the paarshey. Nothing too spicy.'

'Are you going out?' Bhola scratched his head. 'But the car isn't here. Did you ask Avinash-babu to send the car?'

'No, no I'll take a taxi,' she said. But the reference to Avinash made her flush. When she put on her sunglasses and stepped out of the house she felt like a middle-aged adulteress off for a noontime rendezvous while other housewives all over the city were presiding over the day's cooking.

By the time the taxi reached Monmohantala, after crawling through city traffic, it was past eleven. Romola's freshly laundered blouse was sweaty and sticking to her back.

'Turn left at the next cross light,' she said.

'Oh you want to go to Subir Kumar's house?' The driver looked at her through the mirror. Startled, Romola glanced around guiltily as if caught. 'Well, half the city is there according to the radio,' said the driver, shrugging.

He was right. As soon as Romola stepped out of the cab into the muggy midday heat, she could see the swarms of people. Romola suddenly wondered what she was doing here. It had taken everything she had to leave the house today. As she stepped out of the taxi she realized she had no plan. Once she had read about a mysterious woman in black who took a rose every year to the grave of Rudolph Valentino. That was romantic, but Romola wanted more.

Now she wanted to be like Sandhya in *Agnishikha* (Flame), the other woman, the prostitute with the heart of gold who had silently tossed her favourite handkerchief drenched in rosewater on her rich, married lover's body as it passed by the dancing house before hanging up her anklets for ever. Or did she want to be Neelima in *Jeebonrekha* (Lifeline) who had walked into her lover's ancestral home, in full wedding regalia of red and gold (colour had come to the movies by then), clutching the hand of her little boy demanding her rights as the mother of the family's heir – after all, they had been married in the eyes of God that monsoon night when they had taken shelter in the abandoned temple while Hemanta Mukherjee's seductive voice had throbbed in the background?

But she wasn't Neelima or Sandhya. She was a middle-aged woman with greying hair who needed bifocals and was afraid she was going to be run over by buses careening down the street. No one said you are beautiful to her any more. They said you look well. You look so dignified, one of Amit's old school friends had told her recently. And here she was like a half-wit starstruck teenager sneaking away from home, her head stuffed full of wisps of some screenwriter's fantasy.

She took a deep breath, told herself to stop acting so silly, clutched her handbag tighter and plunged into the crowds. She was just going to see his body, pay her respects, and she would leave – it would be as simple as that. But that was if she could fight her way through the swelling crowds. The solid wall of people pressed on her from all sides as if trying to grind her to powder. She had heard of stampedes at holy pilgrimages like the Maha Kumbh Mela, which happened once every 144 years. All the windows were open on the houses lining the street. She could see people squished against each other at every window. Housewives draped themselves over their balconies, shouting down to people on the street. On the rooftop of one house, the maid was hanging out the day's washing but she stood frozen, a green plastic bucket full of wet saris and T-shirts on her hip like a bowl of bedraggled multicoloured birds, her eyes trans-fixed by the flowing mass of humanity below.

Romola remembered once meeting Subir's father, the ven-erable pipe-chewing editor of the *Daily Gazette*. Subir had told her he looked down on him for wanting to act in Bengali films. He only watched American films and European classics. Romola smiled wondering what he would say if he could now see the thousands of people lining the street to catch one last glimpse of his son.

She realized with a start that she didn't really want to be Neelima or Sandhya or any of the other women who for a brief while had found stardom opposite him on the screen. She wanted to be Subir Kumar himself as he was in one of his biggest hits, *Madhumita*. After the heroine died, he burst into her house clutching a poem he had written on a full moon night years ago. As the distraught father exploded in anger and the mother wailed, and the servants dragged him out, Subir read out the poem with tears streaming down his face, his nostrils flaring with emotion. If I am to never see you again, what use this flood of moonlight except to drown in? What use these stars except as cold silent witnesses to my longing? It was such an emotional scene even the actress playing the dead Madhumita couldn't help but be moved. Romola could swear she had seen her bosom heave as Subir uttered one last heart-rending cry of 'Madhumita!'

A car was struggling to get through the street but couldn't move. The driver stuck his head out, cursed and then pleaded. People laughed but didn't budge. Everyone tried to peer in through the tinted windows to see if the passenger was a film star.

Romola felt someone step on her toes as they tried to push by her.

'Ohh,' she exclaimed. 'Bhai, be careful. Stop pushing.'

'Didi,' said a profusely sweating bearded young man in a checked shirt. 'If you don't want pushing you'd best get out of this street today. It's like a river in high tide.'

Usually she had a lot of clout over young men like these. She knew how to give orders and be obeyed. But today she was afraid she would just get crushed underfoot.

Someone started chanting 'Subir Kumar *amar rahe* – Long live Subir Kumar'. More and more people picked up the chant – the noise passing down the street in waves, a bier of sound carried on the shoulders of his mourning fans. It sent shivers down her spine. She felt a little faint and hoped she was not going to get sunstroke. But at the same time, for the first time in many many years, Romola felt a tremor of something forbidden and exciting, a rude weed with deep stubborn roots poking through the rubble, the kind that grew in the cracks between the bricks and mortar of old crumbling homes. She knew she wouldn't be able to share this with anyone else. This would be part of no breakfast conversation with Avinash. But at least she would have it.

When she had seen her wedding invitation she had wondered fleetingly what it would look like if the ornate golden letters had said Subir Lahiri and Romola Dutt instead of Avinash Mitra and Romola Dutt.

When she had first met Avinash, he seemed a decent, responsible man. Her parents had not laid eyes on each other till her father had lifted her mother's wedding veil. But these being much more modern times, and their parents being much more progressive, she had been sent out unchaperoned for a meal with Avinash so they could get to know each other. He was finishing his PhD in America. He did not have a nose as straight and fine as Subir Kumar's but then who did? She could see his hair was already receding but Romola found no real reason to object to him. Her mother was pleased; his mother was keen. She had felt like a little tugboat in the sea, pulled along by other tides.

One day as they were shopping for wedding saris, she suddenly wondered what would happen if Subir Kumar showed up at her doorstep now just like in the movies. If he stood there and shouted for all the world to hear, 'Romola, I cannot live without you.' Would she leave everything and run to him down curved staircases, the marble steps shockingly cold against her bare feet, along miles of courtyard, her sari trailing behind her like a waterfall as the background music swelled, the sitars twanging with such shuddering intensity that the chandeliers shivered as she flung open the door to see him standing there unshaven, his eyes bloodshot from weeping?

'What do you think?' asked her mother. 'Orange or crimson?' Romola looked startled. 'My little daydreamer, she is getting married soon,' her mother said with a fond smile to the lady next to her. 'She is so excited.'

Romola thought, at least he lives in America. She had never been to America and perhaps it would be easier to forget Subir there. Then she laughed at herself. Forget? There was hardly anything to forget. What a lot of schoolgirlish fuss she was making about a couple of chicken sandwiches and some idle afternoons.

And here she was decades later behaving like a giddy schoolgirl while the midday sun beat down on her with increasing intensity. Romola could feel the back of her neck starting to burn. She could smell sweat and cigarette smoke

165

all around her. She felt as if she was trapped in a pressure cooker. She wondered if the garland of bel flowers in her handbag were turning brown in the heat. It was all starting to feel like a stupid idea. In the calm tranquillity of their home, it had seemed like something she had to do. Here on Monmohantala Lane it was something else altogether. People were shoving her in all directions. She had visions of being crushed in a stampede. They'd find nothing left of her except her shoe. Just as she was wondering if she should turn back and hail a taxi, she looked up and saw the birds.

It was a scene right out of *Bhorer Paakhi* (Bird of Dawn), as if the negative itself had been developed against the white glare of the midday sun. There, behind the feathery green fans of a rain tree, smudged with red blossoms motionless in the still noon torpor, was an old house, its green shutters faded by the sun and monsoon rain just as she remembered from the film she had seen three times, not counting the snippets she had caught late at night on television.

As Romola looked up at the house, someone flung open the windows and a pair of doves fluttered up, beige-grey clouds of soft anxiety. That's how every afternoon Subir Kumar used to let his secret lover, the young widow who lived next door, know that he was alone at home – the fluttering doves, startled smoke signals of forbidden romance. Romola, not an overly religious woman, couldn't help feeling this was a sign meant just for her. She decided that it meant she should keep going, fighting through the jostling crowd.

Apart from a fresh coat of paint and some newly installed air conditioners in some of the rooms, Subir's house looked just as she remembered it from when he had shown it to her. She could see a man in a khaki uniform standing at the gates trying desperately to instil some order into the scene. He stabbed at the crowd with a stick attempting to make everyone queue up. But no one paid any attention to him. Like tendrils of some monstrous vine, the crowd curled around him trying to push through the wrought-iron gates. Romola wondered what would happen if the gates collapsed under the sheer weight of the crowds. Inside she could see a courtyard packed with cars, the drivers standing around smoking cigarettes.

'How long are they going to keep the body there?' she asked the man next to her.

He shrugged. 'I heard they are waiting for the chief minister to come to pay his respects. Then it's going to go in a grand procession to the cremation grounds.'

'Will they let people in to see him?' she asked.

'I don't know. Ask that guard – he'll be able to tell you.'

She tried to fight her way over to the guard. He had given up his attempt at crowd control and was just standing behind the gates. The crowd, getting more and more restless, buzzed around her, the numbers seeming to multiply by the minute. The smell of tobacco and sweat was now overpowering. She felt her head swimming. Someone stepped on her foot again and she felt the strap on her sandal snap. Dismayed, she tried to cling on to the shoe but the crowd kept pushing. She grabbed the man next to her to keep her balance. Her sandal slipped off her foot and the teeming crowd swallowed it in a flash.

'Hey, mister,' she said trying to catch the guard's attention. But her voice was lost in the din. She wondered what kind of spectacle she made, her greying hair rapidly unravelling, her creamy cotton sari crumpled, her blouse stained with patches of dark sweat like the map of some lost continent, limping her way through the jostling crowds, one foot bare.

'Let the aunty through,' said the man whose elbow she had clutched. Stung, she looked at him. He was a bearded young man, maybe twenty-five. She put up her hand to pat her hair back into place and almost tripped. The man grabbed her by the elbow to steady her. 'Are you all right?' He was looking at her with some concern. 'You really shouldn't be out here in this madness. You've probably never been in a bus in the last ten years, have you?'

Everything was swimming around her, the noise of the crowd muffled as if she was spinning underwater. Her vision was fogged with sweat. She was getting thirstier by the second and could feel rivulets of sweat running down her back pooling where her sari was bunched up against her skin.

The man grabbed her arm and started hollering, 'Let us through, the lady is fainting. Let us through.' Romola meekly followed, grateful that he was doing the pushing. The next thing she knew they were at the gate and the guard was shaking his head, 'Lady, are you crazy trying to fight through these crowds? Couldn't you just watch on TV?'

Romola had a vision of herself fainting right at the gate. She imagined herself lying there on the baking concrete, the string of bel flowers wilting in the dust, a gasp of fragrance in the unending asphalt. Wasn't that the remake of *Limelight* where Subir Kumar regains his sight and can no longer recognize the flower girl who loved him? But then one day as he passes by in his horse-drawn carriage, he reaches out to buy a bunch of rajanigandha and the touch of her hand and the cool smell of the snowy-white flowers brings it all back to him and he shouts 'Stop' while the flower girl tries to flee. Now that she was there, at the gates of the house, Romola knew she couldn't turn back.

Deep inside she wanted to be acknowledged by the khaki-clad guard, by Amit, by Avinash, by Subir's fat jewellery-laden wife, his television-actress mistress, the young widow next door, the gossip columnist of *Chhaya* magazine. Dammit, she thought, she had sacrificed something too. She had given up Subir Lahiri so he could become Subir Kumar.

In the movie inside her head, Romola was no longer fainting on the sidewalk. In that movie, she was at the front of the crowd, her head bare and unveiled, her hair once again lustrous and black, cascading down her back like a curtain of dark satin. In that movie her pink tissue patola was whole again and the dusty hedges around the walls were all laden with perfumed clusters of snowy flowers – bel, jasmine, rajanigandha. In that movie, her voice was strong and unwavering as it demanded entrance. 'Tell them Romola is here and she has come too far to go back.'

But in reality her tongue felt thick, the words clogged in her throat like leaves in a drain. The guard shook his head once more and offered her his plastic bottle of water. 'Go on, have some,' he said. 'You look like you need it.' For a moment Romola wondered whether it was safe to drink. The bottle seemed a little grimy, the plastic not quite clear any more, as if it had been filled and refilled for years from the neighbourhood tubewell. Then she just took it and gulped two mouthfuls, feeling relieved as the water trickled down her chin. It was lukewarm but it still felt good.

'Are they letting people in to see him?' she asked handing the bottle back to the guard.

'Are you crazy?' he replied. 'Look at these crowds. Only family. And other actors.'

'Can you get me in?' she said. 'I have come a long way.'

'Lady, people have flown in all the way from Delhi,' he said importantly. 'Like I said, are you family?'

'Not really,' she said. 'But I knew him once.'

'Really?' He grinned showing misshapen teeth stained red from chewing paan. 'So does everybody. Everyone is suddenly his long-lost childhood friend. What are you – his girlfriend?'

'How dare you?' she retorted automatically. But inside her head, Romola answered, 'Yes.' For a moment she wanted to tell him, this anonymous man with greasy hair, everything. About that party at the Sanyals', the chicken sandwiches, the bottle-green Plymouth. She wanted to tell him and the bearded man next to her and the fat man mopping his face with an oversized handkerchief next to him. She wanted to tell them that yes, as a matter of fact, she had been his girl-friend for a brief lost summer before many of them had even been born.

But she said none of this. Instead she just looked at the man, swallowed hard and said pleadingly, 'Please, just for a minute.'

The gatekeeper continued grinning impudently. He waved his keys at her and said, 'Lady, just wait by the side of the road like everyone else and you'll see the body when it's brought out. Now if you'll step aside. We have to clear the gate. The chief minister's car should be here any minute.'

Romola wanted to shake him. She wanted to make a scene. She wanted to lie down in front of the gate forcing the chief minister's car to a screeching halt. What if this was it, she thought? What if she made such a scene that she could never go back to the life she once had? Perhaps Avinash would see her on the news that night and recognize her with a start. Would he miss her? she wondered. She would be gone like that Bengali housewife, Sonali something or the other, who had just upped and run off with that Italian filmmaker Roberto Rossellini, leaving ripples of scandal in her wake.

'I am not leaving,' she said with grim determination. 'And if you touch me I will scream.' Some of the men standing next to her were looking at her with a mixture of curiosity and interest. They sensed the beginning of some drama that could while away the tedium of waiting for the body.

The guard shrugged and said, 'Look, I have my orders. And who are you anyway, the Queen of Calcutta?'

'I don't care,' said Romola, hardly believing her own ears. 'Ask whomever you like. I'm not moving.' She was almost starting to enjoy this now. She wished Leela could see her. She imagined telling her the story, embroidered and embellished over time, on the phone to Connecticut. 'And then, can you imagine, he just gave up and opened the door a crack so I could slip in. But he told me to put on my dark glasses so people would think I was some film actress.'

And as she slipped in through the side door, the catty reporter from *Chhaya* magazine would notice her and ask for her story. Of course she wouldn't really tell them. Maybe she would just hint at a mysterious past. But it would be enough, enough so she would count for more than her decision to have rui for dinner and paarshey for lunch.

'I knew your Subir-babu before you were born. So don't push me,' she said with as much confidence as she could muster. 'I can make your life very difficult. I could faint. I could have a heart attack. And it would be your fault.'

The gatekeeper paused. A flicker of uncertainty crept into his face. 'You really know him?' he said.

'Yes, yes, very well.' Romola, sensing her newfound advantage, stressed the 'very'.

'Lady, okay, okay.' The gatekeeper threw up his hands. 'I'll ask someone.'

Romola felt a small sense of triumph creeping up her body, swelling in her breast. In the movie in her head, she was rapidly turning into the Queen of Jhansi leading her loyal citizens into battle against the British, her infant son strapped to her back.

'Who shall I ask? The mistress or the son?' The gatekeeper glowered at her. 'Tell me, who should I say you are.'

And that was when all her bravado evaporated. The movie in her head screeched to a halt, the film flapping like a torn pennant while the spool spun round and round in empty circles.

She realized with a jolt that no one other than Leela far away in cold Connecticut knew anything about 'them'. Even now in her head she put quotes around the 'them' as if it was a mysterious biological specimen that needed to be handled gingerly with forceps. And if Leela were to drop dead one day, she would have a hard time believing that any of this had ever happened, that it hadn't all been a schoolgirl's dream pressed between her memories like a forgotten flower from a party long ago.

The gatekeeper looked at her. 'Lady,' he said not unkindly. 'You had best get out of here before you get hurt. This is not for high-society ladies like you.'

Romola just stood there staring at him. 'Will you put this on his body for me?' she said, finally opening her bag. She had wrapped the bel flowers around the frayed old red diary. She had imagined bending over his flower-bedecked body and tucking that diary in under him. Perhaps it would go up in flames when they cremated him, a handwritten list of his stardom. Or perhaps it would fall out as they prepared the body for the last rites. She had imagined headlines in the newspaper the next day: 'Mysterious Diary of Secret Admirer Found at Subir Kumar's Funeral'.

But the gatekeeper looked at the diary with disdain. 'What's this old book?' he said.

Romola snatched it back and handed him just the flowers. 'Put this on him.'

'All that fuss for this?' said the man taking the string of flowers from her. 'You should see what it's like inside – a goddamn flower shop.'

She said nothing, but as she turned to leave, the man stopped her.

'What?' he said 'I don't get a little money for tea and biscuits? I am going to have to bribe the house-servant you know.' She shook her head and then pulled out some crumpled notes from her handbag.

'That's it?' he said. But he snatched them from her before she could change her mind. 'Go on now,' he laughed. 'Your precious flowers will get there, don't you worry. You might even see them on TV tonight.'

His laughter was still ringing in her ears as she trudged her way back through the crowds – a small fish swimming upstream. Now all she wanted was to go home, step into the shower and forget this day ever happened. With just one sandal she found it hard to walk. In the end she just took it off and carried it with her, hoping she wouldn't step on a rusty nail or a piece of glass. By the time she hailed a taxi, she realized her sari had dark dirty blotches, her hair had lost most of its pins, the soles of her feet were caked with black grime. The driver looked at her curiously but thankfully didn't say anything.

She opened her handbag and retrieved her lace-trimmed handkerchief. It still smelled faintly of the flowers. She patted her face with it trying to blot out the humiliation and breathe in the last whiffs of the morning's fresh fragrance. 'It's okay,' she told herself. 'It was still an adventure.'

The diary lay there in her bag amid a jumble of spare combs and receipts. She touched its plastic cover, stroking it gently. It was just as well she hadn't let it go. She would have missed it. Perhaps when she was dead Amit would find it among her papers and remember that afternoon in the confectionery years ago. And he would realize, with a jolt of surprise, that his mother had had her own life crackling with desire and romance, like fireworks on dark Diwali nights; that she could have been an item in *Chhaya*'s gossip column – Subir Kumar and Romola Dutt.

She rolled the window down drinking in the slight breeze. The city shimmered in the afternoon heat. She felt if she stretched out her hand to touch it, it would just dissolve like sugar in her tea. Nothing was real any more, except the frightened beat of her wilting heart. But by the time she got home, she felt nauseous and could sense the beginning drumbeats of a headache.

'Put my food aside,' she told Bhola. 'I need to take a bath and lie down for a bit before eating. You eat lunch.' Standing in the shower, feeling the water cascading around her, enclosing her in a sheath of coolness, she finally felt her heart stop thudding. She closed her eyes and leaned against the bathroom wall. The tiles felt reassuringly cold and solid against her skin.

When she came out Bhola was waiting for her. 'How do you want the rui done for dinner?' he said.

Towelling her hair dry, Romola was tempted to snap, No fish, no meat. We are in mourning. Instead she said, 'Do what you want.' For a moment she wanted him to ask her where she had been and why she had come home limping, clutching one sandal. But it was as if she had never left the house at all, her escapade had sunk quietly to the bottom of the pool, leaving not even a ripple behind. If Bhola had noticed anything, he didn't dare mention it. So she added, 'Make it with tomatoes and a little yogurt. You know, the way your master likes it. Check to see if there is some yogurt in the refrigerator. And go easy on the oil. The doctor says it's not good for his heart.'

'How was your day?' Avinash asked when he sat down to dinner that night. The television was on, its volume turned down low, the images flickering.

'It was all right,' she said. 'Nothing special.' As she served him a dollop of steaming rice, Avinash said, 'Look, the news is starting. I am sure they will show something about your Subir Kumar.'

Romola served him a piece of fish, the gravy a rich orange-gold pool in his rice. Then she put the lid back on the pot.

'Are you not eating any fish?' asked Avinash. 'What's the matter? Is anything wrong?'

Romola looked at him surprised, even a little touched, that he had noticed. She saw tonight the wrinkles around his eyes.

One day, she thought, he too would be dead. Maybe Amit would make it home in time from America. But there would be no milling crowds for him, no hysterical fans. She could see that scene clearly, as if she had already lived that life. There she was sitting alone at breakfast, measuring out tea for one with one slice of toast, no butter. She shook her head to dispel the vision and touched her wedding bangle lightly with her hand as if to tether herself to her real world. She wondered what he would have done if she had not come home tonight. Now as she looked at him she felt he would have noticed her absence, that in their imperfect, disjointed lives, they too had a rhythm that would have been disturbed. Avinash was still looking at her, an expression of mild concern on his face.

'Are you upset about Subir Kumar? I heard they are going to show his films this weekend at Nandan,' he said. 'We could go together.'

'Oh, it's nothing,' her tone was gentle. 'Here, why don't you have another piece of fish? It's your favourite curry. We made it just for you.'

X

Invitation to a Party

AVINASH DROVE by the Subramaniam marriage hall every day on his way to work but he had never really paid it much attention. The squat nondescript greenish building with the neatly lettered Stick No Bills sign merged into the neighbourhood as if it had always been a part of it. On its left was a pharmacy, the red cross lit up in the evening like a fluorescent admonition. On its right was a clinic, its faded sign promising confidential treatment for all manner of sexual problems from India's 'most famous sexologist'. On nights when the marriage hall was rented out for weddings, Avinash wondered if the groom, bedecked in his pristine silk wedding clothes, felt a burst of reassurance upon glancing at the modest yellow board next to it, its red letters promising 100 per cent satisfaction and deliverance from incontinence, premature ejaculation and lack of virility.

One day, glancing through the newspaper as he drank his morning cup of tea, Avinash read an article about how the Internet had made it easier for gay Indians to come out. Looking up to see if his wife was watching, he carefully removed the page and folded it neatly into his briefcase. That very evening he joined an online group. He looked up the statistics. It said there were 437 other members on the list. He wondered who they were, whether any of them were middle-aged men like him, with greying hair and steel-rimmed glasses, with a wife at home and a son in America.

For six months he lurked on the Internet calling himself FunMan1234. Every day he would see messages pile up in his inbox but he never replied, never posted. He only checked his email at work and was always punctiliously careful to check the box that said 'Do not remember this user'. He would see messages about parties and film nights scroll by, even a discussion group to talk about coming-out issues. Sometimes there would be a personal ad from a young man coming back to town from the US for the holidays, looking to meet other men. Once he had been almost tempted to reply but then as he started composing his message a colleague walked in and he hurriedly closed the browser window.

This was the first time the group was having a party when Romola happened to be out of town. 9 p.m.–1 a.m., Subramaniam Wedding Hall, corner of Clarke Street and C.R. Das Avenue. Dinner, drinks and dancing. 'Can anyone come? Do you need some kind of membership?' he cautiously emailed someone named Khush69.

Khush69 replied within the hour. 'Everyone is welcome, FunMan, though there is an admission charge of Rs 500. Hope to see you there.'

For days Avinash had not been able to think about much else. He wanted to ask Khush69 how many people went to these parties, what they wore, but felt too embarrassed to ask. He checked out the society page of the Sunday newspaper to see what the celebrities were wearing these days. At least half a dozen times a day he decided he couldn't go through with it. Then he would wonder when there would be another party when Romola was away. It was as if the stars were aligning for once.

In the end it was his horoscope that did it for him. 'A new friend will come into your life,' it said. Avinash smiled as he read that, tracing the letters with his finger. It also told him to be careful about his health, and promised a trip abroad in the near future but he ignored the other predictions. Instead he took out his 'special occasion' navy-blue shirt that Amit had got him from San Francisco and sent it to the neighbour-hood press-wallah to be ironed.

By 8 p.m. on Saturday night, he was dressed, freshly shaved and doused in his favourite (and sparingly used) Hugo Boss aftershave that Romola had bought him from the duty-free shop in Dubai a few years before. He wondered whether to tuck in his shirt or leave it out, then decided untucked was more casual. It also hid his paunch better. He trimmed his moustache, cleaned his glasses and had Bhola polish his shoes.

'Are you going to a meeting, babu?' Bhola asked.

'Yes, don't bother to cook dinner tonight,' Avinash said.

The admission price included dinner and he thought that at least he'd get fed even if nothing else worked out. At the last minute, though, he forced himself to eat some leftover rice and dal before he left, just to settle his stomach.

He waited till it was almost ten because he was terrified he would be the first person to arrive. Then he had the taxi drop him off two blocks away. He half expected to see a big rainbow sign saying Gay Party in neon lights over the door. But it looked just as nondescript as ever, sandwiched demurely between the sexologist and the pharmacy. A few young men were loitering around the door smoking cigarettes, chatting. A man in a khaki uniform who looked like a doorman sat on a stool by the entrance. Avinash watched a young man in tight faded jeans saunter up to the door and confidently push it open. For one tantalizing moment he heard a blast of music like the flash of a secret world through a peephole, bringing back memories of a gay bar he had once gone to as a graduate student in America, and then the door swung shut. Taking a deep breath, Avinash pulled up his trousers, checked to make sure he hadn't missed any loops on his belt, sucked in his belly and walked to the door, his heart pounding.

As soon as he walked in Avinash wanted to turn around and flee. The hall was sweltering, packed mostly with men. The disco ball twirling in the middle of the wedding hall painted everyone in shifting stripes of garish pink, blue and gold. The noise was deafening – the loud brassy Bollywood hits ricocheting off the walls. He could smell the dinner – the rich cloying smell of tikka masala and tandoori colliding uneasily with the sharp blasts of copiously applied aftershave and deodorant. Everyone seemed at least twenty years younger than him. He wondered with a lurch if some of Amit's friends might be there. Would they recognize him?

He stood there clutching his dinner coupon, which included one cocktail or two beers or three soft drinks. Two young transvestites in spangled dresses sashayed past him, giggling as they gossiped and pointed at men they fancied. Avinash wondered if they had walked through the streets dressed like that.

He wiped his forehead. He was already sweating – the heat and his nervousness swirling uneasily in his stomach. He walked over to one of the air-conditioning vents and tried to catch the draught but it did not seem to be working. There was a long line at the bar. He kept glancing around, wondering what to do, regretting that he didn't know what Khush69 looked like. He wished he had a cigarette he could light. It would at least give him something to do.

The song changed. The crowd whooped in delight. The boy standing next to him grabbed his friend and dragged him to the dance floor. Avinash watched them being swallowed up in the steaming writhing mass of arms and legs and went and stood in the queue at the bar.

After a few minutes he noticed the young man behind him in line. He kept glancing at him and half-smiling. Avinash turned around to see if he was looking at someone else. But the man was looking at him. He was good-looking, perhaps in his late twenties, dark-skinned with a thin moustache, and when he smiled Avinash noticed his front tooth was chipped. He looked almost familiar but Avinash figured he saw scores of young men like that every day. He was wearing faded blue jeans and a black T-shirt. The T-shirt was shiny and clung to him like a second skin. It had a small alligator over its breast pocket but he was sure it was an imitation.

'Hello,' said Avinash hesitantly.

The man kept smiling, his expression slightly quizzical. Then he replied, 'How are you? What's your name?' He spoke in English but Avinash could tell from his accent that it didn't come naturally to him. Small-town boy, he thought.

'A-Aveek,' said Avinash, stumbling over his new name. Then he switched to Bengali and asked, 'What's yours?'

'Rohit,' said the man. There was something about his eyes that unnerved Avinash. He felt they were looking right through him, that they had caught the hesitation, the little lie. Avinash dropped his gaze.

Before he could say anything more the bartender said, 'What will it be?'

Avinash almost asked for the special, some cocktail called Muggy Night in Calcutta. But in the end he played it safe – a vodka-soda, please. He wondered if he should wait for Rohit to get his drink but he felt too self-conscious and walked away after giving him a little nod. As he left the bar he glanced back to see if Rohit was looking at him but the young man was busy ordering his drink.

Avinash never quite figured out if Rohit came looking for him or whether he just ran into him again. It must have been at least an hour later. He had spent the evening hanging out on the fringes of the party, sipping first one drink, then another, savouring the cold liquor on his tongue, trying to make the buzz last. The party showed no signs of winding down as more and more men arrived, some in tank tops and jeans, some in demurely buttoned shirts, some freshly shaved, some with designer beards, their hair stiffly gelled.

He tried to make conversation with a couple of guys taking a break from dancing. They were polite but they didn't seem too keen to chat with a middle-aged stranger. Everyone appeared to know someone else and would greet each other with loud shouts and hugs. Avinash could feel his shirt sticking to his back. He'd have to get it washed again he thought. He glanced at his watch – 11.21. People were still coming in but he was getting tired. Just as he was about to leave someone tapped him on his shoulder.

Avinash turned around. It was Rohit.

'Having a good time?' he said.

Avinash smiled broadly out of sheer relief at having someone to talk to. He shrugged non-committally and said, 'It's okay. How about you? Do you know many people here?'

'Not really,' replied Rohit. 'A couple, but most of these guys are boys who went to college – you know, English-speaking men. Like you. Our worlds are very different. For a while I went with a young businessman I had met in a park. He introduced me to some of these guys. So I come sometimes.'

Avinash felt a gush of relief that he was not the only one feeling out of place.

Rohit, it turned out, lived out in the suburbs with his mother and sisters. It meant it took him almost an hour and a half in packed local trains every day to get to work. But it was all they could afford on his salary. 'It's not so bad,' he said with a sly smile. 'Sometimes in crowded trains you can have interesting experiences.'

Avinash flushed as an image crept into his mind of Rohit standing in a crowded train, pressed up against him. He tried to shake it off but the image spread inside his head like the stain from a leaking fountain pen.

Rohit was still talking. He had a younger sister who was taking her school-leaving examination. He had started college but after his father died in a factory accident he had dropped out. Now he worked as a chauffeur.

'The pay is better,' he said with a shrug. Avinash complimented him on his English. Rohit said it had helped him get his job. 'I sometimes have to drive foreigners,' he said.

'Oh really?' said Avinash. 'What company do you work for?'

'Just an import–export company,' said Rohit vaguely.

Avinash sensed he was crossing a line and didn't press further. He was a little relieved that Rohit didn't ask him the same question.

There was a moment's awkward silence as they both stared out at the dance floor. Then they both suddenly started speaking at once. Rohit laughed and said, 'You first.'

'Oh nothing,' replied Avinash. 'How did you know about this party? Do you have a computer?' He stopped short, embarrassed. Of course, he wouldn't have a computer at home.

Rohit laughed. 'No, I log in at Internet cafes. They are everywhere.'

Rohit intrigued Avinash. Avinash didn't think he had ever had a real conversation with someone like him. Their lives had no reason to intersect, certainly not at any of the parties Avinash went to. In his everyday world Avinash could have been in the back seat of a car telling someone like Rohit, 'Take me to the Tata Building.' He wouldn't even have paid much attention to his face. But instead here they were tapping their feet to the latest Hindi remixes talking about sexuality and trading growing-up stories.

'Would you like another drink?' said Avinash, feeling generous.

'Maybe later,' said Rohit. Then he looked at Avinash and said, 'Do you want to dance?'

Avinash, startled, said 'Dance? Me? Here?'

'Where else?' said Rohit, chuckling.

As they pushed their way through the crowd, Avinash tried to capture the moment in his head. For a split second he wanted everything to freeze, the laughing faces around him, the boys with their hands in the air, the men dancing with their arms on each other's waists and himself among them, and Rohit's chipped grin.

'You know, you dance quite well,' said Rohit.

'You mean for an older man?' replied Avinash with a smile.

'I like older men,' Rohit said, and touched Avinash's hair. 'I like grey hair. You should stop dyeing it.' Then he leaned over and kissed him on the cheek. Avinash felt the room tilt. I shouldn't have had that second drink, he thought. He moved closer to Rohit and felt Rohit's hand on the small of his back. He liked the way it held him. It was almost possessive.

As the song changed, Rohit looked at him and said, 'What do you say we get out and go somewhere?'

'I don't know,' said Avinash, surprised. 'Where can we go?'

'Surely a man like you has a nice flat with a view,' grinned Rohit. 'Or would the night watchman see me go up and wonder?'

'No, it's not that,' said Avinash sheepishly.

'How about we just go for a walk? It's too noisy in here,' Rohit suggested. 'I know a park.'

You are mad, said a voice in Avinash's head. You are drunk. But Rohit was already walking towards the door. Avinash meekly followed him out of the club and into the dark night. He paused at the door for a moment and looked back. No one was looking at him, no one was marking his departure. Within the disco light of the club-for-a-night he had somehow felt cocooned, as if nestled in the fantasy haven of the Internet where he was still FunMan and this was his wondrous adventure. Now, as he smelled the night air and heard the taxis honking, that dreamscape was evaporating. This is real, he thought. This is happening. He took a deep breath and shut the door behind him. Immediately the noise and laughter disappeared, wiped out by the familiar hum of the city night as efficiently as a wet rag on a blackboard. After the heat of the club, the night air felt cool. He shook his head – even his hair was sweaty. Rohit laughed and pulled out a carefully folded large white handkerchief from his jeans and wiped his forehead.

'Very hot in there, huh?' he said rather redundantly.

As they walked, Avinash felt awkward and self-conscious. He wondered if the city settling down to sleep around them, the cab drivers idling at the street corner were noticing what an odd couple they made. Everything seemed larger than life and he felt he could see himself reflected on every surface. The corner stores were closed. He could see little coal fires burning where people were cooking on the street. The charred smell of chapatti suddenly made him hungry again. 'Babu, a little money?' said a small boy running up to him but without much hope in his voice. He noticed the boy didn't approach Rohit.

'Hey, clear off,' Rohit said, shooing the boy away. He grabbed Avinash's hand and said, 'Come this way.'

As they turned into a narrow alley, Avinash wondered if he should just take Rohit home. He could always pretend he was the new driver or something.

'You know something,' he said, clearing his throat slightly embarrassed. 'My name is not Aveek. It's Avinash, actually.'

Rohit shrugged and smiled. 'Mine is still Rohit.' He let his hands fall to his side, his fingertips gently grazing Avinash's. A young couple passed by on a scooter, the phutphuts loud in the night. Avinash snatched his hand away. He noticed neither of the couple was wearing a helmet.

'Would you ever visit my home?' Rohit said out of the blue.

'You'd want me to?' Avinash could not keep the surprise out of his voice.

'It's not that far. Only a few stops by train. I have my own room,' said Rohit. 'I could show you my books. My sister would like you, I think. You could tell her what to study in college.'

Avinash smiled. His heart was calming down. 'What park are we going to?' he asked. Rohit didn't answer but just whirled around and kissed him. Avinash's eyes opened wide. 'It's okay,' said Rohit. 'There's no one around. No one can see.'

Avinash flushed. There was something sweet, almost romantic, about the way he said that. He wondered with a pang whether he would ever see this young man again after tonight. It would be nice to see his room, he thought to himself. He imagined mentoring his sister, going through her books, while Rohit made tea for them on the stove. He reached for Rohit's hand the way a small animal nuzzles for comfort. Rohit gripped it in return and led him confidently towards the park.

The park, Rohit explained, was actually closed at night but there was a part of the wall that had crumbled and they could sneak in through there. Avinash just followed, letting him take charge. Rohit held his hand out to help him as he stumbled over the bricks and stones.

The park was poorly lit but Rohit clearly knew his way around. Still holding Avinash's hand he guided him down snaking pathways, past flowering bushes, their pearly pink flowers fragrant in the heavy humid night air, over scrubby patches of grass littered with plastic wrappers. Avinash was rapidly losing his sense of direction as Rohit led him into a thicket of trees.

'Careful,' he said. 'It's really dark here.' Avinash almost tripped over the protruding stump of a tree. He could still hear the rumble of the trucks and cars on the main road but it was muffled now like distant thunder. All around him were newer noises, darker sounds, rustling leaves, the scampering of small animals.

'Scared, dear?' Rohit said, laughing.

Avinash shook his head and reached out for him, squeezing his chest through his shirt. Rohit grabbed him and kissed him, pressing up against him, this time, a lot more urgently than at the party. Avinash finally closed his eyes and kissed him back. Now he could really taste Rohit, a mix of cigarette, alcohol and fragrant almost sickly sweet paan masala. The mixture went to his head making him dizzy.

I can't believe this is happening to me, he thought. I am even finding the smell of paan masala sexy. When he was a young man he wouldn't have been caught dead with the stuff. He always thought of it as something terribly un-sophisticated. If he needed a breath freshener he would go for chewing gum.

Rohit kissed him harder, his hands moving under his shirt, touching his bare skin. Avinash followed suit, feeling Rohit's body and the tightness of it. The rough springiness of the hair on his chest made his knees go weak.

'Don't bite my neck,' Avinash said. 'It will leave a mark.' Rohit stopped kissing him and smiled. Then without a word he reached down, took Avinash's hand and placed it on his crotch as he started fumbling with Avinash's belt. Avinash's heart started thudding again but he made no move to stop him.

'Shit,' swore Rohit. 'What complicated belts you people wear.'

Avinash chuckled and unbuckled it for him. He felt Rohit's hand undoing the button of his trousers and tugging down the zipper. Following him, action for action, like a partner in a ballroom dance, Avinash did the same to him, his heart beating wildly as he touched him through his underpants.

Avinash felt his trousers puddle around his feet and he felt Rohit's hands, his fingers rough and callused, pulling his underpants down. Panic welled up within Avinash. It was no longer about just getting caught in the park. Everything was moving too fast. Things were spiralling out of control. He realized he had not thought this far ahead. They had not talked at all about what he was willing to do. Nervously, Avinash tried to slow things down. 'Wait a minute. What do you want to do?' he asked.

Rohit did not answer. Instead he spat into the palm of his own hand and reached behind Avinash, much to his shock. 'No, not that, I don't do that,' Avinash said trying to push his hand away.

But Rohit just laughed and swatted Avinash's hand away as if Avinash's no was just coy protestation to be casually brushed aside.

'No, no, I'm serious,' said Avinash, now genuinely scared. 'Not here.'

'Why not, dear?' breathed Rohit in his ear. 'I want to. And I know you want it. No one can see.'

His tone was still cajoling but now there was a new hint of something steelier as well. He gripped Avinash tighter as Avinash struggled to get out of his embrace.

'We don't have anything,' protested Avinash weakly. 'You know, protection.'

'I am clean,' said Rohit trying to force his tongue into his mouth again.

Avinash tried to push Rohit away. 'I think we should stop. I don't want to do this,' he said, reaching down to pull up his pants. That was a mistake. Even in the dim light he could see Rohit's face change. The flirtatious smile disappeared. He grabbed him and whipped him around, holding Avinash close to him with one arm and locking the other around in his neck. Avinash made choking sounds as he struggled, trying to break away, but Rohit was too strong, holding him in place as he rubbed up against him, thrusting against him roughly.

'You sister-fucking tease,' snarled Rohit. 'You won't take me home and you won't do anything here.'

'Just let me go. I'm sorry,' whimpered Avinash, gasping for breath, almost close to tears.

Rohit slapped him across the face. 'Why did you come with me if you were not going to put out, you old fart? I paid good money to get into that bloody party. You think I have money to piss down the drain? I'm not going home just like that.'

'Not that, not here,' pleaded Avinash. 'I'll do anything else you like.'

Rohit looked at him contemptuously for a second, then put his hands on his shoulders and pushed him roughly to his knees. Avinash knelt in the dirt and opened his mouth, almost relieved. He felt Rohit's penis, thrusting roughly, fill his mouth, making him choke. Rohit's hands were on Avinash's head pushing him forward and into his crotch, sweaty from the dancing and walking. Avinash gagged and felt tears stinging his eyes. Just let him come, he thought. And this will be over.

'Careful with those teeth, fucker,' said Rohit, cuffing him on the head. Avinash closed his eyes and sucked him desperately.

Eventually Rohit came with a grunt. As his body tensed Avinash tried to jerk his head away but Rohit's hands were like iron clamps holding him in place until he was fully spent. When Rohit was done and had loosened his grasp, Avinash spat, wiped his mouth and stood up. His own trousers and underwear were still coiled around his feet. Rohit had already zipped up his jeans. He lit a cigarette, took a deep drag and exhaled with satisfaction. Avinash stood there mutely, still stunned, unsure what to do. 'Want one?' Rohit's tone was mocking as he held the cigarette packet out to him. Avinash shook his head.

'Not a good enough brand for you, eh?' sneered Rohit.

'I have to go,' Avinash mumbled, wiping his mouth with the back of his hand.

'Cut the drama. That wasn't so bad for you, now, was it? I know you wanted it,' snorted Rohit. 'Men like you just pretend they are so respectable and proper. In the end, they all want the same thing.'

Avinash said nothing as he pulled up his trousers.

Rohit looked at him expectantly. 'Well?'

'Well what?' said Avinash.

'Don't I get a little something? A tip?' said Rohit. 'Remember that drink that you offered me back at the party? How about giving me some money for drinks now?'

Avinash continued to stare at him. 'I really don't have any,' he said.

'Don't fucking play games with me,' said Rohit. 'I saw your wallet.' Avinash started backing away but Rohit grabbed him and said, 'I know your type. You just want to come here, have some fun, go back to your air-conditioned apartments. All I am asking of you is some drink money and taxi fare.'

'Just let me go. I have to go home,' pleaded Avinash. 'I'll shout for help.'

'Shout?' laughed Rohit. 'You? Shout? For whom? The police? What will you tell them? You came to this park in the middle of the night to enjoy the night air? Do you even know where you are? Who's here to help you?' Then he put his fingers in his mouth and let out a low whistle. Suddenly over the rustling bushes Avinash heard an answering whistle and then another.

'These are my friends,' said Rohit grabbing Avinash by the collar. 'They can do anything they want with you. Rape you.

Follow you home. Talk to your wife when she goes shopping tomorrow.'

Avinash could hear people in the darkness now, the sounds of leaves being crunched underfoot. He saw the flash of a cigarette lighting somewhere. The park, which had seemed deserted only fifteen minutes ago, was rustling with illicit, shadowy life.

Oh God, he prayed silently. If I get out of this, I'll never do this again.

Rohit moved really close to him still holding on to his collar. 'Just give me what you have and leave,' he said, his breath a blast of paan masala. 'I don't have all night. This is my area. Don't even think about trying anything funny.'

Fumbling with his wallet, Avinash took out all the notes he had and gave them to Rohit. Coins fell from his open wallet on to the grass but he didn't bother to pick them up. 'Just leave me some for my taxi fare,' he begged, praying Rohit wouldn't want his credit cards. But Rohit just stuffed the money into his jeans pocket without even looking at it and let go of Avinash's collar. But before he let him go Rohit pulled out one of Avinash's business cards from the wallet and, waving it in the air said, 'Go on, then. Look, I am being kind, letting you go just like that. So don't think about trying anything smart like going to the police. This was nothing. I could do a lot more damage to you if I really wanted to. You want me to show up at your office?'

He put the card carefully into his pocket. Avinash stared at him unsure as to whether he could actually leave.

'What you waiting for?' Rohit gave him a little push. 'Go on, go home to your wife. Get lost, uncle.' He spat out the last word like a slur.

As he ran, Avinash stumbled and fell. He felt his knee stinging with pain as it scraped against the gravel through his trousers. He picked himself up and ran blindly through the bushes, over the trampled dusty grass. He passed a children's playground he hadn't noticed before, the rusty swing and slide standing like abandoned relics from a different, more normal, world. He ran on, heading towards the sound of traffic and the main road. Now he could make out other shapes in the darkness, other people. But he just ran till he almost crashed into the wall along the edge of the park. He felt his way along the wall, stumbling in the darkness over stones and thorny bushes, searching desperately for the gap they had come through. It felt like for ever until he found it and he fell through it, collapsing weakly on the sidewalk gasping for breath, his heart still racing. Late-night trucks rumbled by, the blast of exhaust making him feel nauseous and relieved all at once. He picked himself up and hobbled away, half afraid that any minute Rohit would come out through the hole in the wall, grab him by the collar and drag him back inside.

As he walked home his knee throbbed with pain. He knew there would be a nasty bruise. It was late but the city was still humming – a low buzz of life that never quite receded. People were sleeping on the pavements. Men sat huddled together smoking. Dogs followed him for a couple of blocks, yapping, and then wandered off.

When he finally reached home and rang the doorbell, a sleepy Bhola opened the door and looked at him in horror.

'Are you all right, babu? What happened?' he cried.

'Just a little . . . Nothing . . . nothing at all. Nothing serious, don't worry.' Avinash said. 'Get me the Dettol from the bathroom. And where do we keep those bandages?'

On Monday as Avinash headed to work, he went by the Subramaniam Wedding Hall as usual. There was no trace at all of the weekend. In the daylight it was just another city corner bustling with life. Auto rickshaws clustered in front of the pharmacy, buzzing like green-and-yellow bumble bees.

Housewives walked down the street from the market, their shopping bags stuffed with fruit and vegetables. A gaggle of schoolgirls in white and blue dresses, their hair neatly braided, clutched their bags and waited to cross the street. A man in a yellowing singlet and checked lungi, a lit beedi between his teeth, was putting up marigolds on a banner above the gate. He had already finished 'ANILA WEDS' in bright orange flowers – each marigold blotting out one more memory of the weekend in a burst of sunny normalcy.

It was amazing, he thought, that only the bruise on his knee remained to remind him it had really happened. He stroked it and winced. But there was a strange erotic reassurance in the pain, throbbing as it did with life. He thought of it as a stamp on a passport, the only reminder of journeys he might never dare make again.

As he walked into his office, he noticed the usual crowd of drivers hanging around the front steps, smoking and drinking tea. He nodded to them absently as he did every morning. They moved aside as usual to let him pass, nodding back and politely hiding their cigarettes behind their backs. But today as he passed he looked at them a little more carefully.

He noticed one of them had made no effort to hide his cigarette. Avinash looked closer. For an instant he thought it was Rohit. Avinash froze, his heart hammering wildly. He stared into the man's eyes as if daring him to grab his briefcase and fling it in the air, laughing, as all his important papers, his very life, rained down like twirling confetti. But the man just stared at him for a few seconds before he slowly lowered his cigarette and said, 'Good morning, sir.' He smiled and Avinash could see his teeth were paan-stained but unchipped.

At the door, his heart still racing, Avinash glanced back to see if any of the other drivers had noticed anything. But they were all chatting among themselves as if he wasn't even there. Only that man was still looking at him as he took a long drag from his cigarette. Avinash dropped his gaze but not before he saw him blow out a perfect ring of smoke that hung lazily in the warm morning air before disappearing without a trace.

XI

The Practical Thing to Do

S HE CALLED as she always did in the foggy chill of a San
Francisco morning before the grey early light had seeped
into Amit's dreams. She thought it was a criminal waste of
money to talk to an answering machine when she was calling
all the way from India. So Romola would painstakingly subtract
the hours (with one hour to spare either way because she could
never quite figure out which way Daylight Saving Time worked)
and call Amit at what she hoped was six in the morning though
he had told her many times he never woke up before 7.30.

It was December and it had been raining. The shrill ring of
the telephone ruptured his early morning dream. Amit stumbled out of bed, disoriented and shivering, and looked around
blindly for the receiver. He blearily picked it up from under
a pile of dirty laundry and realized he was holding it upside
down when he heard the faint tinny voice anxiously repeating
his name over and over again.

'Amit? Amit?'

'Hello?' he said cautiously into the mouthpiece.

As he heard the crackle of static and the familiar faraway
voice, Amit felt his heart clench.

'How are you?' she said. 'Were you asleep?'

The tightness in her voice gave it away. He knew it was bad
news.

'Are you awake?' she said. 'Is June home?' June, the live-in girlfriend who was never acknowledged, not even when she answered the phone ('Hello, is Amit there?' never 'Hello, June, how are you?'), suddenly had a role to play. This, Amit realized, with a sinking feeling, had to be serious.

'Ma.' Amit was suddenly alert. 'What is it?' On the rumpled pillow on the bed he saw June, her brown hair strewn across her face, looking at him questioningly as she rubbed the sleep from her eyes.

'Is everything okay?' she mouthed.

'It's your father,' Romola's voice was trembling. 'A heart attack this morning. By the time the ambulance came it was all over.'

Amit just stared out of the window at the numb grey city where they were cleaning the streets. He could not remember what day it was. He could not remember if he had moved his car. He probably had not. It must have got a ticket by now. The hardwood floor was cold against the soles of his feet, still warm from the bed.

'Are you there?' said Romola anxiously. 'Are you all right?' Amit nodded mutely and realized he couldn't make any sense of what his mother was saying any more. All her words were melding into each other like plastic in front of a heating vent. June had got out of bed and was holding his elbow as if to steady him. But Amit felt as if he was falling.

My father is dead. That makes me half an orphan. I should say something. I should do something. I should know what to do.

'Are you going to be able to come?' He realized Romola had not stopped talking. 'I don't know what to do. Should we wait for you to cremate him?'

'Let me call work and the travel agent. Let me call you back,' said Amit. June was holding his hand and he looked at her blankly.

The day passed in a blur. The travel agent got him a ticket

but the flight was not till the next night. He got leave for three weeks from his office. They even sent over a tasteful arrangement of white calla lilies with a note that said 'With sincere condolences. Our thoughts are with you.' June took the day off and helped him pack. Amit was grateful, yet only dimly aware of it all.

'Amit, talk to me.' June sounded worried as she went through his socks and underwear drawer later that evening. 'What are you thinking?'

'Nothing.' He picked at his T-shirts. 'Just . . . you know.'

'Do you think your mother will want to come back here with you?' said June, not looking at him as she pulled out a handful of underwear.

'Here?' Amit looked at her startled. 'With me? You mean to live with us?'

'Well, I mean she might want to. To just get away. Didn't your friend Raj's mother do that when his father died?'

Amit stared at her, and then at their kitchen, as if he could see his mother standing there right next to the toaster in her old red cardigan. Then he shook his head and said, 'I don't know. I never asked. I mean all the family is there. The house. What would she do here by herself?'

'It was just a thought,' June shrugged. 'I was just wondering. I thought it was sort of the done thing. How many socks do you want to take?'

'I don't know,' he scratched his head. 'I guess you're right. I guess I should bring her back with me. For a little while at least. It would take her mind off things.'

He left his packing half-finished and went online to research visas. He found it extremely comforting to read their bland bureaucratese, the steps neatly laid out one after another.

'I need to take copies of my bank statements for the last six months,' he told June as if he had found a solution to

196

something. 'They ask for that when you need to get a visa for a dependant.'

By the time Amit managed to change two flights and land in Calcutta, his father was just a framed picture on the nightstand. His cousin Rajeev had performed the last rites at the crematorium. As the only son it was Amit's right, his responsibility, to light the pyre. But the plane had a nine-hour layover in Singapore. Romola couldn't bear to keep the body overnight in the house on a block of sawdust-covered ice, melting slowly in the living room. And she shuddered at the thought of Avinash lying there like an unclaimed piece of luggage in the cold dark anonymity of a morgue. Rajeev offered to perform the rites, Romola had told Amit on the phone. Yes, agreed Amit, it was the practical thing to do.

Secretly, Amit was almost relieved. When his great-grandmother died, Amit remembered watching silently as they went about preparing her body for cremation. He remembered the relatives and neighbours crowded around the rooms. The piles of white flowers dripping little puddles of water everywhere. His father dressed in white cotton, his face unshaven. His mother telling him distractedly, 'Did you get something to eat? Go next door and at least have some fruit.' But Amit had shaken his head and clung to her sari, too afraid to let her out of his sight. He had stood at the door behind her when they finally left with the body. They had hoisted the flower-strewn body on their shoulders and set off down the street chanting 'Hari bol, Hari bol.' It scared Amit to think of how they had tied his great-grandmother down with strong twine as if she might try to get off her bier as they carried her down the street. He had stood on the porch and watched them walk down the street scattering puffed rice behind them, her body bobbing under the pile of wreaths.

'Do you know what happens at the burning ghat?' his cousin Rajeev, three years older and infinitely wiser in the ways of the world, had told him that night with ghoulish relish. 'When you light the flames, you have to hit her skull with a stick and break it open so the soul can fly free.'

'You lie,' said Amit, terrified at the image of his father cracking open Great-Grandmother's head. But the image had stuck with him over the years, imprinted somewhere deep inside him. He realized with a start as he packed his suitcase for India that he was past thirty and had never been inside a burning ghat. Sitting in America, he would hear about this uncle and that great-aunt passing. But he'd never been in India when it happened. This time too he was spared. He wondered if Rajeev remembered the story that had haunted him for years. He had no idea if it was true, if Rajeev had indeed cracked his father's skull open.

The first thing he noticed when he stepped into the house in Calcutta was the quiet. His father had not been a boisterous man. Even when he was in the house you barely noticed him. He would sit in his armchair, the one whose stuffing was coming out of the side, reading a newspaper, a cup of tea slowly growing cold in front of him. But for the rustle of the paper and the occasional rasp of him clearing his throat, he made no noise at all. After a while he would get up, fold his newspaper neatly and say, 'I am going for a walk' and quietly leave the house, shutting the door gently behind him.

At one level it felt as if he had just gone for a walk. But as Amit put his suitcase down he could feel the difference. Something intangible had fled the house, wiped away as if with a wet rag, wiped so clean it was hard to tell what had been there in the first place. The house smelled of mourning – wet decaying flowers and heavy, cloying sandalwood incense. People had brought so many flowers that every old vase in the house had been pressed into service. Some stood in a cluster in front of the garlanded portrait of his father. It was an old picture from some official event and he looked somewhat severe in thick black-rimmed glasses and a tie, his moustache just turning grey. The flowers in the garland were already curling at the tips, turning brown.

It was twilight outside. For some reason only the fluorescent lights were on, and they made his mother's skin seem bluish and sickly. She was wearing a white sari, her wrists looked bare without the red and white bangles she'd worn every single day since she got married. Unlike many of his aunts she had never worn a broad red streak of sindoor in her hair like a bloody gash of marital pride. She preferred just a discreet dab of it instead. Amit remembered, every day after her bath, she would sit in front of her dressing table, her wet hair cascading down her back. She would take her old silver comb and dip the end into her little container of sindoor and then very carefully touch it lightly to the parting in her hair, leaving only the slightest hint of red, as hesitant as a comma. Now even that tiny smudge was gone, leaving her scalp shockingly naked. He could see the white hairs fanning out from the parting in her head, bare as an untrodden path, as he folded his arms around her. She looked as if all the colour had been bleached out of her.

'You've come?' she said, her hand clutching the back of his jacket.

The tube light overhead flickered as erratic as the human heart. Blink. Blink. Blink. A sandy brown lizard clung to the wall, perfectly still, only its beady eyes moving as it watched the bugs circling around the light. We need to change the light, Amit thought to himself.

On the long uncomfortable flight from San Francisco, across the endless grey-blue expanse of the Pacific Ocean, he had been dreading this moment most of all, fearing Romola would collapse into a flood of hysterical tears as soon as she saw him and he would somehow come up short, unable to string together the correct words of solace. But instead they just held each other, somewhat awkwardly, as if acknowledging a new relationship between them which she masked by saying, as she always did, 'How was your flight? You must be tired. Have you eaten?'

'I'm all right,' he said and stopped, afraid to say anything more, as if to ask her how she was might snap whatever was holding her together. Amit feared if that happened, he wouldn't know how to prop her up again.

In the end it was only after he had taken off his shoes, washed his face, changed into a pair of his father's old white pyjamas and been served a cup of tea, that Romola finally brought up the topic.

'We did everything we could.' Her hands folded on her lap, her voice quiet. 'But there was nothing to be done.'

'I know,' he said.

'Everyone came,' she continued as if going through a shopping list. 'Madhu Kaka and his wife. Your aunts from Jodhpur Park. The neighbours. Even Ivy-pishi who lives all the way out near the Dunlop Bridge. You should have seen the flowers the office sent. Huge wreaths.'

'Yes.' He tried to imagine the scene as if he could paint himself into it. 'My office sent some flowers as well.'

'And Rajeev. What would I have done without him? He really took charge, like a son.'

'Yes,' said Amit. In his head he could see Rajeev cracking his father's skull wide open. He shuddered, trying to dislodge the image from his head.

When he saw Rajeev later that evening Amit didn't know what to say. Rajeev and his mother came by with a shopping bag. Amit could see oranges and apples stuffed in it. 'What is all this?' protested Romola. 'Why more fruit? You have done so much already.'

'It's nothing,' Rajeev's mother gestured to Rajeev to set the bag down. 'It's important to keep up your strength, Romola. And now Amit is here too.'

'Sorry, old boy,' Rajeev patted him on the back stiffly.

Amit smiled bleakly. 'Ma said she didn't know what she would have done without you.'

Should I thank him for burning my father? Did he really crack his skull? Probably not. Surely they don't do that in the electric crematorium? But it must have all cost money. Should I ask him how much and offer to pay him back?

'It was nothing,' Rajeev's smile made his moustache twitch. He had come from the office and his white shirt had sweat patches under his arms. He had put on weight since the last time they had met. At another time Amit would have teased him about his belly. But he felt it would be inappropriate now. Rajeev pulled out a big plastic bottle of Pepsi from the shopping bag with the air of a magician.

'Here,' he held out the bottle as if it was the scalp of a fox he had just hunted. 'I know you America-returned types can't drink our water any more.'

Amit started to say he only drank Diet Coke because everything else had too much real sugar but then stopped, fearing it would sound ungracious.

Instead he just said, 'Sit' gesturing towards the sofa. But Rajeev had already sat down.

Not there. That's my father's armchair.

They sat facing each other. Amit asked after Rajeev's wife and how old their little one was. Rajeev did not ask about June. Amit had told Rajeev about her on his last visit but Rajeev had only asked two questions. 'Is she American?' and 'Does your mother know?' He had answered yes to both and they had moved on to other subjects. Now they lapsed into silence while Romola and Rajeev's mother kept talking, their voices low, tinged with faint anxiety. Amit watched the lizard poke his head out from behind the fluorescent light.

I would give anything for some Diet Coke. A tall glass with ice at the bottom filled to the brim with fizzy Diet Coke. I wonder if we can get it at the store around the corner.

'So have you thought about what to do with your mother?' Rajeev said balancing a cup of tea on his knee. Romola, who had brought the tea, looked at Amit but said nothing.

'Um, well I don't know, I mean it's up to her, um what she wants,' stammered Amit.

'Of course, she'll go with him,' said Rajeev's mother authoritatively. 'It will be a good change for her. And company for Amit too – he has no one to call his own in San Francisco.'

June. What about June? Why do we pretend she doesn't exist?

But Rajeev's mother was in full flow. 'These are modern times, baba. No one is going to go and shave their heads and sit in Varanasi waiting to die, surviving on scraps of parched rice like crows and pigeons. I am sure Avinash would have wanted her to go with Amit.'

Amit said nothing but glanced at his mother.

'That is for later,' she said soothingly. 'He's just come. There is so much to do. We'll worry about me later.'

'The main thing,' Rajeev's voice sounded professorial, as if he was about to prove a theorem. 'The main thing is to be practical these days. Don't worry about what people will say.'

He's really getting a belly. He should exercise more.

That night as Amit was brushing his teeth Romola came to the bathroom door and said, 'Your old room is a real mess. We had been using it for storage. It's full of dust and papers. We'll have to sort through them and clean it all out.'

'We'll do it later,' mumbled Amit, his mouth full of toothpaste.

'Yes, yes, but what I meant is why don't you just sleep in my room tonight? There is plenty of space in the bed.'

'Your bedroom?' Amit stopped in mid-brushstroke.

'Yes, it feels so big and empty now that it's just me. It keeps me awake at night sometimes,' she replied.

But that's your bed. That's the only bed I remember you and Baba sleeping in ever since I was born. Didn't you get the bed when you got married?

'Remember when you were a little boy and slept between us at night? You used to be scared of the dark,' Romola smiled. It was the first time he had seen her smile since he came back.

Amit slept in one corner of the bed, still in his father's pyjamas, on his old pillow, covered with his childhood blanket embroidered with blue and green fishes. He curled himself into a ball with his back to his mother. He could hear her rustling as she got ready for bed. He knew the ritual by heart. First she would smear on the hand lotion that smelled of English lavender. Then the dabs of Nivea cream to moisturize her face. Then she would tie her hair into a tight plait with a piece of old black ribbon. Finally she would go to the bathroom and change from her sari into an old shapeless nightgown – this one printed with little blue star-shaped flowers. When she was back she would turn on the bedside lamp, put on her reading glasses and sit in her nightgown on the bed writing in her diary.

Even with his eyes shut he could see the entry.

Amit arrived. Rajeev and his mother visited. Brought fruit and Coca-Cola. (She called all dark colas Coca-Cola without differentiation.) *Calls from Bela, Shobha, Mr Sanyal.*

After she was done she turned off the lamp and lay down. 'Are you tired?' she asked.

'Hmmm,' he mumbled as if he was half asleep. The moonlight slanted through the windows, illuminating the empty space between them. When he was a boy that was the space he would sleep in.

Sometime in the middle of the night he woke up with a start. Romola was asleep, snoring gently. Amit lay awake staring at the ceiling. Even in the dark he could make out the tendrils of long cobwebs swaying gently from the corners like seaweed. He wanted to get up and pee but he was afraid he would wake Romola up. He carefully pulled his watch out from under the pillow. 4:30 PM the green letters blinked at him. It was still on California time. He lay there as still as he could, his eyes shut, trying to will himself back to sleep. In the silence of the slumbering house, the only sound he could hear was the tch-tch clucking of the lizard. But the house still hummed in a way it never did in California. Even in sleep the city seemed full of people. He could imagine them asleep all around him, in the neighbouring flats and houses. A city humming with sleeping people. Or perhaps, he thought as he waited for the first pale flush of dawn and the cries of the vegetable sellers, perhaps it's just a noisy refrigerator.

'You know I slept through the night without taking a sleeping pill,' Romola told him the next morning as they had breakfast together. 'It's the first night since your father ...'

Amit said nothing as he buttered his toast.

'It's funny. I never thought I would miss him so much. It's not like he was a great talker. But I guess one gets used to a person in one's life, no matter what.'

'Ma,' Amit suddenly changed the subject. 'Do you get Diet Coke here? Maybe it's called Coca-Cola Light?'

'What's that? I've never seen it,' she replied pouring out his tea. 'Are you on diet-shiet? Is that why you're so thin?'

'I don't know, June. I don't know if I can do this,' he said when he called June to let her know he'd reached India safely. He dropped his voice, after glancing around him. 'I can't imagine my mother living with us in San Francisco. I don't know what I'd do with her.'

'You could try it for a little while,' June replied reasonably. 'It doesn't have to be for ever.'

I am sleeping in her bedroom, on her bed. I don't know how long I can do this. Am I weird to feel like this?

'It's hard enough with the two of us. Imagine her in there as well.'

'We could find a bigger place if we had to,' June replied.

'She won't even let me go buy Diet Coke. She says we have a big bottle of Pepsi sitting in the refrigerator.'

'What are you going on about?' June sounded puzzled. 'Why don't you go buy yourself some Diet Coke, for heaven's sake?'

But there just seemed to be no time to do anything on his own. There was a constant stream of visitors stopping by with boxes of sweets and bags of fruit. Each asked for the details and Amit marvelled at how calmly Romola shared the story with them. Avinash had come back from a walk. He had said he was feeling warm and had taken off his sweater and said he was going to take a shower. Be careful, don't catch a chill now, she had said. Then he said he'd lie down a bit before taking a shower. Amit listened silently, treading and re-treading the now familiar lines. It was almost, he thought, as if he'd been there.

Eventually they'd turn to him. 'How is San Francisco?' they would ask. 'Thinking of settling down? Will you come back?' And finally the question he kept dreading. 'What about your mother? What are you thinking of doing with her?'

Romola sat in the room as if they were talking about an entirely different person, or a piece of furniture, an antique couch too large for a modern apartment.

'Well, I don't know,' Amit was non-committal. 'We'll see what is most practical. There is this house here.'

'Well we could always sell it if we need to,' said Romola suddenly. 'It feels strange here without your father anyway. So empty.'

Amit stared at her in surprise. 'I'll be at work all day. And you've never liked America very much,' he retorted.

'Aah, but she would have you,' Asha-mashi jumped in. 'It'll keep her busy, cooking for you. Otherwise I know what you bachelor boys eat – boiled eggs, sandwiches and Maggi noodles.'

'I don't think she needs to come all the way to San Francisco to cook for me,' Amit replied with a little smile.

'No, no – it's family,' Asha-mashi swept his arguments aside, her bangles jangling. 'You are all she has now. You know that. Just the other day I came by and she was polishing all your old school medals.'

'Those old medals?' Amit looked at his mother. 'I didn't even know we still have them.'

Amit had a vision of his mother carrying his ancient English grammar and drawing medals all the way to America. He imagined her sitting in his apartment in San Francisco with a little kitchen towel polishing those discoloured medals. One of them, he remembered with a twinge of guilt, had been for good conduct.

He had always been a good boy. He had done everything that was expected of him – never one for cigarettes and beers and black-market porn like his school friends. Even Rajeev would sneak out of his house to smoke Wills Filter cigarettes in the park. Amit would hang out with him but when Rajeev offered him a cigarette he'd just shake his head. 'Afraid your mother will find out?' Rajeev would say mockingly, blowing out a cloud of smoke. 'You are such a good boy, Amit.'

The maid came into the room with a glass of Pepsi and some sweets on a plate for Asha-mashi.

'Please have some,' said Romola.

'No sweets, no no,' protested Asha automatically. 'I have to go home and have lunch anyway. Your brother-in-law is home today and is waiting for me.'

'At least have the Coca-Cola' insisted Romola. 'Something cold—'

'Oh no,' Asha-mashi shook her head vigorously. 'I can't drink all this Coca-Cola. Makes me burp too much. Here, Amit, you have it. You are the American after all.'

Why don't Indians drink their sodas with ice even in America? One Coke, no ice please. Just water, no ice please. I want Diet Coke from a soda fountain in a gas station. I want to fill a paper cup with a small avalanche of ice and then press the Diet Coke button. I want to fill it to the brim. Wait for the bubbles to slowly die down and then fill it up again until it overflows. Not like here. Where the soda machine is out of reach behind the counter. And an old man fills a small plastic cup with miserly exactitude before handing it over.

Amit sipped his soda. Just as he had expected, it was refrigerator-cold but flat.

'My grandson wants Coca-Cola all the time,' Asha-mashi burbled on.

The phone rang and Amit left the room to answer it. When he walked back he heard them still talking about the house. He paused near the door listening to his mother.

'If I had my way I'd say, Amit, come back here, find a job, and move back,' Romola was saying. 'But I know that's not possible. You can't just drop everything and come back because your mother is alone. I know that. We'll just have to do what's feasible.'

'Your Amit has always been a good boy. He will do the right thing.'

'I never liked America but perhaps now I wouldn't mind it. To be closer to him.' He could hear the smile in Romola's voice. 'Sometimes I feel he has gone so far away. It's good to have him home.'

Amit cleared his throat and walked into the room. The women stopped talking and looked at him, still smiling. 'Who was that on the phone?' asked his mother.

'No one,' said Amit. 'Wrong number.' He didn't know why

he lied. It was Rajeev calling to say he was coming over to discuss whether to serve samosas and sweets or just sweets at the funeral. Somehow Amit didn't feel like talking about it.

'Ma,' he said casually. 'I'm going out for a walk.'

'Walk? Now? Why? It's almost lunchtime,' protested Romola automatically. 'Have you had your bath?'

'No,' said Amit as calmly as he could. 'I'll be back soon. I just need to get some fresh air.' His ears were ringing and he felt as if his knees might buckle under him if he had to speak another word.

I need personal space. Oh my God, listen to me. Personal space and Diet Coke. How much more American can I get?

As soon as he walked outside, though, his spirits lifted. It was a clear winter morning, the sunlight buttery around him. He walked down the street to the market at the end of the road and with every step he took it seemed as if the ringing noise in his ears started to recede, replaced by an old, familiar clamour: crows, bicycles bells, vendors.

The sides of their little market street were piled high with winter vegetables – stubby carrots and cabbages and cauliflowers, some no bigger than a clenched fist, others as large as footballs. Women sold them squatting on the pavements, their saris hitched up around their knees, silver blades flashing in the sun like steely minnows as they lopped off the leaves and threw them casually into the gutter. As if on cue, an old cow appeared, more grimy brown than white, its ribs showing, and began chewing the leaves. No one paid it any attention. Amit just stood in the middle of the street staring at it all with a half-smile.

'Ei,' yelled the cauliflower-woman smacking the cow's nose when it nudged too close to her pile of vegetables. The cow barely moved half an inch, tail flicking idly, as it went back to the discarded leaves. Amit smiled at the cow, feeling, for the first time since he had arrived, that he was really home, that things hadn't changed so irrevocably in his life, leaving him stranded without a compass.

'Do you need a cauliflower?' said the woman seeing him staring. 'These are from my village, from my own soil. Not those big ones they grow on the sewage dumps of Dhapa.'

Amit shook his head. The woman shrugged and dismissed him. A boy weaving through the street on his bicycle yelled at him, 'Dada, watch out. This isn't your uncle's road.' Amit, startled out of his reverie, laughed and stepped aside.

In front of him he could see the old corner cigarette and paan store. It still looked the same – a cramped cubbyhole of a store, just big enough for one man to crouch in. But even that had a touch of something new – a garland of Frito Lays now hung from the ceiling. There was a picture of an Indian film star on the little packets with flavours he'd never heard of – Bindaas Bhel, Mast Masala, Tangy Treat, even something called American Cream and Onion. Amit suddenly felt hungry as he looked at the packets – red, green, blue, shiny with salty promise.

He wondered which one he should get. He felt almost-guilty, as if he was personally turning India into a fast-food nation. June had once brought home a book from the library that was all about how economic globalization was making multinational corporations the new colonial masters.

But he felt an irresistible urge to try some Bindaas Bhel. 'Can I have that, please?' he said gesturing at the orange packet.

The man behind the counter peered down at him from his little perch and said, 'Oh, Amit? When did you come back? So sorry to hear about your father. Such a gentleman – I'd see him go to market every day in his white shirt and with a shopping bag.'

Amit flushed guiltily, as if he had been caught violating some obscure rule of mourning, buying Bindaas Bhel potato chips. He couldn't remember the paan-wallah's name. He didn't know if he'd ever known his name. The man had always been Paan-babu. Rajeev had bought his first clandestine cigarette from him, a single cigarette he had lit with the long coconut fibre rope with its glowing fiery end tied to a post next to the store. He'd stand there in the corner, next to the store, puffing urgently at his cigarette before they went home to their good-boy lives. 'Have some paan masala,' Paan-babu would tell them, grinning knowingly, his teeth stained dark red. 'It will hide the smell.'

But that was years ago. Amit hadn't known that the paan-wallah even knew which house he lived in. He wished he could just pay for his chips and leave. But the man, now balder and fatter, his droopy moustache streaked with silver, was in a chatty mood.

'Would you like a paan?' he offered as he took one of the glossy dark heart-shaped leaves and smeared white lime-paste on it.

'No,' Amit shook his head. 'Just the chips.'

'The American chips, eh?' the man chuckled. 'All the kids love them. They see them on TV, no? So when did you come? How is your mother? Is she going back with you?'

'Umm, I don't know,' Amit muttered. 'Not yet. Probably.'

'Well, it will be hard for her to be alone. But we'll all be here, don't worry,' the man said earnestly. 'But how will she manage that house?'

Amit wondered if he could suddenly just pretend he'd forgotten an important phone call and turn and run. Instead he carefully pulled off one Frito Lay packet and handed it wordlessly to the man.

'You know,' said the man leaning forward confidentially. 'My brother-in-law is a promoter. Very good business he is doing these days. They tear down these old houses and turn them into flats. Just like that. Everyone's happy. You get half the flats. Keep one, sell the others if you want. He does the same. Everyone makes a little money.'

'That's good,' said Amit, hoping to hurry the transaction along.

'Yes,' said the man nodding vigorously as he carefully folded the paan. 'It's the thing these days. This neighbourhood is just gold now, you know. Remember the Sanyal house that used to be in the corner there? It's gone. It's become six flats. I reckon the same thing is going to happen with the judge's house now that he's dead. But I hear the sons are all fighting over it.'

'Right,' Amit nodded, desperate to flee the conversation.

'You, of course, are an only son. You don't have to worry about all that. But the trick is you have to find someone you can trust, you know. Otherwise they might just leave you with a half-finished building.' The man held up the paan, inspected it and said, 'What do you say? Are you sure you don't want one of my special paans?'

'Yes, sure,' Amit said with a faint smile. 'Before lunch, you know. Just these chips.'

'Ten rupees,' said the paan-wallah as he popped the paan into his mouth. He looked satisfied as he chewed, his lips stained a dark blood red from the betel juice. 'But think about it. If you like, I can put in a quick word. My brother-in-law lives quite close by. You remember my sister, don't you?'

Amit didn't but didn't want to admit it. He handed the paan-wallah ten rupees and said, 'All right, I will think about it.'

Amit shook his head, smiling. It was the kind of story he could tell his friends in San Francisco. In India the paan-wallah doesn't just sell paan and cigarettes. He dispenses real-estate advice. As he walked away he glanced up at what used to be the Sanyal house. It was now a three-storey boxy apartment building, the balconies grilled in like cages. He could see wet underwear and saris hanging from blue nylon clotheslines strung on the balconies. He remembered the house that had been there. It had been an old mansion with a great driveway with huge old columns on either side. There had been a big banana tree on one side and an old mango tree on the other. Every summer it would be laden with sour little green mangos. The windows had been as big as doors and he remembered old Mrs Sanyal sitting on a stool near the window yelling at the potato-wallah to run over and hand her a half a kilo of potatoes. He wondered who lived there now. A young woman walked out holding the hand of a little boy. She didn't look familiar at all.

As he walked past the house he tore open his Bindaas Bhel chips and ate every single one. They were dusted with some lethal-looking red powder that exploded in his mouth with bursts of spiciness. It made him thirsty. He remembered he'd meant to see if the paan-wallah stocked Diet Coke but he didn't want to go back to him again. Instead he just walked back, licking the last grains of salt from his fingers so that not a trace would remain by the time he got home.

As he passed by the cauliflower woman he paused and almost on a whim picked up a cauliflower.

'How much?' he asked.

She told him. 'Okay,' he said and handed her the money. The woman stared at him in surprise as if she had expected him to bargain. Then she shrugged and handed him his change, still looking at him as if he was slightly daft.

When he got home his mother said, 'What? A cauliflower. Why did you get a cauliflower? We already have two.'

'Oh,' he said. 'I suddenly had an urge to eat fried cauliflower.'

'You should have just told me,' she said. 'Silly boy. Did you have Indian money on you? How much did you pay?'

'No, Ma, I paid with dollars,' he joked. But he didn't tell her how much he had paid. Whatever it was, he knew he had paid too much.

That day when he went for a shower Amit masturbated for the first time since he had arrived in Calcutta. They were in the middle of thirteen days of mourning – no meat, no fish, no leather shoes, no sex. He was sure masturbation was forbidden as well. But as he stood under the shower, the water turned on to full blast, smearing his head with thick golden creamy Sunsilk shampoo, almost absently, as if programmed by some faraway brain, he reached down to his crotch. He watched the water splash on the bathroom wall and heard it gurgle down the drain as he tugged at himself, trying to fill his head with erotic thoughts. June, he whispered to himself, as if attempting to rub a genie to life. But her chestnut brown hair remained stubbornly foreign in his mother's bathroom. He shut his eyes instead and tried to remember himself at fourteen in that very bathroom ejaculating to lingerie ads in his mother's women's magazines.

'Are you done, Amit?' his mother suddenly shouted from outside the door. 'Rajeev just came over. He wants to discuss something before he heads back to his office. What are you doing in there so long anyway?'

Amit leaned back wearily against the wall, his eyes still shut, his crotch soapy.

'Coming,' he said finally. 'I'll be out in a minute.' He tried half-heartedly to climax but the moment was gone. He just turned off the shower and watched the water gurgle into the drain and then, resigned, towelled himself dry.

Rajeev, of course, wanted to make arrangements about the food for the funeral. A hundred and twenty-five guests – one samosa, one kochuri and two sweets in a box per guest. What did Amit think about that?

'Sounds good,' Amit shrugged, trying to concentrate. The arithmetic seemed too much to wrap his brain around. 'Have we got a shop in mind?'

'Why don't I talk to the sweetshop in my neighbourhood?'

Rajeev replied. 'If you go to them they are bound to try and rip you off because they'll know you live in America.'

'Yes,' shrugged Amit. 'Why don't you?'

Like you've taken care of everything else. I don't know why I am here. You could just shave your head and perform the funeral too and no one would say a word.

'Kakima, that's settled then. Will you call my mother and let her know? She'll just tell the sweetshop,' said Rajeev. He waited till Romola left the room, then leaned forward and said in a low voice, 'Amit, you'll be leaving soon. Everyone is wondering what you've decided.'

'About what?' said Amit.

'Your mother, of course,' Rajeev threw up his hands. 'You know, she's not going to bring it up unless you do. You can't leave her here alone.'

But I can't take her with me to California. I just can't, but how can I tell her that?

'This house is just too big,' continued Rajeev. 'Look at the ceiling. I can see some plaster peeling in that corner. I bet it'll start to leak this monsoon. The next day the windows won't shut. How will she manage all of this on her own?'

But my house in San Francisco is too small. The walls are too thin. I will never be able to have sex any more.

'Amit, you are going to have to decide. She'll go along with whatever you want. She loves you.'

Too much. Rajeev, can you love someone too much?

'I mean, I'll do whatever you need. But this is your mother. It's your decision now that your father's gone. I'm always here but you know our flat is so far away. I am not going to be able to drop by all the time like I am doing now.'

That was when Amit had the brainwave. It was so simple, so obvious, he started to believe in fate after all, as if a path had been laid out in front of him all along, just waiting for him to open his eyes and walk down it.

'What if we turn this house into an apartment building?' said Amit. 'I hear everyone is doing it these days. We'd get good money. And then Ma would have to deal with only one flat. Much more practical, no?'

'Flats?' Rajeev looked at him thoughtfully.

'Yes, flats.' Amit was on a roll. 'I think we could make eight apartments here, don't you? It's prime real estate, people tell me. I am sure developers would salivate at the prospect. Don't you have friends who are developers?'

'Yes,' Rajeev nodded. 'My old schoolmate Alok Dastidar. Remember him? He was in the football team.'

'Yes, yes,' Amit could barely contain his excitement. 'I could give you power of attorney so you could deal with all the paperwork. And once the apartments are done you could keep one. It would be much closer to your work as well.'

'Do you really mean that?' Rajeev sounded genuinely surprised.

'It's the least I could do, Rajeev,' Amit said not insincerely. 'You've been like a son to my mother. She would feel so relieved having you all close to her. And she loves your little boy. It would help her pass her time.'

'Think about it,' said Amit. But he didn't want him to. In his head he could already see the apartments stacked on top of each other. He could see Romola and Rajeev and Rajeev's mother and wife and son. He could see every one of them in his tidy domestic tableau, organized as neatly as the Christmas manger scene at his Jesuit school. Everyone neatly in place, except for him. Once that would have filled him with quiet desolation but right now he felt only fizzy relief.

'I don't know,' Rajeev said scratching his head. But Amit could see the idea was slowly taking root.

'I'll talk to Ma,' he told him.

But it was harder to tell Romola than he thought it would be. Every time he was ready to bring it up, something stopped him. Once it was the phone ringing. Then it was a power cut. And the next time he just couldn't find the words.

Finally one day when they had sat down to lunch Romola mentioned something about repairs. Amit realized this was the moment. He swallowed a mouthful of rice, chased it down with a glass of water and said, 'Ma, have you ever thought about tearing down the house and building flats?'

'Tear down the house? This house?' said Romola. 'What do you mean?'

'I think it would be a good idea. I have been talking to a few people. I see the Sanyals down the street have done it.'

'When did you come up with all these ideas?' Romola sounded alarmed.

'Well, I talked to Rajeev.' He held Rajeev out as if he were an amulet. 'It was hard to get any time with you, what with the funeral and all. Rajeev agrees it makes the most sense.'

'But this house, it's where you were born. I came here as a bride. We can't just tear it down like that. Do you know how much history is in this house? Your great-grandfather built it with his own hands.'

'That's why it's springing leaks everywhere. The ceilings are so high we can't even keep the cobwebs off it. And you said you were okay selling it off. This way once the flats are done you can keep one for yourself. It will be smaller and much easier to maintain.'

'But who's going to deal with all the paperwork and lawyers and builders and contractors?'

'Aha, I thought of all that. Rajeev. I asked him if he would take charge of this. And then when the flats are done we could give him one from our share as well. He jumped at the idea. I mean, their house is so small and so far away from his office. And it's rented anyway.'

'Rajeev? But it's our house, not Rajeev's.'

'Ma, I am only thinking about you here,' Amit's voice was

suddenly sharp as he tried to hold his carefully stitched plan together. 'And you are the one who said Rajeev was just like your son.'

'Like my son, yes,' Romola's voice was sharp as well. 'But that's just a way of speaking. You are my son. I don't want to depend on Rajeev. He has his own mother and wife. I thought you wanted me to come to America, if not now, then perhaps in a few months.'

Amit dropped his eyes. 'Of course, you can come for a visit whenever you like. But I don't think you should move just like that. It might be all too much change to deal with right now. And there's June. But don't worry. I mean, I'll send money for you every month.' As soon as he said that Amit felt his heart sink. But it was too late.

I didn't mean that. I didn't mean it that way. It's not about the money. I know that.

But his mother's face had lost all colour. She sat quietly for a minute, her fingers still flecked with grains of rice and dal. Then she said quietly, 'Don't worry about me. I think your father left enough for me to take care of myself. I won't be rich but I'll be fine. You just be happy, Amit, wherever you are.'

'Ma, this house is yours too. I mean, you don't have to do anything you don't want to. I just thought this would be more manageable for you. And you'd have Rajeev nearby . . .' Amit's voice trailed off.

'You could have just asked me what I wanted,' Romola said without looking at him. 'I was right here, wasn't I? For once someone could have asked me what I wanted. That's all I ever do – try to guess what everyone else wants.' Then she got up and went to the kitchen to put away the leftovers.

But I couldn't, Mother. I was afraid if I asked you, you would tell me.

Amit sat on the chair staring sightlessly at the newspaper until he felt the rice drying on his fingers.

For the rest of his trip she never referred to the house again. And every day like clockwork she produced one of his favourite dishes, going to the vegetable seller three markets away to get out-of-season banana blossom so she could make some banana-blossom curry.

On the day he left for San Francisco, Romola hired a driver to take them to the airport. 'I can take you both,' Rajeev told them. 'I'll just leave the office a little early.'

'You've done more than enough, Rajeev,' Romola replied firmly. 'Don't worry. I'll take him myself. I don't want you to rush from work. You don't need to come so far out of your way.'

At the airport they sat in silence watching little knots of families cluster around their departing members. Occasionally the disembodied crackling voice of a woman announced the arrival and departure of unseen flights in Bengali, Hindi and English. In the harsh fluorescent light of the Calcutta airport, Romola looked tired. Hunched on the hard plastic orange seat she clutched Amit's carry-on as if she was holding him. A little bored boy was roaming around the airport staring at the flickering goldfish in the aquarium. His father tried to entertain him with sodden paper cups of Coke.

'Do you want something to drink?' said Amit. 'Tea?'

'No, no, it's too late. It will keep me up all night.'

'I'll get something,' said Amit standing up.

'Here, let me give you some money.' Romola opened her handbag and started fumbling inside.

'It's all right,' said Amit. 'I have some.'

'I know you do,' she said with a wan smile, holding out a note. 'But let me get it for you.'

Amit took the money from her. It was a fresh note, crisp with unused promise. At the soda counter, he suddenly folded the note and put it back in his wallet as if it was a letter, or a piece of paper with an important phone number. Pulling out one of his own crumpled notes, he asked the man if he had any Diet Coke.

'No, sorry sir,' he replied. 'Only Pepsi. Mirinda. 7Up.'

He got himself a cup of neon-orange Mirinda. The man filled it carefully to the brim as if he was decanting a chemistry experiment and then handed it gingerly to Amit. It was fizzy at least, though it coated his mouth with instant cloying sweetness. He chugged it down sitting next to his mother.

'When will you reach San Francisco?' she asked.

'It will be two in the morning for you, I think,' he said.

They fell silent. It was almost a relief when the announcer's plastic voice told all passengers of Flight 227 to Singapore to proceed for their security check.

'I should go,' said Amit standing up, gently prying the carry-on bag away from her fingers.

Romola clutched his hands instead, her eyes brimming with unshed tears, her lips trembling with the effort to keep them in.

'Call me when you reach San Francisco,' she said slowly as if reciting a prayer even though he'd just told her it would be 2 a.m. for her. Next to him a young newly-wed bride, her forehead awash in bright red sindoor, was preparing to go on the same flight and was weeping loudly, being passed from one snuffling family member to another, while her husband stood by awkwardly next to a small mound of luggage. For a moment Amit wanted to touch Romola's feet to ask for her blessings. But they'd never been a family into demonstrations like that.

'I'll call,' he said awkwardly wrapping his arms around her just as he had when he had first walked into the house. 'Eat properly. Take care of yourself.'

After he checked his bags in, right before he walked into the security area, he looked over. She was still standing there just as he'd left her holding the rail. For a second he wondered

219

what she'd do if he went running back and said it was all a misunderstanding, of course she was coming to San Francisco to live with him, forget the house. Or that he was coming back to live with her.

But instead he just raised his hand in tentative goodbye.

Then he turned and walked down the long empty hallway without turning back. And with every step he took, he felt Romola recede from him, growing smaller and smaller until she was just a pinprick of light in the indigo darkness swallowing up the city behind him.

It was only when he turned the corner and knew she could no longer see him that his shoulders suddenly sagged and his knees buckled. For the first time since he had come to India after his father died Amit began to weep, his tears coming in such great nauseous heaves, he was afraid he would throw up the Mirinda he'd just drunk. He could almost taste it in his mouth again, the plastic sweetness now tart with the taste of his betrayal. He held on to the wall for support as he rummaged in his pockets for some tissue.

The passengers boarding the flight filed past him quietly, weighed down by overstuffed carry-on bags, their gazes turned away, studiously avoiding him as if he was contagious. Only the weeping bride, merely sniffling now, her eyes still red, the eyeliner smudged, paused near him uncertainly. But then her husband nudged her elbow and she too moved on towards the airplane, looking back just once, her moist dark eyes luminous with gentle commiseration that he felt he didn't deserve, but was nevertheless grateful for.

XII

The Scene of the Crime

The dream-child moving through a land
Of wonders wild and new,
In friendly chat with bird or beast –
And half believe it true.
    – Lewis Carroll, *Alice in Wonderland*

ROMOLA HAD never wanted to come back to Carbondale. It had been Amit's idea entirely. 'It will be a change,' he said cheerily one day after he had come home from work. 'Why don't we all take a trip together?' Romola, who had been sitting on the loveseat in the afternoon sun, looked up at him perplexed. Outside another warm October evening in California was gliding to a leisurely close. The neighbour's sons were riding their bicycles up and down the sidewalk, whooping and hollering, ringing their bells with mad glee.

'Where, Dad?' said Neel. He was sitting on the carpet near Romola trying to build a monster Lego truck and watch cartoons at the same time. Romola, who wanted to watch a talk show on television, was beginning to get very tired of sitting by her grandson on the loveseat, and of having nothing to do: once or twice she had peeped into the Lego manual, but it had complicated pictures and instructions. She leafed through the newspaper though she had already read it in the morning.

'We'll go to a small town in the middle of Illinois,' Amit told his son. 'It's very pretty. It's where your grandfather went to college. Did you know your grandmother lived there once as well?'

'Is that where I am going to study?' asked Neel, pausing in his construction work.

'Oh no,' his grandmother quickly said, taking off her gold-rimmed reading glasses. 'You, my prince, will go to somewhere like Stanford. Or Harvard. Stanford is closer to home, na? But Amit, why do you want to go to Carbondale?'

'I thought it would be nice to show Neel Baba's old university,' said Amit. 'And aren't you curious about what the town looks like now? It must be what, over thirty-five years since you saw it?'

'There is nothing to see,' Romola said sharply. 'It's just a university town. It's not like it has monuments and temples. Or the Himalaya mountains. Or Disneyland.'

'Yes,' Neel thumped on the floor with his half-finished truck. 'Let's go to Disneyland.'

June was taking Tupperware containers of food out of the refrigerator and putting them into the microwave. From her silence, Romola understood this was something that had already been discussed and decided, though Amit had framed it as a question.

'Plus I think it would be good for you, Ma,' said Amit gravely. 'You know, for your, um—' he cast a sideways glance at Neel, 'your condition.' His tone formed little quote marks in the air slotting Romola's condition, quaintly, as unmentionable.

Romola had just been diagnosed with what the doctor called a mild case of depression. Amit would leave her pills out on the granite kitchen counter every morning before he went to work with a glass of water and a little yellow Post-it note that said 'TAKE ME' on it in large ballpoint letters. Romola didn't know why she was supposed to take pills for something as natural as missing her own bed in Calcutta and being rather bored in California. Every morning she took the blue pill and popped it into a plastic Ziploc bag she kept tucked away at the bottom of her handbag. She wasn't sure why she didn't just flush it down the toilet, its water already bright blue from the Clorox toilet-bowl cleaner June used. Romola was a hoarder by nature and it seemed a waste to flush the pills away. Sometimes when she was stressed she put her hand in the bag and ran her fingers over the nubbly shapes. Their mere presence was strangely comforting, like prayer beads. Her mother used to like to go to bed with sleeping pills under her pillow, pills she never ever took but liked to keep close by. Her grandmother-in-law used to store jars of home-made mango chutney under her bed just in case she got sick and bed-bound. Perhaps some day her pills would come in handy too, thought Romola.

Since Romola had arrived in America for an 'extended stay' several years after Amit's father's death, she knew her son was trying to keep her busy and engaged. None of it was working that well. First he tried to teach her how to get online so she could email her nephews and nieces in India but Romola found it too confusing. He then took her to the Indian senior centre somewhere in Silicon Valley. Everyone there seemed to talk in either Gujarati or Telugu, neither of which she understood. Aren't there any Bengalis here, she thought irritably. Someone asked her if she would like to come to the temple on Sunday and Romola, who had only visited temples in Calcutta when forced to by her grandmother-in-law, had a panic-stricken vision of being strapped into the back seat of the family sedan and forced to go on pilgrimage through the beige suburbia of Livermore. By the time the last senior yoga stretching exercise was over and the extra-perky middle-aged woman with a saccharine voice and streaky hair-dye job had led them through the 'breath release', Romola was beside herself. For a few days Amit kept asking her when she wanted to go back to the centre and Romola kept inventing excuses to avoid it. Eventually he gave up.

Perhaps it was that guilt that prevented her from protesting too strongly about the trip to Carbondale. Perhaps in the deepest recesses of her heart she was curious. Though she rarely mentioned it, she had thought of Carbondale often, of coming there as a young bride, of her first taste of America and how it had made her recoil.

'It will be like going back to find our roots,' laughed Amit.

It's like going back to visit the scene of the crime, thought Romola but she kept it to herself.

Carbondale had not changed too much from how she remembered it, even though almost four decades had passed. As they drove into town in their rental car, Amit said, 'So, Ma, what do you think? Does it look familiar at all?'

Romola stared out of the window at the little rows of white houses on small streets with names like Poplar and Laurel. It was autumn already, or what they called 'fall' here. Some of the trees were starting to change colour, the leaves turning gold with hints of burned orange. She recalled whole streets turning into a blazing bonfire of red and gold, something that never happened in Silicon Valley. She remembered a perfect brick-red poplar leaf she had picked up from the street and stuck in her diary. It was her first autumn in America. 'What will you do with that dead leaf?' Avinash had asked.

'I'll save it,' she had replied. 'Autumn leaves, like in that song.'

She had been wearing an ugly puffy blue jacket they had bought at the discount store that day. Its zipper would always get stuck. It had been her first 'winter purchase'. She had left the jacket behind in America. But years later, back in Calcutta, she had found that leaf in her diary, still whole but brittle, like memory.

How young they had been, she thought, younger than Amit and June, scarcely older than the students sitting on the steps of the little houses and chatting, some of them smoking, holding bottles of beer. They drove slowly down the street, braking for a young man in denim cut-offs who ran out to retrieve an errant Frisbee.

'Do you remember the street where you lived when you first came here, Romola?' said June.

'No, that was so long ago,' Romola replied. 'It wasn't a sweet little house like these. It was an ugly modern apartment building. Who knows if it even exists anymore?'

But she did remember. If she closed her eyes she could picture it perfectly. It used to be called the Nile Apartments. The town had an Egyptian fixation. Their school newspaper was named the *Daily Egyptian*. There was nothing Egyptian about the Nile Apartments, though – squat, nondescript blue-grey blocks of identical buildings each with a pocket-handkerchief-sized threadbare lawn in front. Many of the international students ended up there, especially ones with families. The place always smelled of curries, as if years of homesickness had seeped into the walls. She remembered how her heart had sunk when she'd first seen it, this place she was going to have to call home. For a while she had tried to bravely make a home out of it – organizing her kitchen, buying brightly coloured cushions at yard sales, putting up wall hangings she had received as wedding presents. The day after she discovered Avinash's illicit affair, it became the place she needed to escape.

She remembered standing at the window of the apartment every day combing her hair after a shower. Her hair had been long and black then, falling almost to her waist. The up-and-down rhythms of her hairbrush would calm her down, allaying her homesickness for one more day. Now her hair was grey, thinning at the top, the ends straggly. June had given her a trim the other day and it barely reached her shoulders now. 'It looks trendy,' Amit had said with an approving chuckle. Yes, of course, she remembered that apartment as if it had only been yesterday when Avinash turned the key in the lock and brought his new wife and their heap of luggage inside. Her mother-in-law had tied red ribbons, saved from their wedding presents, around the bulky suitcases, so they would have no trouble recognizing them at the airport.

'No,' she lied to her son. 'I can't remember where it was at all.'

But all day long she kept returning to it in her head, as if tripping over a child's toy someone had left lying in her path. She remembered Michael Koh, the studious Malaysian physics PhD student who lived below them, and his brother George, who was taking courses in electrical engineering. She wondered whatever happened to them. When she and Avinash had finally left Carbondale, the Kohs had helped them load their suitcases into the taxi. As the taxi rounded the corner, Romola had turned back to wave to them – two men in floppy shorts silhouetted against the midday sun, their hands raised in farewell.

She had resolved at the time to never come back to America. She had said she didn't want to be marooned in some small town in America alone with a baby and to her surprise Avinash had acceded with little fuss. She had thought that once she went back to India and started a family everything would be okay again. And it did turn out all right, she thought. Avinash proved to be a good husband, all things considered. And Amit turned out to be a good son, decent and caring. Sometimes, however, she wondered if Avinash had

226

resented her for going back. What would it have been like, she thought, to have raised a family in America, to hear Amit call her 'Mom' as Neel called June? But in the end, she thought with a wry smile, what did it matter? Here she was with her son and his American wife and their little American boy in a small Midwestern town just as if she and Avinash had never left after all.

Romola realized she was snapping and unsnapping her handbag, running the tips of her fingers over the blue pills inside. Determined to be more engaged on a trip that was being made in her honour, she put the bag aside and said, 'I remember there used to be an international store we would go to for spices. I used to write down the names of the spices in English before I went there. Coriander for dhoney, cumin for jeerey. But fenugreek was a hard one. I could never remember it.'

By the time evening rolled around, her enthusiasm was flagging. They had walked all over campus. Amit pointed out the church with the clock tower. There seemed to be dozens of new buildings but the pond was still there. Romola watched a young couple on a rowboat glide by, trailed by two ducks. Amit took a photograph of her. 'Cheese,' he said. She obliged, holding her grandson in front of her. They walked up and down Main Street, still called Main Street. But she recognized none of the shops. Where there used to be a Chinese restaurant they went to for special occasions, there was now a print and copy shop. The old post office had turned into an ice-cream store where Neel insisted on getting a waffle cone. Amit eagerly embraced his role as tour guide bombarding her with questions until June quietly said, 'I think your mother is getting tired, dear. It's been a long day.' They decided to head back to the motel.

But at night Romola couldn't sleep. She told Amit she wasn't hungry and went up to her room. For a while her grandson kept her company while his parents finished their dinner. When Amit and June came by to say their goodnights, she sent Neel off with them and sat at her window watching the streetlights come on. 657 Holly Street, Apt 202 – her first American address. How many times had she written that on the lower left-hand corner of envelopes? How many times had she run down to the mailbox, hoping for a letter from India with that handwritten address under the familiar reassurance of the stamps with Mahatma Gandhi's bald head? She remembered the window from which she had her own postcard-sized view of America. She had looked out of it once in despair, wondering how she would ever find her way back home. She could hardly believe she had now found her way back to Carbondale after all these years. Outside the town slowly settled down to sleep, the way small towns do. She remembered that hushed feeling well, the suddenly empty streets, the flickering television screens in locked-up houses, and the welling feeling of trapped loneliness she had fought down night after night with mango pickle and rice.

At ten o'clock, wide awake and restless, Romola wrapped a shawl around her and quietly let herself out of the room. Tiptoeing past Amit's room she wondered what she would say if he suddenly came out. Where was she sneaking off to at night? But his curtains were drawn and the room was dark. They seemed to have gone to bed. Only the glowing eye of the soda-vending machine at the far end of the corridor watched her unblinkingly. The bored young woman sitting at the reception reading a magazine barely looked up as Romola walked out the door.

The October night was still pleasant though the first hint of a winter chill was already in the air. A young man with a backpack was approaching her.

'Excuse me,' said Romola. 'Do you know where Holly Street is?'

He did not. She had to ask three other people before a young Chinese woman told her how to get there. It was a longer walk than she had thought it would be and she had to ask her way a few more times. To her astonishment her old apartment building was still there, as ugly as ever. It wasn't blue-grey any more. It had been painted what seemed to be a rather bilious pistachio green but everything else was the same. She half expected to stumble on another bicycle someone had left on the path but there was nothing there. It was already close to eleven and the street was deserted. Romola stood in front of the driveway wondering who lived there now, whether their lives were any happier than hers had been. She had an urge to go up to the front door, ring the bell and run away.

Two young men, one walking with a bicycle, came up the street towards her, looking at her curiously. 'Are you okay, ma'am?' said one politely. 'Do you need help?' Romola shook her head, suddenly aware of how odd she must look, standing there, huddled in a shawl, in her cream synthetic sari with its green floral pattern. She started backing away from the house slowly. Somewhere a dog barked, making her jump. Romola started walking faster, pulling her shawl more tightly around her. It was a mistake coming here, it was just a stupid ugly building, she told herself, what had she been afraid of? They could have just come in the morning, she, Amit, June and Neel, and she would have told them silly funny stories of her life in America, of how she had once tried to make pizza in the old oven in her kitchen and it had come out hard and black. 'Yes, that's what I'll do,' she resolved. 'Tomorrow I'll suddenly remember the name of the street. And we can come see the house and then I can close this chapter for good.' By now it was past eleven and she hoped Amit had not got up to check in on her.

It was at that moment she realized she was completely lost.

She had somehow wandered into a part of town with very few people. The stores were shut. There were a few car lots, lights blazing, the cars on sale gleaming but not a soul in sight. American flags fluttered in the evening breeze over Japanese cars. Giant poinsettias of red, white and blue adorned some of them, their prices scrawled in fluorescent yellow across their windshields, advertising wondrous sales of slashed prices. The cars looked ready to go somewhere, as if at the stroke of midnight they awoke to life and freedom. It reminded her of the stories she used to read as a girl where the toys suddenly burst into life after the children went to bed. But despite the lights and the cheerful signs advertising Halloween Specials, there were no people around. Cars whooshed by her as Romola trudged on, hoping she was walking in the right direction, starting to fight back the first ripples of panic until she spotted a bar on a side street.

It was called Wonderland. A funny name, thought Romola as she pushed open the door, hoping someone inside would be able to guide her back to the motel. It looked quite ordinary. It was not very full and rather dimly lit but it seemed everyone stopped talking to turn and stare at her as she stood uncertainly at the door. There were a lot of men, many of them looking like college students drinking beer. She spotted a couple of women standing in a corner near a pool table. There were video-game machines lined up against the wall and the music was so loud it made her head spin. Romola stood at the door, unsure about what to do next. After the brief lull, the conversations picked up around her again as if nothing had happened. And she might have just pushed the door and gone back out into the night again, if someone had not suddenly materialized from the shadows and said, 'Excuse me, are you Indian?'

The voice was low and masculine but when Romola looked up she saw the most perfectly made-up woman she had ever seen. The high cheekbones were chiselled, the plucked eye-brows perfectly arched, the skin a 'fair and lovely' olive, the wine-red lips pursed in a glamour-doll pout. She wore a sheath-like satiny purple dress and tottered on impossibly high heels.

The apparition looked impatient. One eyebrow rose even higher. 'Well?' she demanded. 'Are you? I mean, you are wearing that gorgeous sari.'

'Oh,' laughed Romola smoothing her pleats, a flush of pleasure sweeping over her, bringing colour to her face. 'I didn't realize you were talking to me.'

'Who else would I be talking to?' Glossy red talon-like claws fished out a little mirror from her bag like a fabulous bird of prey.

'Who are you?' said Romola, ignoring the question altogether.

'Oh, how terribly rude of me. Excuse me. I am Lady Bang la Dish. But you can just call me BLD for short. A bit like the sandwich.' She looked at Romola expectantly as if waiting for her to laugh. Then seeing Romola's blank expression, she shrugged and carried on. 'I wanted to go to that Indian Students' Association on campus but at the last moment I freaked out. But I really need to know what kind of outfit an Indian princess should wear.'

'An Indian princess?' Romola, dumbfounded, repeated.

'Yes, yes, for my dance performance,' BLD said. 'I am a performer, you know. Nothing big. Just some shows here and there. But one must keep it authentic.' Someone yelled at her from across the bar. BLD threw up her hands. 'Oh, won't she be savage if I keep her waiting. But don't go anywhere. Sit on that stool. What would you like to drink? How about a gin and tonic? I'll be right back.'

Romola was about to say she didn't want a drink. She just needed to know if BLD knew where the Best Western motel was but she had vanished, leaving behind a cloud of perfume. Someone came over and thrust a gin and tonic in Romola's hand before she could protest.

How strange everything is today! thought Romola as she took a tentative sip. Her eyes widened. It was strong.

All around her men were laughing and talking to one another. She spotted a young man who looked like he could be Indian. For one moment he reminded her of Avinash as an earnest young graduate student, the neatly parted hair, the moustache that had never been shaved, the square glasses. She tried to catch his eye, sure he would know where the Best Western was. But he looked at her as if he had seen a ghost and quickly walked over to the other end of the bar. Within minutes he was gone.

Romola took another sip of her drink. She warily looked around her. There was a bank of video games near her and a pile of free magazines. She opened one and quickly put it down. She couldn't see very well without her reading glasses but she didn't need them to realize it was full of pictures of men without shirts, some of them showing their butts as well. Romola clapped her hand over her mouth as she realized where she was. She was wondering if she should just slide off the barstool and quietly let herself out of the door when BLD reappeared and admonished her, 'You've hardly drunk a drop.'

Romola took a big gulp of the gin and tonic. It felt really refreshing. So she took another, crunching the ice cube between her teeth. 'It's Bombay Gin,' said BLD with a chuckle. 'Get it? Bombay Gin for you?'

This time Romola did get it. She was going to say she was actually from Calcutta, not Bombay, but decided it didn't really matter.

'What brings you to our town?' said BLD. 'What's your name, dear?'

'Romola. Romola Mitra. I used to live here almost forty years ago,' she said.

'You don't say.' BLD's eyebrows arched and almost disappeared into her hair.

'Was this, um, this place, here then?' Romola wondered if Avinash had ever come here on his own. She tried to picture him standing there ordering his screwdriver. That had always been his favourite drink.

'Oh honey, this has been here for ever. Though it's had different names, Lonely Hearts, Faces, Wunderbar . . .' said BLD. 'But forty years, that's a long long time in gay bar years. You know, I don't even know if they had gay bars down here then, though I should know. I've lived around here for over forty years now but don't tell any of these queens that. I'm not admitting to being a day over thirty-five.'

Romola smiled. There was something about BLD's frankness that was attractive. Or perhaps it was the gin and tonic. She'd drunk most of it and now felt as if she was floating down a deep well. She looked around. One of the men standing at the bar and talking caught her eye. He smiled and raised his drink to her. She blushed and raised her glass back.

'Do you know,' she told BLD, 'you have the most beautiful cheekbones?'

'You don't say,' BLD seemed genuinely taken aback at the compliment. 'That calls for another drink. Especially coming from someone as elegant as you. You are the most elegant creature in this whole place.'

Romola smiled bashfully. It had been a long time since she'd heard a compliment like that. A waiter brought over their drinks. 'This here is my new friend, Romola. She lived here almost forty years ago. She is back visiting,' BLD said.

'I thought the whole idea was to get out of Carbondale and never come back,' the waiter said.

'Oh shush,' said BLD. 'It isn't so bad. Actually, it is,' she said conspiratorially to Romola. 'But what's a girl to do?'

Between the throb of the music, the drink sloshing in her head, and BLD's accent, Romola could understand approximately one word in three. But it didn't matter – BLD was unloading the story of her life as if they were old friends meeting after many years.

Bang la Dish's mother had been born in Dhaka, Bangladesh, but had grown up in some small American suburban town in the middle of cornfields with one Dairy Queen ('I thought I'd call myself Dairy Queen for a while,' laughed Bang la Dish). Her father was the son of German–Irish parents. 'Standard European mutt, you know,' BLD said, knocking back her drink. Romola didn't know. It all sounded terribly exotic to her – the German–Irish accountant, son of a plumber, meeting the Bangladeshi–American girl who preferred peanut butter and jelly sandwiches to rice and dal.

'Believe me, honey, it was anything but exotic,' replied BLD, laughing uproariously.

Soon they were swapping stories as if they were high-school girlfriends. Once Romola looked nervously at her watch. 'Oh don't you worry,' said BLD. 'I'll take you home. I have a car. And your son must be asleep anyway. What will you do at Best Western? Buy non-stick cookware from late-night cable television?'

BLD wanted to move to New York or San Francisco but didn't know how she could afford it. 'Have you been to those Indian stores in Fremont?' she asked eagerly. 'I went there once with my mother. Oh my. They smelled divine.'

'Yes,' said Romola eagerly. 'You must come. We'll go shopping. And then we can go rent a Bollywood film.'

'I want to practise a dance number. You must teach me.'

'Oh,' laughed Romola. 'I don't know all those jhin-chak cabaret dances. What kind of a woman do you think I am?'

'I don't know,' BLD raised an eyebrow. 'What kind of a woman are you, Romola?'

Romola blushed again and laughed nervously. She thought that maybe they could rent that old seventies film, *Jewel Thief*. She'd always liked the vamp in it, the way she flashed thigh and cleavage, the shiny golden dress that made her breasts point out like twin propellers. She imagined them rewinding and playing the songs over and over again, matching hip-shake for hip-shake. She could just see BLD sashaying in between the convertible sofa-cum-bed and the matching loveseat wearing white kid gloves and fluttering Amit's *Economist* magazine in front of her like a fan.

BLD asked her if she wanted a cigarette.

'Oh, I don't smoke,' said Romola. 'Well I used to sometimes at a party but that was years ago,' she lied.

'It's a terrible habit, but have a puff – all the Hindi film vamps do. Anyway, they won't allow smoking in here soon. So it's our last chance to be real vamps.'

As BLD lit up her cigarette using her Betty Boop lighter, Romola said, 'Do you know, this is the best time I've ever had in Carbondale?'

'Really?' said BLD. 'What is your story? I've just been prattling on about myself. Tell me about you, your husband and everything else.'

So Romola told her about landing in America, the apartment on Holly Street, about the shock of finding out that Avinash had had a male lover.

'You don't say. And then what happened?' BLD's eyes were wide.

'Nothing. I couldn't tell anyone. I didn't know what to do, where to go. I just wanted to go home.'

'Did you ever tell him you knew?'

'I couldn't,' she replied. 'I didn't know what to say. I hoped it was just something in the past. I just said I didn't want to raise a child here. He was a very decent man, you know. I never told anyone. Especially not my son. You are the first person I have ever talked to about it. It must be the gin.'

'But what about the sex?' BLD leaned forward. 'What was that like? Could he do it properly?'

Romola burst out laughing. 'What did I know about properly? We were not reading *Cosmopolitan*-sholitan then.'

'Men,' BLD shook her head and blew out a smoke ring. 'Men are bastards. Why do you think I got tired of being one?' She threw her head back and cackled. Romola stared at her for a second and then joined in.

'Wait here,' said BLD suddenly. 'I have an idea.' She slid down from the stool and disappeared behind the bar with her handbag. Romola looked at her watch. It was almost one. She shrugged. It was too late now anyway. She just hoped they didn't lock the front door at the motel.

She noticed the music around her had died down. A voice announced, 'Ladies and gentlemen, a special impromptu treat for us tonight. The one and only Lady Bang la Dish.' A spotlight hovered uncertainly on the bare wooden stage. A hand pushed aside the tatty red velvet curtains, a sinuous leg arched itself around the drapes and then Lady Bang la Dish herself was onstage.

'Ladies and gentlemen, and everyone in between, you are here on a very special night,' she crooned into the mike, her voice extra-sultry. 'We are going to make history at Wonderland. Our first-ever Bollywood number. For my new friend Romola, all the way from Calcutta.' She winked.

Romola's mouth fell open.

'Mera Naam Chin Chin Choo' blasted through the club suddenly sweeping aside the Top 20 pop music from minutes ago. Everyone around her seemed startled for a moment but as BLD thrust her bosom out and shook her hips, they started hooting and hollering. Romola started laughing like she had not laughed in years. She had the sensation of thousands of coloured feathers cascading down from the ceiling, an endlessly exploding piñata. She could see herself running through the feather storm, her face raised up, drowning in the softness of the falling feathers. When BLD stepped down from the stage and came towards her, hand outstretched, Romola laughed and protested, but only mildly. 'Oh no, no, I don't know how to do all this.' By now everyone was cheering and clapping along and Romola let BLD pull her off the barstool and drag her on to the stage.

They bumped hips and danced around the stage, Romola holding her sari out in front of her, trying to match her steps to a song she had once listened to on a little cassette recorder – *The Golden Hits of Asha Bhosle – Vol. 1.*

'*Mera naam chin chin choo, chin chin choo,*' trilled the sexy Asha Bhosle over the sound system. 'Chin chin choo' repeated BLD, laughing seductively. Romola giggled too, trying to do the hip flourishes she remembered from the old film. BLD fished out her sunglasses from somewhere and stuck them on Romola. Feeling impossibly glamorous, though she could see almost nothing, Romola sang along '*Chin chin choo, baba chin chin choo*'. She was dimly aware that the whole bar had joined in, a chorus of men going '*Chin chin choo*', the wings of a vampy song from 1958 lifting them all up.

When the number ended, the place erupted in thundering applause. Romola, her heart pounding like a steam engine, clung on to BLD for support. BLD reached over and kissed her on the cheek leaving a perfect wine-red imprint of her lips. 'Thank goodness I was carrying my Bollywood mix with me. You are the best, Romola,' she laughed. 'We could become partners. An act. What do you say?'

'And we'll get some new music,' said Romola breathlessly. 'I'll find the latest hits for you. Maybe we can make you a new outfit. I could cut up my wedding sari.' June had once asked if she would mind if she took one of Romola's heavy silk saris and made a skirt. Romola had said she would most certainly mind. But she quickly put that thought out of her head.

'Last call!' shouted the bartender sending another gin and tonic over their way.

'Oh, too much,' laughed Romola taking a big gulp.

'Chin chin,' said BLD touching her glass to Romola's and collapsing into laughter at her own joke.

When they eventually staggered out, they were still giggling as they made their way towards BLD's battered burgundy Oldsmobile. 'Good night darling,' said a man in a leather jacket to BLD. 'You were just fabulous. Namaste,' he told Romola. She smiled and waved her hands airily as if she danced to cabaret numbers in gay bars all the time.

'Let's get you home before they send out a search party,' said BLD unlocking the car door for her. The car felt like a ship. BLD swept aside a jumble of CDs and tissues and Romola slid into the front seat. BLD lit a cigarette, stuck in her Hindi film CD and cranked up the volume. They drove through the quiet streets lined with the names of American trees while Lata Mangeshkar's nightingale voice, achingly perfect, filled the night around them.

A little Bengali poem she'd learned as a child buzzed in Romola's head. She would sing it for Amit when he was a baby, strapping him on to her knees and bouncing him up and down.

'*Ghugu shoi, khoka koi, ghughu shoi, khoka koi.*'

But she could not remember the next line. That, suddenly, became very important to her. She wondered if BLD's mother had ever sung that to her. She glanced over at BLD who winked at her and squeezed her hand.

When they finally pulled up to the motel, its sign still resolutely on as if it was a lighthouse guiding her to shore, BLD hugged Romola and slipped a piece of paper into her hand.

'It has my email and phone. I always keep one handy. You never know if you'll meet Mr Right at the bar, though all I get are Mr Right Nows,' she chuckled. 'But don't disappear on me, darling. You are the bomb, Romola. Come back anytime and we'll have a proper Bollywood girls' night on the town.'

Romola hugged her back. She smelled of stale perfume and gin. Romola wondered what it would be like if BLD lived in California. She imagined waking up in the morning and calling her after Amit and June left for work and Neel had gone to school. She would pull up in that burgundy car, and they would go to thrift stores and the mall and for picnics in the park all the while listening to old film songs.

'You take care,' she told BLD as she had heard the Americans say and then sashayed to the door. When she turned around to wave goodbye BLD blew her a kiss.

As soon as Romola walked into the motel she realized she was in trouble. The receptionist who had seemed half asleep when she had left was now wide awake.

Amit was sitting in the lobby talking agitatedly to a police officer. For a moment as she looked at him, his anxious profile, she thought it was Avinash – the same hairline, the furrowed brow, the glasses.

'Ma,' Amit cried springing up from the sofa where he had been sitting. 'What's going on? Where have you been?'

'Oh, I'll explain later,' Romola said wearily. 'I got a little lost but this kind person helped me get back. I didn't want you to worry. I am so sorry.'

Amit was still wearing the sweatpants he had gone to sleep in. His face was taut with stress. 'Ma, are you crazy? I've been beside myself,' Amit said. 'Neel woke up as well. June is upstairs trying to get him to sleep again. He keeps asking for you. How could you disappear just like that in the middle of the night? Didn't you even think?'

Amit, it turned out, had woken up, found his mother missing, panicked and called the police. The Carbondale police were on the lookout for an elderly Indian woman in a sari. Romola had the hardest time explaining that she had not been kidnapped.

'But where did you go?' Amit asked, agitated, over and over again as if it was a piece of a jigsaw that just would not fit. Romola tried to describe her evening but the story got hopelessly tangled in its telling. She led them outside as if to retrace her path home but the Oldsmobile and BLD were long gone.

'No, no officer,' she said loudly as if explaining something to a particularly dull child. 'Miss la Dish is a good friend. She brought me home just fine so no one needs to worry.'

'Miss Ladish, huh?' said the officer. 'Like a radish, huh? Do you even know this person's name?'

She could tell that the officer, a young man in his twenties, was not buying any of her story.

Romola began to laugh.

'Excuse me, ma'am?' said the officer while June, who had come downstairs by then, tried to shush her.

'Oh, I just realized why she calls herself Bang la Dish,' Romola snorted. 'Bangladesh. I get it!'

Amit stared at her.

'She's half-Bengali,' said Romola as if that explained everything. Amit said nothing but looked at her as if she was some stranger who had wandered in from the road and into their family.

'I'm very sorry, officer,' June said politely. 'Thank you so much for all your help. I guess everything is okay now. We really do apologize for the trouble. My mother-in-law got a little confused. After all it's a strange town, you know. She moved to the US recently from India.'

'But I lived here before any of you were born,' Romola said indignantly but no one paid her any attention.

It was past 2.30 in the morning when everything was finally sorted out and the policeman left.

'You smell of cigarettes,' scolded Amit. 'Have you been drinking? Oh God, Ma, if you want a drink, just tell me. You don't have to sneak off to strange bars.'

'Do you remember that rhyme "Ghugu shoi" I would sing to you?' Romola asked.

Amit stood there looking stunned.

'Let's just get your mother to bed,' said June hurriedly.

Romola nodded meekly, knowing there was nothing more to say. She glanced outside. For a moment she thought BLD was still standing there, her satiny dress glimmering in the light of a street lamp. Then she realized she was only imagining it. As Romola walked upstairs she wondered whether she'd have a hangover the next day.

'God knows what kind of people you could meet there. You could have been robbed,' Amit muttered. 'What were you thinking? Are you crazy? I don't even know what to tell Neel.'

Nothing, thought Romola. Tell him nothing. It will be our secret. In a family of secrets, what was one more? But she said nothing. Her mind was far away. There was so much she needed to learn. She was already composing a letter to BLD in her head. Not a real letter, of course, she would have to send an email. She would have to finally sit down and learn how to do that. At least Amit would be pleased about that, she thought.

The next day, when it was time to leave Carbondale, Amit was still stonily silent. June said little, hiding behind her sunglasses, sipping her coffee, unwilling to mediate between her husband and his mother. Neel sat on the back seat next to Romola chattering away as usual. Romola did have a slight hangover but did not want to mention that to anyone. She rolled down the window to feel the fresh air on her face, the night's events now just part of some make-believe adventure.

She opened her handbag and rummaged for the little piece of paper with BLD's email. She felt her bag of pills next to her pen and her reading glasses. But she could not find the paper. She closed her eyes and half-believed she was still in Wonderland, though she knew she had to but open them again, and all would change to dull reality. As the car pulled out of the motel's parking lot, Romola, her eyes still shut, casually lifted her hand up to the open window, dropping the little blue pills one by one, leaving a trail for BLD, all the way across America.

> Don't let him know she liked them best
> For this must ever be
> A secret, kept from all the rest,
> Between yourself and me.
> – Lewis Carroll, *Alice in Wonderland*

ACKNOWLEDGEMENTS

A PECULIAR set of coincidences and strange encounters conspired to make this particular book happen.

This book would have remained in the recesses of my hard drive if Diya Kar Hazra at Bloomsbury had not called out of the blue. Diya called because the novelist Manil Suri told her he liked a short story of mine in the anthology *Out! Stories from the New Queer India*. That story snuck into the anthology because Minal Hajratwala, its editor, remembered it from our writing group in San Francisco. That writing group happened because Pueng Vongs bullied me into it. Pueng would not have been my friend and colleague had not the remarkable Sandy Close shared a glass of red wine with me at Pied Piper on Market Street in San Francisco and offered me a job at the Pacific News Service. I would not have made that crazy leap of faith from my software job to a news service if Gregory Roberts had not reassured me we wouldn't end up homeless on the streets of San Francisco. This daisy chain could go on and on but suffice to say the fingerprints of all of them are all over this book and I am grateful for that.

A few of these stories appeared in early versions elsewhere. 'Ring of Spices' appeared in an early form in *Contours of my Heart* edited by Sunaina Maira and Rajini Srikanth. 'White Christmas' is inspired by 'Black and Blue' from the anthology

Men on Men 6 edited by David Bergman. 'The Games Boys Play' is a reincarnation of 'Auld Lang Syne' from *Story-wallah!* edited by Shyam Selvadurai. A version of 'Great-Grandmother's Mango Chutney' won the Katha Prize for Indian American fiction in *India Currents* magazine. To all of those editors who saw something in those stories, my gratitude.

Minal, Pueng, Daisy Hernandez and Sunita Dhurandhur were part of the writing group that made me go back to these stories again and again. We didn't have frisee salads with pomegranate seeds but it was the best group ever. My grati-tude to Jennie Dorny who went out of her way to scrutinize the fine print of the contract, to Anna Ghosh, Nayan Shah and Lakshmi Chaudhry who gave me invaluable advice. To Alexandra Pringle and the entire Bloomsbury team who have shepherded this book into being. And to Bishan Samaddar who reassured me when I flailed, pushed me when I procras-tinated, and gives me much more than he realizes. And finally, a Jesuit priest named Camille Bouché who taught me the only lesson I've ever had about writing: Write simply. Don't show off. Big words are not necessarily the right words.

Many people, friends, relatives, acquaintances, have asked me over the years, 'Are you going to write a book?' And I'd always smile noncommittally. Now there's no wriggling out. Whether or not it's the one they hoped I would write, this is the book.

A NOTE ON THE AUTHOR

Sandip Roy is a Senior Editor for the popular news portal Firstpost.com and blogs for the *Huffington Post* and is an Associate Editor with New America Media. He has been a long-time commentator on National Public Radio's *Morning Edition*, one of the most listened-to radio programmes in the US and has a weekly radio postcard on KALW 91.7 FM in the San Francisco Bay Area. He has contributed to various anthologies including *New California Writing 2011, Story-wallah!, Contours of the Heart, Out! Stories from the New Queer India, Mobile Cultures, Because I Have a Voice: Queer Politics in India* and *The Phobic and the Erotic: The Politics of Sexualities in Contemporary India*. He currently lives in Kolkata.

A NOTE ON THE TYPE

The text of this book is set in Berling roman, a modern face designed by K. E. Forsberg between 1951 and 1958. In spite of its youth it does carry the characteristics of an old face. The serifs are inclined and blunt, and the g has a straight ear.